• • •

The
Unpolished Life
of
Eleanor Whitfield

• • •

a novel

Rachel Hanna

CHAPTER 1

The teenager sitting in front of me is chewing her gum like her life depends on it. The smell of watermelon wafts across my face. Actually, she is not just chewing. She is masticating with the kind of aggressive enthusiasm I would assume is usually reserved for eating competitions where gluttonous humans shove ample amounts of hot dogs in their faces.

Each snap of her jaw sends a wave of the artificial watermelon scent flying across my pristine studio. I can feel my left eye beginning to twitch.

"Madison." I keep my voice very measured and pleasant. The voice of my mother perfected over forty years of teaching Atlanta's elite how to exist in polite society. "We discussed what appropriate behavior is in formal settings. Would you like to dispose of that gum before we continue?"

Madison, sixteen, highlighted hair and an expression suggesting she would literally like to be anywhere else on earth, rolls her eyes so hard that I am genuinely concerned about the structural integrity of her optic nerves.

"My mom said I had to come here. She did not say I had to, you know, like, participate."

The other two girls sitting on either side of her, Kaylee and Brittany, are equally uninterested, and they snicker behind their manicured hands.

I take a deep breath, then another. This studio is beautiful, with tall windows and hardwood floors polished to a mirror-bright shine, and cream-colored walls adorned with tasteful botanical prints and antique mirrors so students can observe their posture. It looks exactly like what it is, a museum dedicated to a dying art form.

"Very well." I smooth my hands down the front of my navy sheath dress. "Let's attempt the curtsy one more time, and remember, this is not about subservience. It is about grace and acknowledgement. You are not bowing to someone's superiority. You are showing your own refinement."

"But, like, when would I ever even curtsy?" Brittany asks, examining the split ends of her hair. "I'm not meeting the Queen or, like, whatever."

"The Queen kicked the bucket," Kaylee adds, trying to be helpful. "And she wasn't our queen anyway."

"Exactly." Brittany nods. "So, like, what is the point?"

The point? The point?

I want to tell them that the point is heritage, tradition, and the preservation of social graces that separate us from absolute chaos. I want to explain that my mother built this business from nothing because she truly believed that proper etiquette would open doors, build confidence, and transform awkward girls into poised young ladies ready to take on the world.

Instead, I just say, "The curtsy teaches awareness and control of your body, and these skills translate into confidence in every situation, like job interviews, formal events, or meeting your future in-laws."

"My mom says I am not allowed to have in-laws until I'm thirty," Madison announces, finally removing her gum and sticking it right under her chair.

Under the chair. The antique Chippendale chair that my mother purchased at an auction in 1987. The chair that has supported the derrieres of debutantes, society matrons, and one memorable visit from a minor European princess.

I close my eyes briefly and try to summon whatever patience I have in reserve. I am running dangerously low these days. I doubt it's appropriate for the only etiquette teacher left in Atlanta to strangle one of her students.

"Okay, ladies, let's take a different approach." I move to the front of the room and position myself in front of the full-length mirror. "Watch me first, and then we will try together."

I demonstrate a proper curtsy, right foot behind left, slight bend of the knees, subtle inclination of the head. It is all muscle memory for me at this point, drilled into me before I could even read. My mom used to say that I curtsied before I could walk, and I am fairly certain that is anatomically impossible, but it does speak to her priorities. She was always very proud when she said it.

When I rise, I catch my reflection. Thirty-four years old. Brown hair pinned up into a French twist that is so tight it gives me a headache every single day, and yet I continue to do it. Posture that would make a ballerina weep with envy. I look exactly like my mother.

The thought brings a familiar ache, the one I have been trying to ignore for two years now.

"Oh, that was actually kind of pretty," Kaylee admits, which might be the highest compliment I have received all year.

"Thank you. Now, everyone up. We will practice this together."

The girls shuffle to their feet with all the enthusiasm of death row inmates heading toward the execution chamber.

We spend the next twenty minutes trying curtsies that range from "acceptable" to "did you just have a small seizure?" By the end, Madison has complained about her knees seventeen times. Brittany has checked her phone twice despite my no phones policy, and Kaylee somehow managed to curtsy directly into a side table, knocking over a vase of silk flowers.

When their mothers finally arrive, a trio of Buckhead housewives in coordinating Lilly Pulitzer outfits, I paste on my most professional smile and assure them that their daughters are "making wonderful progress."

"Eleanor, you are such a treasure," Mrs. Anglin, Madison's mother, says, doing air kisses on both of my cheeks like we're in Europe and not next to a Starbucks in Atlanta. "Your mom would be so proud of you carrying on her legacy."

The words hit me somewhere soft and unprotected, but I maintain my smile through sheer force of will.

"Thanks, Patricia. It means so much."

After they leave, the studio falls silent. I lock the door, flip the sign to closed as if anyone is going to show up anyway, and finally let my shoulders drop from their permanent position somewhere near my earlobes.

The check in my hand is for three hundred dollars. Three sessions at one hundred each.

I move to my desk, a gorgeous antique secretary that my mother found at an estate sale, and put the check on a pitifully small pile waiting for deposit. Then I pull out the folder I have been avoiding all week.

Bills. So many bills.

The rent for the studio space is $4,000 a month. It is in a prime Buckhead location because my mom thought that location was everything, that you could not teach refinement in a strip mall. She was not wrong, but she also signed a lease before rent increases made the neighborhood financially impossible.

Utilities, insurance, the quarterly payment on the equipment loan that my mother took out when she renovated the space five years ago, and the credit card bill I have been slowly drowning under since the funeral expenses.

I do the math I have done a hundred times before, hoping that the numbers will somehow rearrange themselves into something I can manage, but they do not. They never do.

The truth is unforgiving and stark. Whitfield Etiquette is dying. Has been dying for years, really. A slow decline that my mom refused to acknowledge, and I have been desperately trying to reverse. But the world has changed. Nobody wants to learn how to address an envelope or which fork to use with fish.

The debutante balls still happen, but the girls who attend them would rather watch a YouTube tutorial than sit through my mother's carefully crafted curriculum.

I had six students last month. Six. Down from a peak of forty when I was a teenager, helping my mother demonstrate proper posture while she lectured on the importance of a firm handshake.

"Don't shake like you have a dead fish in your hand," she would say.

I sink into my desk chair and let my head fall to my hands, not caring that I am probably ruining my hairdo. The silence of the studio presses in around me. This beautiful, expensive space is empty except for my failure.

My phone buzzes, and I grab it with embarrassing desperation. Maybe it's a new client. Maybe it's someone who saw my website, my Instagram posts, or my increasingly apathetic attempts at marketing. Unfortunately, it's a text from my former fiancé.

Archie: Saw your post about the spring session. Hope business picks up. Let me know if you want to grab coffee sometime.

I stare at the message, trying to decode what it means.

Archie and I ended things over six months ago, after being engaged for two years. There had been a growing distance between us. He wanted a wife who would host dinner parties and charm all his clients, someone who would fit seamlessly into the world of investment banking and country-club memberships. But I wanted, well, I am still not entirely sure what I wanted. Just not the constant pressure of being Archie Farnsworth's perfect fiancée.

The breakup was civilized, of course. Everything in this world was civilized. We are both too well-bred for scenes. He got his ring back, and we moved on, or so I thought. We agreed to "remain friends," in a way that means we will awkwardly avoid each other at social functions for the next ten years or so.

I do not respond to his text. I do not even have the energy for whatever game he is playing.

Instead, I stand up and walk through my studio, running my fingers along the smooth surface of the practice table where students learn proper place settings. Twelve forks, twelve knives, twelve spoons, all arranged in perfect formation. My mother could identify every piece with her eyes closed. She could explain the history and purpose of each one with the passion of a museum curator.

I stop at the wall of photographs.

My mother at twenty-five, opening the studio with a ribbon-cutting ceremony attended by the mayor's wife. My mother at forty, receiving an award from the Junior League. My mother at sixty, teaching a class of bright-eyed girls who actually wanted to be there.

And then me, at all my various ages. Five years old in a tiny dress, practicing my curtsy. Sixteen, showing how to do a proper tea service. Twenty-two, officially joining the business as my mother's partner.

I look at that last photo of my mother and me standing in front of this very desk, both of us smiling. She is wearing her signature pearls, the ones that I keep in a velvet box because I just cannot bear to wear them. Her posture is perfect, her expression serene and confident. She never doubted herself, not a day in her life. If she did, she never let it show.

"I'm trying, Mother," I whisper to the empty room. "I'm trying so, so hard."

The studio does not answer. It just sits there, beautiful and useless, a monument to a world that no longer exists.

I am in the small kitchen at the back of the studio, stress eating the shortbread cookies I baked at three a.m. last Tuesday, when my phone rings and scares me.

I glance at the screen, thinking it will be Archie again or maybe one of my few remaining clients, but the number is unfamiliar. A Georgia area code, but definitely not Atlanta.

I swallow the last of the cookie and answer with my professional voice.

"Whitfield Etiquette, this is Eleanor speaking."

"Ms. Whitfield? Ms. Eleanor Whitfield?"

The voice is male, older, and with an accent that sounds like honey poured over gravel. Deep South, but not Atlanta South.

"Yes, this is she."

"Well, I am mighty glad I reached you. My name is Harlan Tucker, and I'm an attorney up here in Copper Creek, Georgia, calling you about your great aunt Mavis Flanigan."

I blink, searching the memory bank of my brain.

Mavis. The name sounds familiar, but only barely, like a shadow at the edge of family gatherings or maybe a name my mother mentioned with pursed lips and careful disapproval, as she did most people.

"I'm sorry, did you say Mavis Flanigan?"

"Yes, ma'am. Your grandmother's sister, if I've got my genealogy right. She passed away last week, and I'm the executor of her estate. She's left you something in her will, but I'm afraid you will need to come on up here to Copper Creek to sort it all out."

I sink onto the small stool that we keep in the kitchen, my mind racing. Great Aunt Mavis. I think I met her once, maybe twice, when I was really young. I remember her big hair, loud laughter, and my mother hustling me away with an unusual urgency.

"I am very sorry for your loss," I say automatically, the words feeling strange. "But I am not sure I understand. My mother never really spoke about her."

Harlan chuckles, a warm sound that crackles through the phone.

"Oh no, I don't imagine she did. Mavis was, well, she was something else. Your grandmother's family was not too pleased when she moved up here to the mountains and bought herself a bar."

"A bar?"

"Well, more of a honky tonk. The Rusty Spur. Been a fixture of Copper Creek for going on almost fifty years now. Mavis bought it about thirty-five years ago and ran it right up to the very end."

I have no idea what to say about any of this. I feel like I am in some sort of fever dream. My great-aunt, whom I barely remember, lived in a town I had never heard of and ran a bar. Sounds like the setup to a joke, except Harlan's voice is gentle and serious.

"Mr. Tucker, I do appreciate your calling, but I do not think this has anything to do with me. I mean, surely Aunt Mavis had other family or people who were closer to her."

"She did not, actually," he interrupts. "Mavis never married and never had children. Your grandmother, of course, passed on years ago, and your mother." He pauses delicately. "Well, Mavis kept track even if they did not speak. She knew that your mother passed. Sent flowers to the funeral, though I suspect you never even saw the card."

I did not. My mother's funeral was a blur of white lilies and murmured condolences. I was much too numb to notice anything.

"Ms. Whitfield, I do not want to get into too many details over the phone, but Mavis left you her entire estate - the bar, the property, everything. There are some conditions attached, which is why I need you to come up here in person. So, can you make it to Copper Creek sometime this week?"

I look around the kitchen, at the pile of bills on my desk, at the empty studio that is slowly bankrupting me. What do I have to lose? A nice little trip to the mountains might reset my brain and give me some new ideas.

"I can come tomorrow," I hear myself say. "What is the address?"

～

That night, I could not sleep. I lie in my bed, this queen-sized four-poster piece of furniture that came with my apartment and is too formal for any actual comfort, and I stare at the ceiling.

My mind keeps circling back to the phone call, to the name that apparently was buried in my memory for decades. Mavis Flanigan. The wild one. The black sheep.

I remember now. Fragments are resurfacing like debris after a shipwreck.

My mother's voice, tight with disapproval. "We don't discuss Aunt Mavis, Eleanor. She made her choices, and those weren't choices that a lady makes."

I was maybe seven years old, asking why we never visited the great aunt who sent me birthday cards with five-dollar bills tucked inside. My mother had taken the card from my hands, looked at it with distaste, and dropped it in the trash.

"Your grandmother's sister decided that propriety wasn't important to her. She left a perfectly good life in Atlanta to run some sort of 'establishment' in the mountains, and we don't associate with people who make those kinds of choices."

So I never asked again. My mother's word was law, and her disapproval was a force of nature that shaped my entire existence. So if she said we did not talk about Aunt Mavis, then Aunt Mavis simply did not exist.

But apparently Aunt Mavis did exist quite thoroughly. Enough to run a bar for thirty-five years. Enough to build a life in a town called Copper Creek. Enough to remember her great-niece in a will despite decades of family silence.

I get out of bed and walk to my laptop, opening it on the kitchen counter. I do a quick search for Copper Creek, Georgia, which brings up a modest Wikipedia entry.

Population one thousand eight hundred forty-seven. Located in the Blue Ridge Mountains. Known for its annual Bluegrass Festival and "charming small-town atmosphere."

I search for The Rusty Spur and find a Facebook page whose cover photo makes me physically recoil. It is an old wooden building with a big neon sign featuring a cowboy boot and a spur, the kind of place that probably has peanut shells on the floor and plays country music at volumes that violate noise ordinances.

The most recent post advertises a "Two-Step Tuesday," with a photo of people wearing jeans and cowboy boots line dancing.

Oh my goodness. My mother would have had a stroke.

I close my laptop and pour myself a glass of wine, a respectable Sancerre, because even at midnight, alone, I am my mother's daughter.

I walk to the window and look out at the Atlanta skyline, familiar and glittering.

What could Aunt Mavis possibly have left me? I mean, just the bar itself. I cannot imagine what I am going to do with a honky tonk in the mountains.

Sell it, probably. I can use the money to pay off my debts, keep the studio afloat for maybe another year while I figure out a new business model.

The thought brings a small flicker of hope, the first I have felt in many months.

Maybe this is the universe throwing me a lifeline. Maybe Great Aunt Mavis, in her death, will save me from the slow-motion disaster that my life has become.

I finish my glass of wine and go back to bed, but sleep still eludes me.

Instead, I find myself thinking about the birthday cards. The ones that my mother threw away. Five dollars every year, plus a note in handwriting I can barely remember.

What did those notes say? What did Aunt Mavis think about year after year as she sent cards to a great-niece she would never see?

I will never know.

She is gone, this woman I never really knew. And all

that is left is whatever she decided to leave behind
for me.

Tomorrow, I will drive to Copper Creek. I will meet
with Harlan Tucker, sign whatever papers are needed,
and figure out how to turn Aunt Mavis's legacy into
something useful.

A few days. A week at most. And then I will be back
in Atlanta. Back to the stack of bills and the empty
studio and the slow, genteel failure of everything my
mother built.

I can feel her criticism from beyond the grave.

I mean, it is a plan. It's not a good plan, but at least
it's something. It is more than I had when I woke up
this morning.

I finally fall asleep around three a.m., and I dream
about my mother.

She is standing in the studio, arranging flowers in a
vase and shaking her head slowly.

"Really, Eleanor?" she says in that voice that could
cut glass. "A bar? After everything I taught you?"

"I'm just going to sell it," I tell her, but she is already
turning away, disappearing into the shadows of the
studio.

And when I wake up, my pillow is damp. I cannot
remember if I was crying.

CHAPTER 2

I spend the morning packing a small bag, just enough for a few days, and canceling all of my appointments. It doesn't take long, since I have only two appointments scheduled all week.

I choose my outfit carefully: a cream silk blouse, navy slacks, and low heels. I want to be professional without looking ostentatious. I do not have any idea what one wears to inherit a honky tonk, but I refuse to show up looking anything less than put together.

Before I leave, I stand in the doorway of my studio one more time. The morning light catches the crystal chandelier my mother installed in 1995, sending little rainbows dancing across the walls. It is beautiful. It has always been beautiful, but it is also a cage, I realize suddenly. It is a gilded, elegant cage that I have been trapped in my whole life, trying to live up to standards set by a woman who never once told me I was enough.

I shake off the thought. This has to be grief talking, or exhaustion, or the stress of impending financial ruin in front of all of Buckhead's elite. My mother loved me. She just showed it through correction rather than praise, through pushing me to be better rather than just accepting me for who I was.

And who am I really?

I lock the door and head to my car, a sensible three-year-old Lexus sedan that's almost paid off. I enter Copper Creek, Georgia into my GPS and watch as the route pops up on the screen. Two hours north into the mountains, away from everything I know.

I have only been to the North Georgia mountains once, many years ago, when we had a meeting there at a winery. I do not remember much about it other than the beautiful blue hills off in the distance and the subpar wine that I drank.

"In five hundred feet, turn right," the GPS announces.

I take a breath, check my mirrors, and pull out of the parking lot.

Whatever is waiting for me in Copper Creek, I will handle it with the grace and efficiency I have been bred to exude, just like my mother taught me. I will sign the papers, sell the bar, and return to my real life. Simple, straightforward, completely under control.

The GPS guides me toward the highway, and I do not let myself think too much about those birthday cards that were in the trash, or the great aunt who remembered me when no one else really did, or the dream about my mother turning away.

I just drive.

~

The GPS has obviously lost its mind.

"In one mile, turn right onto Possum Hollow Road," the pleasant robotic female voice announces.

I grip my steering wheel tighter, convinced that I have somehow driven into an alternate dimension where road names are generated by some kind of random hillbilly word generator.

I have been driving for almost two hours, watching Atlanta's gleaming skyline shrink in my rearview mirror until it disappears entirely, replaced by rural scenery. The highway gave way to a state route, which gave way to a county road, which is now apparently giving way to something called Possum Hollow Road.

My Lexus feels very out of place here. The last twenty minutes have just been a parade of pickup trucks, some rusted, some lifted on enormous tires, but all of them making my sedan look like a lost tourist. Which I suppose I am.

I make the turn onto Possum Hollow Road and immediately hit a pothole that rattles my teeth. The road narrows, winding through the forest so thick that the trees form a canopy, dappling the pavement with shadows.

It is beautiful, I admit begrudgingly. The Blue Ridge Mountains rise in the distance, their peaks softened by a haze that makes them look like a watercolor painting.

I round a curve and nearly rear-end a tractor. Yes, an actual tractor. Moving approximately three miles per hour. It is driven by an elderly man in overalls who waves cheerfully at me as I slam on my brakes, my heart hammering against my chest.

There is no room to pass. The road is too narrow, the curve too blind.

I have no choice but to follow the tractor that would make a snail impatient.

"Recalculating," my GPS says, with what I swear is a tone of judgment.

"I'm not lost," I tell it, as if it understands me. "Just trapped behind agricultural equipment."

The GPS, of course, does not respond. It has probably given up on me.

Eventually, after what feels like seventy years, the tractor turns onto a dirt path, and the driver tips his John Deere cap at me as I finally accelerate past him. I wave back, my mother's training kicking in even when I am irritated beyond reason.

The road begins to descend, and suddenly I can see it. Copper Creek, Georgia, nestled in a valley below, like a toy village arranged on a Christmas train set.

It is small. Impossibly small.

I can see the whole downtown from up here, maybe three blocks of buildings clustered around what looks like a central square, surrounded by scattered little houses, and beyond those nothing but trees and mountains.

"You have arrived at your destination," the GPS announces as I enter the city limits.

I have *not* arrived at my destination. I have arrived at what appears to be the set of a Hallmark movie, complete with American flags hanging from every lamppost and flower baskets so aggressively cheerful they border on hostile.

The main street is called, with stunning originality, *Main Street.*

I drive slowly, looking at all the storefronts. Dixie's Diner. Sweet Tea Bakery. Mountain Hardware and Feed. The Clip Joint, which is a barber shop with an actual spinning pole. And something called Grits and Grind, which I assume is a coffee shop.

Every parking spot on Main Street is occupied by a pickup truck. Every single one.

I circle the block twice before I find a spot in front of the hardware store, and even then, I have to squeeze between a Ford F-150 and a Chevy truck that are both parked at angles suggesting that their drivers have never even heard of parallel parking.

I turn off the engine and sit there for a minute, staring at the town through my windshield.

A woman in a floral dress walks by carrying a casserole dish, waving at someone across the street. Two men in flannel shirts lean against the hardware store, drinking coffee from paper cups and laughing. A dog, unleashed, because apparently leash laws are suggestions here, trots down the sidewalk with a tennis ball in its mouth.

Everyone is moving slowly, deliberately, as if time itself is just taking a coffee break.

I check my reflection in my rearview mirror, smooth a non-existent flyaway from my French twist, and step out of my car.

The air hits me first. It is clean and cool, scented with pine. It is so different from Atlanta's humid exhaust that I actually pause to breathe it in.

"Nice car," someone says.

I turn to find an elderly woman looking at my Lexus with curiosity. She is wearing a purple track-suit and sneakers, her white hair permed into tight curls.

"You lost, honey?"

"No, I, well, I have an appointment with Harlan Tucker, the attorney."

The woman's face lights up.

"Oh, you must be Mavis's great-niece, the one from Atlanta." She says "Atlanta" the way someone might say "Mars." "Harlan's office is right up those stairs there, just above the hardware store. Go on up, the door's never locked."

"Thank you, I—"

But she has already moved on, waving at somebody else, leaving me standing on the sidewalk with the feeling that everybody in this town will know my business before I can even finish climbing the stairs.

I find the door she pointed to, a narrow entrance wedged between the hardware store and something called Birdie's Alterations, and climb a steep staircase that creaks under my low heels.

At the top, a frosted glass door reads Harlan Tucker, Attorney at Law, in gold lettering that is peeling at the edges.

I knock, and a voice calls out, "Come on in, it ain't locked."

The office is exactly what I expected and nothing like what I expected all at the same time. It is small, barely bigger than my studio's supply closet, and every available surface is covered with papers, books, and file folders. It looks like somebody's file cabinet exploded in here.

Bookshelves line three walls, stuffed with legal volumes and what appear to be local history books. A ceiling fan rotates lazily overhead, desperately needing dusting and stirring the warm air. The single window looks over Main Street, and through it I can see the town square with its white gazebo and towering oak trees.

Behind the massive wooden desk sits a man who looks like he was ordered out of a catalog of Southern lawyers. He looks to be in his sixties, with a shock of white hair that seems to have its own weather system, wild eyebrows that move expressively as he looks up at me, and a rumpled seersucker suit that has seen better decades. Reading glasses are perched on the top of his head, apparently forgotten as he squints at me.

"Ms. Whitfield." He rises, extending a hand with genuine warmth. "Well, I'd recognize those cheekbones anywhere. You look just like your great-aunt did at your age. God rest her soul. Please, sit down."

I shake his hand, firm grip, calloused palms, nothing like the limp fish handshakes of Atlanta's professional class, and settle into the chair across from his desk. It is surprisingly comfortable, worn leather that has molded to accommodate countless clients before me.

"Thank you for seeing me, Mr. Tucker. I have to admit, this was all very unexpected."

"Harlan, please. We don't stand on ceremony much around here." He settles back into his chair, which creaks in protest. "I imagine it was unexpected. Mavis told me you probably didn't know much about her."

"I didn't know anything about her, really. My mother…" I pause, trying to choose my words carefully. "My mother just didn't discuss her."

Harlan nods. "Your grandmother's family was what we might call particular about propriety. When Mavis left Atlanta back in '89 to buy a bar in the mountains, well, it did cause quite the scandal. They more or less pretended she ceased to exist."

"But she kept sending me birthday cards."

His eyebrows rise slightly. "Did she now? I didn't know that, but it sounds like Mavis. Stubborn as a mule about the people she loved, even when they didn't love her back."

Something in my chest tightens. "I mean, I never got to read them. I'm embarrassed to say that my mother threw them away."

Harlan makes a sound that conveys sympathy, understanding, and judgment toward my mother all at once.

"Well, Mavis knew that, knew the situation. She didn't hold it against you, dear, if that's what you're wondering. She kept track of you over the years. Your graduation, your engagement, your mother's passing. She was real proud of you, even from a distance."

I don't even know what to say to this. A woman I never knew was proud of me? It feels like receiving a gift I did not earn and cannot return.

"Mr. Tucker. Harlan. You mentioned on the phone that there were conditions attached to this inheritance."

"Well, straight to business. I appreciate that." He reaches into a drawer and pulls out a file considerably thicker than I expected. "Before we get into the particulars, I want you to understand something about Mavis. She was not just some bar owner. She was the heart of this community. When she bought The Rusty Spur, it was a failing roadhouse with a reputation for trouble. Well, she turned it into something quite special, a place where everybody was welcome, where folks came together, and where music and laughter meant something."

I nod politely, wondering where this is headed.

"When Mavis got sick—cancer—it moved fast. She spent a lot of time thinking about what would happen to the Spur after she was gone. She had no children, not even a spouse. Her closest living relative was you."

"But we never even met. Not really."

"No, you did not, and Mavis knew that. She knew you might not want anything to do with her bar or her town, but she also knew," he pauses, looking like he is choosing his words carefully, "she knew that sometimes people need a chance to become who they are supposed to be. She thought maybe you needed that chance."

I have no idea what he is talking about. I suspect my expression makes this clear.

Harlan chuckles. "Let me just read you the relevant portions of the will. Then you'll understand."

He opens the folder and pulls out a document covered in dense legal text.

"I will skip the boilerplate. Here is what matters. *I, Mavis Louise Flanigan, being of sound mind and ornery disposition.*" He glances up. "She insisted on that wording."

"Of course she did."

"Do hereby bequeath to my great-niece, Eleanor Grace Whitfield, the following: the property and business known as The Rusty Spur, located at 247 Mountain Road, Copper

Creek, Georgia, including all fixtures, equipment, inventory, and the residential apartment located on the second floor of said property."

I blink. "The apartment?"

"Mavis lived above the bar. It's a nice space, actually. She renovated it about ten years ago."

"I see." I am trying to calculate property values, wondering what a bar and an apartment in a tiny mountain town might be worth. Enough to pay off my debt? Enough to save the studio?

"There's more," Harlan says. Something in his tone makes my stomach clench.

"This bequest is made with the following conditions: Eleanor must maintain ownership of The Rusty Spur for a period of no less than six months from the date of my death. During this period, the bar must remain operational, maintaining regular business hours and honoring all existing commitments, including but not limited to, scheduled entertainment and community events."

"Six months?" My voice comes out higher than intended. "I have to keep the bar open for six months?"

"That is correct."

"But I do not know anything about running a bar. I teach etiquette classes."

"Well, that was an anticipated concern. *The current staff of The Rusty Spur, including the bar manager, Mr. Wyatt Rivers, will be retained and granted full authority to manage day-to-day operations. Eleanor's role is to maintain ownership and presence, but not to single-handedly operate the establishment.*"

"Presence? What does that mean?"

"It means you need to be here, in Copper Creek, for six months."

The room tilts slightly. I grip the arms of my chair, trying to process what he's saying to me.

Six months. Six months in this tiny town. This place with roads named for possums and tractor traffic, running a honky-tonk bar I have never even seen.

"What happens if I refuse? I mean, if I just don't accept this inheritance?"

Harlan's expression softens. "Well, then the property will go to First Baptist Church of Copper Creek to be sold and the proceeds used for their building fund. And Pastor Dale is a good man. He'd put the money to good use, but the bar would almost certainly be torn down. Developers been sniffing around this area for years, wanting to put up vacation condos."

"And if I accept, but don't fulfill the conditions? If I leave before the six months are over, or close the bar down?"

"Same result. Property goes to the church."

I stand up abruptly, moving to the window because I need to move around. I need to do something to abate the panic rising in my chest. Below me, Main Street is continuing its lazy afternoon existence, completely indifferent to the fact that my entire life is being upended.

"Harlan, I have a business in Atlanta. A studio. Clients."

These lies taste bitter on my tongue. I have three bored teenagers and a pile of unpaid bills. It is hardly a thriving enterprise.

"I can't just abandon everything for six months."

"I understand this is a lot to take in." His voice is patient. "Mavis knew it would be. That's why she left you the apartment rent-free. The bar is profitable, not wildly so, but it turns a decent income, so you wouldn't be struggling financially."

I turn back to face him. "Why? Why would she do this? She didn't even know me. I didn't know her. Why would she leave me everything and then trap me here for months?"

He is quiet for a long moment. "All I can say is that Mavis was a wise woman. She did this for reasons only she knew, but I believe they were good ones."

"I need to see it," I hear myself say. "The bar. Before I make any decisions, I would like to see what I'm dealing with."

He nods, as if he expected it. "The Rusty Spur's about a mile outside of town on Mountain Road. Can't miss it. Just follow the road, pass the church, and look for a neon boot. It's closed right now, but Wyatt should be there prepping for tonight. I'll call ahead and let him know you're coming."

"Wyatt. The manager."

"That's right. Good man, Wyatt Rivers. Mavis trusted him completely. You can, too."

I gather what's left of my composure and stick out my hand. "Thank you, Harlan. I'll be in touch."

His handshake is warm. "Take your time, Ms. Whitfield. This is a big decision. But if I might offer some unsolicited advice from an old country lawyer—"

"Please."

"Sometimes the things that scare us the most are exactly what we need. Mavis believed that. She lived it. Maybe she saw something in you that made her think you needed to learn it, too."

CHAPTER 3

Mountain Road is unsurprisingly a road that goes up a mountain. I drive slowly because the curves are sharp and unfamiliar, but also because I am delaying the inevitable. The forest presses close on both sides, broken occasionally by driveways that disappear into trees, leading to houses I cannot see.

I pass the First Baptist Church, white clapboard, tall steeple, and a sign out front reading: FREE COFFEE + ETERNAL LIFE.

I continue climbing. And then I see it.

The Rusty Spur announces itself with a giant neon sign that is visible even in daylight, a cowboy boot with a spinning spur, outlined in red and blue lights. The building itself is a very large wooden structure, weathered to a silvery gray, with a wide front porch and a parking lot that could hold at most thirty cars. There are string lights strung across the porch, unlit now, but promising evening festivity.

I pull into the parking lot and sit in my car, staring. How did I get here?

It is worse than I imagined, but somehow better. The building has a certain ramshackle charm, like a beloved old dog that has seen better days but still wags its tail. There are flower boxes on the porch. They look like they have been tended, with red geraniums spilling over the edges. A hand-painted sign on the door reads "WELCOME Y'ALL" in letters that are a little bit crooked, but enthusiastic.

I can hear music from inside. Country, of course. Something with steel guitar and lyrics about a truck or heartbreak or maybe both.

I take a deep breath, check my reflection one more time, and get out of the car. The porch steps creak under my heels. The front door is heavy, real wood, with a brass handle worn smooth by how many hands have touched it over the years.

I push it open and step inside.

The interior is dim, lit only by afternoon light filtering through the windows. They sure could use a good cleaning. My eyes adjust, and I begin to make out the details. A long wooden bar running along one wall, bottles of liquor glinting on shelves. Tables and chairs scattered around a scuffed wooden floor. A small stage in the corner, complete with a drum kit and a microphone stand. Mounted deer heads and vintage beer signs, string lights, and, inexplicably, a disco ball.

It smells like old wood and spilled beer and something else that I cannot quite identify. It definitely doesn't smell like my studio back in Atlanta.

Standing behind the bar, watching me with an expression I cannot read, is quite possibly the most attractive man I have ever seen in my life. He is tall, well over six feet, with broad shoulders that strain against a gray Henley shirt, sleeves pushed up to reveal forearms tanned, muscular, and tattooed. Dark hair with a slight curl at the ends. Square jaw covered in stubble. Blue eyes, startlingly so, that are currently examining me with a mixture of curiosity and something that might be amusement.

"Well, you must be Eleanor," he says. His voice is deep, with just enough Southern drawl to make my name sound like something musical. "Harlan called. Said you'd be coming by."

I straighten my spine, summon my mother's voice in my head. *Poised, Eleanor. Presence. Never let them see you sweat.*

"And you must be Wyatt Rivers," I say. "The manager."

"That's me." He sets down the glass he was polishing and walks around the bar, moving with such an easy confidence that shows he is completely comfortable in his own skin. What must that be like?

He is wearing worn jeans and work boots, and he looks like he belongs here in a way that I never will.

Wyatt extends his hand. "Welcome to The Rusty Spur."

I shake it, noting the calluses, the strength, the warmth. "Um, thank you. I'm here to assess this situation."

One corner of his mouth quirks up. "Assess the situation? That sounds official."

"Well, I've just come from Mr. Tucker's office. He explained the terms of the will."

"Oh, the six months thing," he says, nodding. "Yeah, Mavis told me about that before she passed. She wanted to make sure you'd give the place a real chance."

"A real chance of what exactly?"

He shrugs, his impressive shoulders rising and falling. "Well, that's something you'd have to figure out for yourself, I reckon. Mavis wasn't a woman who liked to explain herself. She just trusted that the reasons would make sense eventually."

I look around the bar again, trying to see it through objective eyes. Obviously, the floor needs refinishing. The windows definitely need cleaning, and the disco ball is just a crime against aesthetics. I don't think I've ever even seen a disco ball in person.

"How many people work here?"

"Four, including me. Dolly's been waitressing here for over thirty years. Boone handles security. He's a big guy, gentle as a lamb unless you give him a reason not to be. And Presley waits tables and tends the bar with me when she's not writing songs."

"Songs?"

"Well, she's a singer. Performs here sometimes. Mavis encouraged it."

Something flickers across his face. Grief, maybe? I do not know what to say to that. This man clearly loved my great aunt, and I am standing here in her bar, looking at property values and exit strategies. I didn't know her. This stranger knew her, and I didn't. It's so strange.

"The apartment upstairs," I say, changing the subject. "Can I see it?"

"Sure. Follow me."

He leads me through a door at the back of the bar, up a narrow staircase that is very clean and well-lit. At the top, he opens another door and steps aside to let me enter, but I am not prepared for what I find.

The apartment is wonderful. Completely, unexpectedly wonderful.

It is open and airy, with exposed wooden beams and large windows overlooking the mountains. The furniture is definitely eclectic. A velvet sofa in deep turquoise, mismatched armchairs, and a coffee table made from what looks like an old barn door. The walls are covered with art, vintage concert posters, local landscapes, photographs of people laughing and dancing, and everywhere, little touches of someone's personality.

I'm assuming my great aunt's.

A collection of cowboy boots is displayed on a shelf. A guitar is propped in the corner. Books are stacked on almost every surface. A kitchen with copper pots hanging from a rack and herbs growing in the window.

It looks like someone actually lived here. Someone who was very happy. It is like I walked into the middle of someone's life. It feels comfortable and uncomfortable at the same time.

"Mavis had good taste," Wyatt says from the doorway. "Different than probably what you're used to in Atlanta, but good."

I look at him. "You knew her well."

"She gave me a job when I needed one. Gave me a purpose when I had lost mine. She was," he pauses, and I see him swallow hard, "she was the best person I ever knew."

The sincerity in his voice makes something crack inside my carefully constructed composure. This is not just a bar to him. It is not just a job. It is a home, a family, and a life.

And I am jealous of him in this moment, that he knew my great aunt so well, and I knew nothing.

How did I miss out on knowing the greatest person someone ever knew?

I am just the outsider who has inherited all of this.

"I haven't decided yet," I tell him, because I need him to know that, to be honest about at least this much. "I mean, whether I'll stay, whether I'll accept the conditions."

He nods slowly. "That's your choice to make, ma'am. But if you do decide to walk away," he meets my eyes, "just know that what you're walking away from is more than a building. It's more than a business. It's over thirty-five years of Mavis's heart and the hearts of everyone who loved her."

He turns and walks back down the stairs, leaving me alone in my great-aunt's apartment, surrounded by the life of a woman I never knew.

I sit on the turquoise sofa and look out the window at the mountains. I try to imagine spending six months in this place. Months of pickup trucks and twangy accents and a bar called The Rusty Spur. Months of small-town nosiness and country music, and a blue-eyed manager who looks at me like he is trying to figure out if I am worth trusting.

Months of being someone other than Eleanor Whitfield, etiquette instructor, keeper of her mother's legacy, and professional failure.

The thought is terrifying.

It is also, I realize with surprise, the first thing that has made me feel anything at all in years.

I have some big decisions to make.

For now, I will just sit in Mavis's apartment, watch the sun set over the Blue Ridge Mountains, and wonder what on earth I have gotten myself into.

I have made a terrible mistake.

That is the thought that is running through my mind over and over as I stand in the doorway at The Rusty Spur on a Friday night, frozen like a deer caught in the headlights of approximately forty pickup trucks' worth of patrons.

This bar is packed, wall-to-wall with people wearing denim and flannel and cowboy boots, laughing and shouting over music so loud I can feel the bass vibrating in my chest. The disco ball I noticed yesterday is spinning now, casting fractured light across the dance floor, where couples are doing something complicated with their feet that I could not replicate if my life depended on it. It is certainly not the waltz.

And every single person in this establishment is staring at me.

I am wearing a pencil skirt. *A pencil skirt.* Navy blue, perfectly tailored, paired with a cream silk blouse and my mother's pearls. I spent forty-five minutes on my hair, pinning it into an elegant chignon that says, "Professional businesswoman here to assess her inheritance." But what it actually says, apparently, is "Lost tourist who wandered in looking for the nearest Whole Foods."

A woman at a nearby table leans over to her companion and says in a voice that carries perfectly despite the noise, "Well, bless her heart, she must be from the city."

I have been in Georgia long enough to know that "bless her heart" is rarely a compliment.

The smart thing to do would be to leave, go back to the little bed-and-breakfast where I spent last night. It is the only available accommodation in Copper Creek, run by a woman named Mabel who asked me seventeen questions about my marital status over breakfast. Regroup. Return tomorrow during daylight hours when I can conduct a proper inspection without an audience.

But I am Eleanor Whitfield, and Whitfields do not retreat.

I straighten my spine, lift my chin, and walk into the chaos.

The crowd parts for me like I am Moses approaching the Red Sea, if Moses had been wearing Ferragamo pumps and attracting bewildered stares.

I walk toward the bar, where I can see Wyatt pulling beers from the tap with the easy efficiency of someone who has done it about ten thousand times. I've never even touched a beer or a tap.

He sees me coming. Of course he does. Those blue eyes track my progress across the room, and I watch his expression shift from surprise to what appears to be concern.

"Ms. Whitfield." He sets down the beers he has just poured and leans against the bar, his arms crossed over his chest. The Henley he wears tonight is black, and it does nothing to diminish the breadth of his shoulders. I must stop noticing such things. Maybe the mountain air is affecting me. "I didn't expect to see you here tonight."

"I own this place," I remind him, raising my voice to be heard over the music. "I have every right to be here."

"Well, I never said you didn't." The hint of a smile plays at the corner of his mouth again. "Just figured you'd want to ease into things. Friday nights at the Spur are a lot."

As if to illustrate his point, someone behind me lets out a whoop that could probably be heard in the next county, followed by very enthusiastic applause as the band on stage launches into a new song.

"I can handle 'a lot'," I say, with air quotes and more confidence than I actually feel. "I'd like to observe the operations, see how things run."

"All right, suit yourself." Wyatt gestures to an empty stool at the end of the bar. "Have a seat. I'd offer you a drink, but I'm guessing you're not a Bud Light kind of woman."

"I don't drink beer." I sound snooty. Actually, I sound like my mother.

"Color me shocked," he says, putting his hand on his chest. He is now smiling, and I cannot tell if I am irritated or something else. "So what's your poison?"

"I'll have a glass of Sancerre, if you have it."

Wyatt raises an eyebrow. He looks at the young

woman working the bar beside him, early twenties, auburn hair in a messy braid, wearing a vintage Dolly Parton t-shirt.

"Hey, Presley, we got any fancy French wine?"

The young woman, Presley, apparently, looks at me with curiosity. "We've got a Chardonnay that comes in a box. That close enough?"

I open my mouth to decline, but something in their expressions stops me. They are not being mean. Not exactly. They are just testing me, seeing what I am made of.

"That will be fine," I say. I've never drunk wine from a box, but I suppose there's a first time for everything.

Presley grins, and then her face transforms from pretty to genuinely beautiful. "Coming right up. You must be Mavis's niece, the one from Atlanta."

"Great-niece, and yes."

"I'm Presley Tucker. Harlan's my uncle."

She pours wine into a glass that is definitely not a proper wine glass. It is a mason jar, because of course it is, and slides it across the bar to me. I've also never drunk anything from a mason jar. Wow, so many firsts tonight.

"Mavis talked about you sometimes. Said you were fancy."

"I'm not," I start, and then stop. By every measure that these people would use, I am absolutely fancy. Denying it would make me look foolish. "I guess I am, by some standards."

"Well, there's nothing wrong with fancy," Presley says. "It's just different, is all. Mavis always said different was good. Kept things interesting."

Before I can respond, a large hand lands on the bar beside me, and I turn to find myself face to face with the biggest human being I have ever seen in my entire life. He is easily six and a half feet tall, broad as a barn door, with a shaved head and a full beard, but his eyes are surprisingly gentle.

"You're the new owner." It is not a question. It is a statement. And even if I wasn't the new owner, I would say I was because this man could squish me with his pinky finger.

"I am. Eleanor Whitfield."

"Boone Davidson." He puts out his hand that could probably crush my skull like a grape, and I shake it. His grip is carefully controlled. "I handle security. Anything you need, you let me know."

"Thank you, Boone. I appreciate that."

He nods once, satisfied with the exchange, and moves away to resume his position near the door. I watch him go, marveling at how somebody so massive can move so quietly.

"Don't let his size fool you," Wyatt says. "Boone's the gentlest soul in this county. Mavis used to say he was proof that God had a sense of humor, because he put the heart of a poet in the body of a linebacker."

"He writes poetry?"

"Reads it mostly, but yeah, he's written a few. Won't

show them to anybody, though." Wyatt pours another round of beers for a customer. "Mavis was the only one he ever let read them."

There it is again, the shadow that crosses his face whenever he mentions my great aunt, the grief that is still clearly fresh for him.

"You all loved her very much," I say, as quietly as I can over the music.

Wyatt's hands are still on the tap, and for a moment, he does not even look at me. When he does, his expression is unreadable.

"She was family, not by blood but by choice. And that means a lot around here."

"I'm beginning to see that."

"Are you?" He holds my gaze, and there is a challenge in his eyes. "Because from where I am standing, you're here to figure out how to get through the next six months with minimum involvement so you can sell this place and go back to your real life."

The accuracy of his assessment stings a little more than it should.

"I haven't decided anything yet," I say, which is technically true. "I'm still assessing."

"Assessing." He says the word like it tastes bad. "Right. Well, you assess away, Ms. Whitfield. Just try not to get in anyone's way."

He moves down the bar to serve another customer, leaving me on my stool with my mason jar of boxed wine and the feeling that I just failed a test I didn't know I was taking.

The next hour is an education.

I sit at my post at the end of the bar, drinking my wine, which is not terrible, and watching The Rusty Spur in action. It is total chaos, but it's an organized chaos. Everybody seems to know their role, moving around each other like dancers in a choreographed routine.

Wyatt handles the bar with quiet authority, mixing drinks and pouring beers, and somehow managing to have a conversation with every customer who approaches. He remembers their names, asks about their families, and laughs at jokes I cannot hear over the music. The patrons clearly adore him.

Presley works beside him, faster and flashier, spinning bottles and flirting harmlessly. She has a natural charm that draws people in. And I notice she knows the words to every single song the band plays, singing along as she works.

Then there is Dolly.

I notice her about twenty minutes into my observation. A woman in her sixties with platinum blonde hair teased to impressive heights, rhinestone reading glasses hanging from a beaded chain around her neck, and an energy level that puts people half her age to shame. She walks through the crowded tables with trays of drinks and plates of food, never spilling a drop, no matter how much chaos is around her.

But what strikes me most is how she interacts with the customers. Every table gets a smile and a touch on the shoulder, a moment of genuine connection. She calls everybody darlin' and sugar and honey, and it does not sound performative. It sounds like she means it.

At one point, she walks up to an elderly man sitting alone at a corner table, and I watch her crouch down to his level, taking his weathered hand in hers. They talk for a long moment, and when she stands, she is dabbing at her eyes. She squeezes his shoulder, says something that makes him laugh, and then moves on to the next table.

"That's Earl," Wyatt says, appearing beside me. I didn't even see him walk up. "His wife passed away last month. They used to come in here on Friday nights and dance the night away. Now, he comes in every Friday because he can't stand being alone. And Dolly makes sure he doesn't have to be."

I look over at Earl, his hunched shoulders and the way he is clutching his beer like a lifeline. And then I look at Dolly, who is already charming another table into ordering dessert.

"She's really remarkable," I say.

"She is." Wyatt's voice softens. "She's been working here for so long. Mavis hired her when nobody else would. Single mom with a GED and a deadbeat ex. Gave her a chance when she needed one."

It's a theme, I'm realizing. Mavis giving people chances, building her own family out of people who needed one when her own family abandoned her. Collecting weary souls and knitting them together into something beautiful.

"Why are you telling me all this?"

Wyatt meets my eyes. "Because you should know what you're dealing with. This isn't just some business. It's not just numbers on a spreadsheet or a property you need to 'assess'. This is people's lives. Their livelihoods. Their home."

"I understand that."

"Do you?" He shakes his head. "I'm not trying to be harsh. I just need you to see it. I mean, really see it before you make any decisions."

Before I can respond, a commotion near the door draws our attention. Two men square off, chests puffed, voices rising above the music. One shoves the other, and suddenly the bar's happy chaos has an edge of danger.

Wyatt is moving before I can blink, crossing the room in long strides that eat up the distance. I expect him to wade in with his fists. He certainly has the build for it.

But instead, he steps between them, his hands raised, his voice calm. Boone stands on the outskirts, obviously waiting for Wyatt to say the word before stepping in.

I cannot hear what Wyatt is saying over the music, but I can see the effect. The tension in both men's shoulders eases. One of them actually laughs, shaking his head.

Wyatt claps them both on the back, gestures toward the bar, and just like that, a potential fight dissolves into handshakes and what looks like an offer to buy each other drinks.

"He's good at that," Presley says, walking closer. "Wyatt, I mean. Diffusing things. Mavis always said he could talk a tornado into changing direction."

"And where do you think he learned that?"

"Army, mostly. He did three tours overseas. Came back a bit broken. Mavis helped with that, too." Presley's eyes are on Wyatt as he guides the two former combatants over to the bar. "She helped all of us one way or another."

I watch Wyatt pour shots for the men. Watch them clink glasses and drink. Watch the whole incident fade into nothing. He catches me looking and raises an eyebrow as if to say, see, this is what it takes.

I raise my mason jar of wine in acknowledgment.

His lips twitch, almost a smile, before he turns back to his customers.

CHAPTER 4

The band takes a break around ten o'clock, and the energy in the bar shifts. People drift toward the bar for refills, cluster in groups to chat, or head outside to get some fresh air. The sudden relative quiet feels kind of strange after hours of constant noise.

Dolly appears at my end of the bar, sliding onto the stool beside me with a sigh of relief.

"Lord, have mercy, my feet are staging a rebellion."

She kicks off one shoe and rubs the arch of her foot, completely unselfconscious about it.

"You must be Eleanor. I'm Dolly."

"I figured. It's nice to meet you."

"Uh-huh." She looks me up and down with a frank assessment. "Mavis said you'd be pretty. She was right. Got those family cheekbones."

"Yeah, everybody keeps saying that. I didn't realize our cheekbones were a known feature."

"Mavis told us all about your family and even showed us pictures a time or two. Your grandmother and Mavis sure looked a lot alike." Dolly points to Presley for a glass of sweet tea. "Mavis used to say her sister traded her soul for a Buckhead address. I mean, no offense."

"None taken. I'm actually fascinated. No one in my family ever talked about Mavis. What was she like?" I ask. "Mavis, I mean. Everybody talks about her, but I never…" I trail off, not really sure how to finish that sentence.

Dolly's expression softens.

"Oh, she was a force of nature. That's what she was. Stubborn as a mule, generous as a saint, but absolutely terrible at minding her own business."

She laughs, a warm sound that crinkles the corners of her eyes.

"You know, that woman would give you the shirt off her back and then tell you exactly what she thought of your life choices while helping you put it on."

"Well, that sounds… intense."

"Oh, it was. But here's the thing you need to know about Mavis. She never told you anything she wouldn't tell herself. She was much harder on herself than anyone else. She held herself to the same standards she held everyone else to."

Dolly takes a long sip of her tea.

"When she got sick, she didn't want anyone to know. Kept working right up until she couldn't anymore. Wyatt had to practically carry her upstairs those last few weeks."

I think about Wyatt's face when he talks about Mavis, the grief that still looks so raw.

"He loved her."

"Sugar, we all did. But Wyatt…" Dolly shakes her head. "He came back from overseas all broken up inside. Not physically. I mean, some of that too. But in his heart. In his spirit. And Mavis saw it. She gave him a job, a purpose, a reason to keep going. She saved his life, and he knows it."

The band is returning to the stage, instruments being tuned and adjusted, and the noise level is rising again.

"Dolly, why are you telling me all this?"

She looks at me with eyes that have seen decades of joy and sorrow.

"Because Mavis believed in you. I don't know why, 'cause she never explained it, but she was convinced you were supposed to be here. That you needed this place as much as it needed you." She pats my hand with fingers that are surprisingly soft, despite years of hard work. "I'm just trying to help you see what she saw. The rest of it's up to you."

The band launches into their next set, and Dolly slips off her stool, sliding her feet back into her work shoes with a grimace.

"Duty calls, honey. You need anything, just holler."

She is gone before I can respond, weaving through the crowd with her tray held high.

❧

By midnight, I am exhausted in a way I have not been in years. I have spent the past four hours watching, listening, and trying to understand this place I have somehow inherited.

I have seen Wyatt break up two more potential fights, each time with that same calm authority. I have watched Presley perform a song during one of the band's breaks, her voice clear and haunting, and understood why Mavis encouraged her to pursue her passion. I have seen Boone gently escort a drunk patron outside and then make sure he had a safe ride home. I have watched Dolly comfort and charm her way through dozens of interactions.

And I have seen the customers. The regulars who greet each other like family. The couples on the dance floor who have clearly been doing this for decades. The young people who are learning the steps from their elders. I have seen birthday celebrations and anniversary toasts, and what I am pretty sure was some kind of informal engagement. I mean, the woman said yes, the bar erupted into cheers, and Wyatt poured free shots for everyone.

It is not what I expected. It is not the rough, dangerous roadhouse I imagined when I heard I had inherited a honky-tonk bar. It is something else entirely. Something I do not even have a word for.

The crowd is starting to thin out when Wyatt appears beside me again.

"Closing time is in thirty minutes. You've been here for hours. You must be tired."

"I'm fine," I say. And then yawn, my jaw cracking loudly.

He almost smiles. "Okay. Right. Fine. You know, you can go upstairs whenever you want. The apartment is yours."

I had almost forgotten about the apartment. The charming, eclectic space that was Mavis's home. That is apparently now mine, at least for the next six months.

"I should probably just stay at the bed and breakfast," I say. "I don't want to impose."

"Um, it's not imposing, because it's *your* apartment," Wyatt says, shrugging. "But suit yourself. Mabel's biscuits are worth the interrogation about your love life."

"She asked me if I had a 'special fella' three times during breakfast."

He laughs. "Only three? She must like you. She asked me seven times at church last Sunday."

The image of this rugged, tattooed man sitting in a little church pew while an elderly woman grills him about his romantic prospects is so absurd, so unexpected, that I actually laugh out loud.

"You should do that more often," Wyatt says quietly.

"Do what?"

"Laugh. You look different when you laugh. Less like you're waiting for someone to grade you."

The observation cuts a little too close to home. I look away, focusing on the last few customers gathering their things to leave.

"I should go," I say. "It's late."

"It is."

He does not move to let me pass.

"Ms. Whitfield. I mean, Eleanor. I know I've been hard on you tonight. I just, I need you to understand what's at stake here."

"I think I'm beginning to."

"Good."

He steps aside, finally giving me room to slide off my stool.

"For what it's worth, Mavis was never wrong about people. And if she thought you belonged here, then maybe you should consider she knew something that you don't."

I do not know how to respond to that, so I just nod and make my way toward the door.

The night air hits me as I step outside, cool and clean, heavy with the scent of pine. The parking lot is nearly empty now, my Lexus looking lonely among the remaining trucks.

I am halfway to my car when I hear it, music coming from inside. It is not the band. They have packed up and gone home. This is softer, simpler. It is just a guitar and a voice.

I turn back and look through the window.

Inside the bar, it's mostly dark, with chairs upturned on tables. But on the small stage, illuminated by one single light, sits Presley with a guitar, playing something slow and sad. Wyatt is behind the bar, wiping down the counter, but he has stopped to listen.

The song is about leaving home and finding your way back, and the people who wait for you, who keep the light on, who love you even when you don't deserve it.

I stand in the parking lot of my great-aunt's bar, in a town I had never even heard of a week ago, and feel something crack open in my chest.

I do not know what Mavis saw in me. I do not know why she thought I belonged here.

But standing here in the dark, under the shadow of the Blue Ridge Mountains, listening to Presley sing about home, I feel something I have not felt in a very long time.

Hope.

The Copper Creek Bed and Breakfast has betrayed me.

"I'm so sorry, honey," Mabel says, wringing her hands as if she is genuinely distressed. "The bluegrass festival starts tomorrow, and I've got folks coming in from three states. Every single room is booked solid through Sunday."

I stand in her doily-covered parlor, my overnight bag at my feet, trying to process what she is saying. It is Saturday morning, and I have been in Copper Creek for less than forty-eight hours, but I am already homeless.

"Isn't there another hotel? A motel, maybe?"

Mabel shakes her head, her silver curls bouncing. "Nearest one's forty-five minutes down the mountain, and honey, they'll be full up too. This festival brings in folks from all over. It's our biggest weekend of the year."

Of course it is. Of course, the one weekend I desperately need accommodation is the one weekend where every available bed within a fifty-mile radius is occupied by banjo enthusiasts.

"Okay, what about a vacation rental? Airbnb?"

"A what now?"

I close my eyes and try to count to ten in my head. When I open them, Mabel is looking at me with a sympathy usually reserved for lost puppies or people who have received bad medical news.

"You know," she says slowly, "Mavis's apartment is empty, and it's yours now, isn't it? It seems a shame to let it go to waste when you need a place to stay."

The apartment. The charming, eclectic, aggressively

quirky apartment above the bar that I am not sure I want to own. The apartment where my great aunt lived for thirty-five years, surrounded by cowboy boots, concert posters, and a life I cannot begin to understand.

"I couldn't possibly."

"Why not?" Mabel interrupts, tilting her head like a curious bird. "It's got everything you need. A bed, a bathroom, a kitchen. And again, it's yours, legally speaking. Harlan drew up those papers himself, didn't he?"

She isn't wrong. I mean, the apartment is mine, at least for the next six months. And my other options appear to be sleeping in my car or driving forty-five minutes to a motel that is probably full.

"I suppose," I say slowly. "It would be the practical choice."

Mabel smiles like she has just solved world hunger. "That's the spirit. And don't you worry about a thing. I'll send some of my blueberry muffins over with Pastor Dale's wife. She's heading your direction anyway."

Before I can protest or ask why Pastor Dale's wife would be heading toward a honky-tonk bar, Mabel is ushering me right out the door with promises of baked goods and assurances that everything will work out just fine.

I sit in my car for a long moment, staring at the façade of the bed and breakfast that has just evicted me. Then I pull out my phone and do something I have been avoiding since I arrived.

I call my best friend.

Cynthia answers on the second ring.

"Eleanor, finally! I've been dying to hear about this mysterious inheritance. Is it fabulous? Oh my gosh, please tell me it's fabulous. Is it like a villa in Tuscany? Maybe a penthouse in Manhattan?"

"It's a honky-tonk bar in the Blue Ridge Mountains with a giant neon boot outside."

Silence.

Then, "Oh. I'm sorry. I think I misheard you. It sounded like you said—"

"Yes. A honky-tonk bar called The Rusty Spur, complete with a neon cowboy boot sign and a disco ball."

More silence.

Then Cynthia starts laughing. Great, howling laughs that make me hold the phone away from my ear for fear of eardrum rupture.

"Oh my gosh," she gasps. "Oh my gosh. Eleanor, your mother must be spinning in her grave."

"That's not funny."

"Well, it's a little funny." She is still giggling. "Eleanor Whitfield, etiquette instructor to Atlanta's elite, owner of a honky-tonk bar. You just can't make this stuff up."

"Oh, there's more." I take a breath. "I have to keep it

for six months. Live here. Keep it operational. Or it goes to the local church."

The laughter stops.

"Wait. You have to live there for six months?"

"That's what the will says."

"But what about the studio and your clients?"

I think about my three bored teenagers, my empty appointment book, and my pile of unpaid bills.

"I'll figure something out."

"Eleanor." Cynthia's voice has gone serious, which is a rarity. "Are you okay? This is a lot."

"I'm fine," I say automatically. "I'm just adjusting."

"Adjusting to what? Country music and cowboy boots?"

"Something like that."

I watch a pickup truck rumble past, its bed loaded with musical instrument cases.

"I'd better go. I need to move into my apartment."

"Your apartment above the bar?"

"Yep."

"The honky-tonk bar?"

"Yes, Cynthia."

She is quiet for a moment.

"Call me tonight. I want to hear everything. And Eleanor?"

"What?"

"Maybe it isn't the worst thing that could ever happen. I mean, maybe it's what you need."

She hangs up before I can ask her what she means.

~

The Rusty Spur looks very different in daylight, without the neon sign blazing and the parking lot full of trucks. It is almost a peaceful place. The weathered wood of the building glows in the warm morning sun, and I can hear birds singing in the trees that border the property. A creek, I am assuming Copper Creek, runs behind the building, its gentle burbling audible in the quiet.

I park my Lexus in the empty lot and sit for a minute, trying to gather my courage. I grab my overnight bag and head for the side entrance Wyatt showed me yesterday, the one that leads directly to the apartment stairs. The door is unlocked, because of course it is. I am learning that locked doors are apparently an optional thing in Copper Creek.

I called Cynthia again this morning, and she will be mailing some of my belongings to me. Just enough to get through six months. I won't need all of my things because the odds of my staying here are slim to none.

I climb the stairs slowly, my heels clicking on the wooden steps. At the top, I pause with my hand on the doorknob, suddenly feeling a rush of reluctance to enter. This was Mavis's space, her home. Walking in feels like I am trespassing, even though I technically own it now.

I push open the door anyway.

The apartment is just as I remember it from my

brief visit, eclectic, colorful, and utterly unlike anything I have ever lived in. The turquoise velvet sofa looks even more inviting in daylight, piled with throw pillows in various patterns that really should not work together, but somehow do.

I set my bag down and start to explore properly.

The kitchen is small but well-equipped, with copper pots hanging over a rack that I vaguely remember from my first visit. There is a collection of cast-iron skillets that look older than I am. The refrigerator is empty except for a box of baking soda and a bottle of hot sauce, but the pantry is actually stocked with basics like flour, sugar, and spices in mismatched jars.

The bathroom is a riot of turquoise tile and vintage fixtures, including a big clawfoot tub that makes me want to take a bath right now, even though I showered this morning. Fluffy towels in sunset hues hang from brass hooks, and a collection of bath products on a shelf smells of lavender and honey.

The bedroom stops me in my tracks.

It is dominated by a queen-sized bed with an iron frame, its quilt homemade-looking. Handmade. Intricate patterns in deep reds and blues and golds stitched together with such obvious care.

For a moment, it reminds me that my mother would never have done such a thing. Make a quilt? Absolutely not.

There are more pillows, more colors, more person-ality than my entire Atlanta apartment combined.

But what catches my attention is the wall above the bed.

It is covered in photographs.

There are dozens of them, maybe hundreds, arranged in an overlapping collage that takes over the entire wall. Photos of people laughing, dancing, and hugging. Photos of the bar through the years. I can see it evolving from a rough roadhouse into the welcoming space it is today. Photos of Mavis herself at various ages, surrounded by people, always smiling.

It strikes me for a moment how little I ever saw my mother or grandmother smile.

Why were they so different from Mavis?

I step closer and study the faces. There is Dolly looking younger, with the same impressive hair. Boone is slightly less massive but has the same gentle eyes. And Wyatt, in what looks like some kind of military uniform, is standing stiff and serious next to a beaming Mavis.

Then, in the corner, almost hidden among the others, I see a photo I recognize.

It's me.

Maybe eight years old, in a pink dress with a white collar, my hair in pigtails, standing in front of a Christmas tree, holding a wrapped present, and smiling at the camera with gap-toothed enthusiasm.

I do not recall this photo being taken. I certainly do not remember sending it to anyone.

But somehow, Mavis has it.

Somehow, she kept it all these years, displayed among her most treasured memories.

My throat tightens, so I reach out and touch the edge of the photo, feeling the slight curl of the aged paper.

She knew me. Not personally, and not really, but she knew me. She watched me grow up from a distance, collected evidence of my existence, and cared enough to keep a photo of a great-niece she had never been allowed to know.

And I never even knew her name until a week ago.

The guilt is sudden and overwhelming.

I sink onto the edge of the bed, staring at the wall of memories, and feel the weight of everything I missed. Every birthday card my mother threw away. Every connection severed before it could even form. Every chance to know this woman who apparently loved me anyway.

"She started that wall the year she bought the bar."

I spin around, heart hammering in my chest, and see Wyatt standing in the doorway of the bedroom, looking slightly uncomfortable.

"I knocked," he says. "Downstairs. You didn't answer."

"I was… distracted." I gesture vaguely at the wall.

He nods and steps into the room, but keeps a respectful distance.

"She added to it every year. Said it helped her remember why she did what she did. All those people, all those moments, that's what the bar was really about."

"There's a photo of me." My voice comes out strange and thick. "I didn't know she had it. I don't remember it."

"She had a lot of things." Wyatt moves to stand beside me, looking at the wall. "Letters. Photos. Newspaper clippings. She kept track of you best she could. Your graduations. Your engagement announcement. Your mother's obituary."He pauses. "She cried when your mom died. Even after everything, she cried."

"They never spoke. My mother and Mavis. Not once in all the years I was alive, that I know of."

"No, but that didn't mean Mavis stopped loving her or you. Mavis had more love in her heart than anyone I've ever known. If you take away nothing else from this experience, just know what a phenomenal human she was."

He turns to look at me, and his expression is softer than I have seen it.

"She talked about you sometimes. Wondered what you were like and if you were happy. She worried about you."

"She didn't even know me."

"She knew enough." Wyatt shrugs. "You see, Mavis

had this gift for seeing people. Like really seeing them. Not just what they showed the world. She saw something in you that made her believe you needed to be here."

I think about what Dolly said last night. What Harlan said. What everyone keeps saying. That Mavis believed in me. That she thought I belonged here. That she was never wrong about people.

"What if she was wrong this time?" I ask quietly. "Like, what if I'm not what she thought I was?"

Wyatt is quiet for a long moment.

Then he says, "Well, there's only one way to find out."

CHAPTER 5

After Wyatt leaves - he came by to drop off a spare key and check that I had everything I needed - I spend the afternoon settling in.

I unpack my small amount of belongings, hanging my clothes in a closet that is still full of Mavis's things. It feels kind of strange. Her wardrobe is as eclectic as her decor. She has vintage Western shirts, flowing bohemian dresses, and a surprising number of sequin items that I can only assume were for theme nights at the bar. I push them to the side, making room for my pencil skirts and silk blouses, and try not to feel imposter syndrome.

I make a quick grocery list based on what is in the pantry and then realize I have no idea where the grocery store is, so I add 'find grocery store' to the list.

I try to connect to the Wi-Fi only to discover that the password is MavisRocks1989, and the connection is slower than anything I have ever experienced since the dial-up era.

By late afternoon, I am restless and frustrated and desperately in need of something productive to do. And that is when I remember the bar's financial records.

Harlan mentioned that the bar was profitable, and Wyatt confirmed it had been running smoothly, but I am a businesswoman, or I was before my business failed, so I need to see the numbers for myself.

I find the office downstairs, a small room behind the bar, crammed with filing cabinets and a desk that has seen better days. The computer is ancient, running some version of Windows I didn't know still existed, but it turns on, and that's what matters.

The financial records are, in a word, a mess.

Not in a bad way, exactly. More in a 'this system was designed by someone who valued intuition over organization' way.

There are spreadsheets, but they are labeled things like 'Money Stuff 2023' and 'That Thing Harlan Needed'. There are folders full of receipts, some organized by date, some by vendor, and some apparently just by vibe.

But as I dig deeper, a picture starts to emerge.

The Rusty Spur is definitely profitable. Not wildly so. I mean, it is not a gold mine, but it is solidly and consistently profitable. Revenue has grown steadily, but slowly, over the past decade. Expenses seem reasonable, and the staff is paid fairly.

There is even a small emergency fund that Mavis called the *'Oh Crap Account'*.

More interesting than the numbers, though, are the notes.

Mavis kept notes on everything. She scribbled in margins, stuck Post-its everywhere, and typed in random documents scattered across the desktop.

Notes about customers, such as *'Earl's wife is sick, comp his drinks this month'*.

There were notes about staff, like, *'Presley's birthday is March 15, and she likes carrot cake'*.

There were, of course, notes about business, like, *'Theme night idea: Redneck wedding reception - tacky decorations, bouquet toss, and fake ceremonies'*.

I find a document titled, *'IF I DIE'*, and my heart clinches before I even open it.

It's a letter to me.

Eleanor,

If you are reading this, I am dead, and you are probably confused as heck. I am sorry about that. I was never very good at explaining myself.

I know you do not know me. Your mama and your grandmama made sure of that. I don't like to speak ill of the dead, but since I am one now, I feel like that rule no longer applies.

I don't blame either one of them. We were all such

different people who wanted different things, and they thought they were protecting you. Maybe they were.

Here is the thing. I have watched you from a distance your whole life, and I have seen something your mama could not see. You are not happy. You might be successful at times. You are polished, for sure. You are everything she wanted you to be, but you are not happy.

I know because I was you once, trying to be what everybody expected, following rules I did not make, suffocating in a life that looked perfect from the outside. Then I came here, and I found something different. I found a place where I could be myself, that messy, loud, and perfect real person. I found people who love me not because I was proper or refined, but because I showed up and cared.

I'm leaving you the bar because I think you need what I found. And if I don't leave it to you, well, you just might never find it yourself. It is a chance to figure out who you are when you are not performing for anyone. A place to be graceless and still be loved.

Just give it those six months, honey. That is all I ask. Six months to try something different.

Of course, if you hate it, if you are miserable, you can sell it and go back to your life. But give yourself the chance to find out.

And Eleanor, please be kind to Wyatt. He has been through more than you know, and he is going to be prickly about you at first, I think. But he is the best man I have ever known. And if you let him, he will show you what this place is really about.

I love you, even though we have never met. And I hope you find what you're looking for.

Your Aunt Mavis

P.S. The secret to my barbecue sauce is a splash of bourbon and a tablespoon of instant coffee. Do not tell anyone. I will haunt you.

I read the letter three times, and then I close it and sit in the cramped office surrounded by her chaotic filing system and let the tears fall for a woman I never met.

I am still in the office when Wyatt finds me. It is after ten p.m., and the bar closed for the night because apparently Saturdays are slower than Fridays during festival weekend, when everyone is at the outdoor concerts. I have been going through files for hours, trying to understand the business, trying to understand Mavis, trying to understand why a woman I never knew believed in me more than I do.

"You're still here."

Wyatt leans against the doorframe, his arms crossed. He has changed out of his work clothes into jeans and a soft flannel shirt, and he looks tired in a way that goes deeper than physical exhaustion.

"I found her letter." I gesture at the computer. "The one she left for me."

"Oh." He moves into the room and sits in a worn

armchair in the corner. "Yeah. She worked on that for a few weeks. Kept rewriting it, trying to get it right."

"You knew about it?"

"She read me some parts of it. Wanted to make sure she didn't sound crazy." He smiles, just a little. "I told her it sounded exactly like her, which is to say completely crazy, but also completely right."

I swivel in the desk chair and face him.

"She wrote about you and said you'd be prickly."

"Oh, did she now?"

"She also said you're the best man she ever knew."

"Mavis had low standards."

"I don't think she did." I study him in the dim light of the office. "I think she saw people very clearly. That's what everybody keeps telling me, anyway."

He is quiet for a long moment.

"What else did she write?"

"That she thought I wasn't happy. That she wanted to give me a chance to figure out who I am." I pause. "Was she right? I mean, could she really tell that from a distance?"

"I don't know. You tell me." His eyes meet mine, and there is no judgment in them. "Are you happy? I mean, were you before all this?"

The question catches me off guard. I open my mouth to say yes, of course, I had a successful business and a nice apartment and a perfectly adequate life, but the words will not come out.

"I don't know," I admit finally. "I thought I was. Or I

thought I was supposed to be, which felt like the same thing."

"It's not."

"No. I'm starting to realize that now."

He leans forward, his elbows on his knees.

"When I came back from overseas, I thought I knew what my life was supposed to look like. Get a job, settle down, be normal, you know? I couldn't do it. Couldn't sleep, couldn't focus, couldn't stop waiting for something bad to happen. PTSD, among other things." He shrugs like it is no big deal. "Mavis found me one night, sitting in my truck outside the bar, having a panic attack. She didn't ask any questions. Didn't try to fix me. Just sat with me until it passed and then offered me a job."

"And that helped you?"

"Well, it gave me something to do. Something to focus on besides my own head. The bar needed me. The staff needed me. The customers needed me. It's real hard to spiral when people are depending on you."

I think about my empty studio and my dwindling client list, and the growing sense that I was becoming irrelevant.

"I understand that more than you might think."

"Yeah. I figured you might."

We sit in comfortable silence for a moment. Outside, I can hear the creek burbling in the distance and the faint sound of music from the festival.

"Tell me about her," I say suddenly. "About Mavis. I

mean, not the legend. Not the saint everyone keeps describing. The real person."

Wyatt considers the question for a moment.

"Well, she cheated at poker. Badly. Everybody knew it. No one ever called her out because watching her try to be subtle was just way too entertaining."

I laugh. "Really?"

"She also couldn't cook to save her life, despite what she told everybody. And that barbecue sauce recipe she's so proud of? Dolly's grandmother's. Mavis just added the bourbon."

"The letter mentioned the bourbon and the coffee."

"Oh, the coffee was also her contribution. That was the only good idea she ever had in the kitchen."

He is almost smiling now, lost in the memory.

"She sang off-key. She argued with the TV during football games. And once she got into a fist fight with a woman who insulted Dolly's hair."

"A fist fight?"

"Well, more of a slap fight. Neither of them could throw a punch worth a dang. But it's the thought that counts."

I am fully laughing now, and it feels strange and wonderful, like stretching a muscle I forgot I had.

"She sounds like a handful."

"Oh, she was." His voice softens. "She was also the kindest, most generous, but stubbornly loving person I've ever known. She took in strays. People who didn't fit in anywhere else, who needed a place to belong. She gave us all a home."

"And now she's given it to me."

"Yep." He meets my eyes. "Question is, what are you going to do with it?"

I don't have an answer. Not yet. But sitting here in her cluttered office, surrounded by evidence of a life well lived, I feel something I have not felt in a long time.

I feel curious about what comes next.

Later, after Wyatt has gone home and I have climbed the stairs to my new apartment, I stand in front of the photo wall again. I find the picture of me as a child, gap-toothed and beaming, and trace its edges with my finger.

"I'm here," I whisper to the empty room. "I don't know if I'm what you hoped for, but I'm here. I'm gonna try."

Of course, the apartment doesn't answer, but I swear I feel something. A presence. A warmth. A sense of being.

I pull Mavis's letter from my pocket. I printed it out because I cannot leave it trapped in her ancient computer, and read the last line again.

"I hope you find what you're looking for."

"Me too," I say to no one.

Then I change into the most casual pajamas I own, which are silk because I am still me after all, and climb into Mavis's bed with its handmade quilt and fall asleep surrounded by the memories of a woman who loved me before we ever met.

I have made a decision.

After days of observing, exploring, and reading through Mavis's chaotic filing system, I have decided that the best way to understand the business is to just participate in it. Not watch from the sidelines with my mason jar of boxed wine, but actually help. Roll up my sleeves, as it were, and contribute.

This is, I will later realize, the worst decision I have made since agreeing to let Archie's mother plan our engagement party. Who has one-hundred doves at an engagement party?

On this particular evening, I walk down the stairs of the apartment in what I thought was appropriate attire. Dark slacks, a tasteful blouse, and sensible flats. And I am filled with optimism.

I have skills. I have experience managing a business. I have years of training in proper social interaction.

How hard can running a bar actually be?

"Absolutely not," Wyatt says when I announce my intentions.

He is behind the bar, setting up for the evening rush, and he does not even look up from the glasses he is washing.

His dismissal is so casual that it takes me a moment to process it.

"Excuse me?"

"You heard me."

Now he looks up, blue eyes assessing me with something between concern and amusement.

"Tonight is our second busiest night of the week. It's not the time for training anyone, especially you."

"Well, I'm not asking to be trained. I'm offering to help." I straighten my spine, trying to channel my mother's most authoritative tone. "Besides, I own this place. And I should understand how it operates."

"You can understand how it operates by watching. Exactly what you've been doing. And that's fine."

"Well, watching isn't the same as doing."

Wyatt sets down the glass he's holding and braces his hands on the bar.

"Ms. Whitfield. Eleanor." He says my name like it costs him something. "Have you ever worked in a bar before?"

"Well, no…"

"Have you ever worked in any service industry at all?"

"I run an etiquette school. That's a service."

He rolls his eyes.

"Teaching rich kids which fork to use isn't the same thing as serving drinks to a packed house while live music plays and people are line dancing and someone's inevitably going to spill beer on someone else's girlfriend."

"Well, I understand that, but I am a quick learner and I—"

"You'll get in the way," he interrupts. His voice is not unkind. It's just firm. "You'll slow us down, confuse the customers, and probably end up getting hurt. No offense."

"None taken," I say, even though I take plenty. "But I'm not asking for your permission. I'm informing you of my decision."

We stare at each other across the bar. It is a battle of wills, and I refuse to be the one who blinks first.

He finally sighs.

"Fine. But you're shadowing Dolly, and you do exactly what she says. If she says stop, you stop. If she says leave, you leave. Understood?"

"Understood."

"And don't say I didn't warn you."

CHAPTER 6

The first hour isn't really that bad.

Dolly takes me under her wing with the patience of someone who has definitely dealt with worse. She shows me how to carry a tray. *"Balance is everything, sugar. You lose the tray, you lose your tips."* How to navigate the crowded floor.

"Hips first. Always lead with your hips." And how to take orders correctly. *"Write it down. I don't care if you think you'll remember. Write it down."*

I follow her through the bustling crowd, my notepad in hand, watching her work. She's amazing, greeting customers by name, recalling their drink orders, and smoothly redirecting a handsy customer with a joke that makes him laugh. She definitely knows what she's doing with each customer, and I start taking notes.

"You're doing good, darlin'," Dolly says during a brief break. "Just keep watching and—"

"I'd like to try to take an order," I interrupt. "Just one table, to see if I can do it."

Dolly's eyebrows rise toward her impressive hairline.

"Honey, I don't think—"

"Please. I need to know if I can do this."

She studies me for a long moment and then sighs in a way that suggests she is already regretting it.

"Fine. Table seven. It's old Mr. Patterson and his buddies. They're harmless."

Table seven is occupied by four elderly men in various states of flannel, drinking beer, and engaged in what appears to be a heated debate over fishing lures. I approach with my notepad and my most professional smile in place.

"Good evening, gentlemen. Can I get you another round?"

Four pairs of eyes swivel toward me, looking confused.

"Well, well," one of them says, Mr. Patterson, I assume. "You must be Mavis's niece, the one from Atlanta."

"Great-niece, and yes. Eleanor Whitfield."

I extend my hand automatically, and he shakes it with a grip that is surprisingly strong for his age.

"Good handshake," he says. "Firm. None of that dead fish nonsense."

"Thank you. My mother always said a proper handshake was the foundation of any interaction."

"Smart woman."

He gestures to his nearly empty glass.

"I'll take another Bud Light, and so will these reprobates."

I write this down carefully, four Bud Lights, and feel a small surge of triumph.

I can do this.

It is just taking orders and delivering drinks. I mean, how hard can something like that be?

"I'll have those right up to you," I say, and turn to head toward the bar.

That's when I notice the menus.

They're tucked into the little wooden holders on each table, handwritten on chalkboard-style paper. And as I pass table eight, I can't help but look at one.

I stop dead in my tracks.

The menu says: *Nachos, piled high with all the fixins. Wings, hot, medium, and if your chicken. And loaded potato skins, your gonna love them.*

Your? **Your** gonna love them?

And if *your* chicken. **Y O U R.**

That does not even make sense.

It's clearly supposed to be if **you're** chicken, as in if you are too cowardly to try the hot wings.

I pick up the menu and stare at it in horror.

There are more errors, like mozzarella sticks with an unnecessary apostrophe, and queso dip made fresh *everyday* when it should be every day with a space, two words. And desserts with an apostrophe, which is just, well, no.

"Is there a problem?"

The woman at table eight is looking at me.

"The menu," I say. "There are grammatical errors. Several of them."

"Oh." She looks at her companion, a man in a trucker hat who is more interested in his basket of wings than any editorial concerns. "I guess I never noticed."

"How could you not notice? *'Your gonna love them'* is missing both an apostrophe and the proper form of 'you're.' And *'mozzarella stick's'*? That apostrophe has no business being there. It is plural, not a possessive."

The woman blinks.

"Um, okay."

"I have to speak to somebody about this," I assure her, tucking the menu under my arm. "This is completely unacceptable for a business establishment."

I march toward the bar where Wyatt is mixing drinks.

"We need to talk about the menus."

He does not look up.

"What about them?"

"They are riddled with errors. Grammatical errors. Spelling errors. The apostrophe usage alone is a crime against the English language."

He does look up this time, and there is that expression again, like he is questioning every life choice that led to this moment.

"The menus have been the same for at least fifteen years."

"Well, then they have been wrong for fifteen years."

"Nobody's complained."

"I'm complaining."

"You're not a customer."

"I'm the owner."

The words come out of my mouth way louder than I intended, and I now realize that lots of people at the bar are watching me with interest.

Wyatt's jaw tenses.

"Can we discuss this later?" His voice is low and controlled. "When we're not in the middle of a night rush?"

"Fine." I clutch the menu to my chest. "But just know this isn't over."

"Yeah, I'm sure it isn't."

I turn to deliver my drink order, which I had nearly forgotten about because of my grammatical outrage, and nearly collide with Dolly, who has appeared at my side like a rhinestone ghost.

"Sugar, what is going on?"

"The menus are wrong. The grammar is atrocious."

Dolly looks at me, then at the menu, then back at me.

"Honey, nobody here cares about grammar."

"I care about grammar," I say, putting my hand on my chest.

"I can see that." She gently takes the menu from my grip. "Why don't you go deliver those drinks to Mr. Patterson's table, and then we can talk about menus tomorrow."

"But tomorrow—"

Her voice is still sweet, but there is steel underneath it.

"Right now, we have customers to serve."

She's right. I know she's right. It's like my mother's ghost has overtaken my body, forcing me to yell about apostrophes and grammar.

I take a breath, nod, and head back to the bar to pick up the beers I ordered approximately seventeen crises ago.

The next hour is even worse.

I deliver the beers to Mr. Patterson's table without incident, but that small success goes straight to my head. I start noticing other things. Things that need improvement. Things a professional establishment simply should not tolerate.

The tables are not arranged efficiently. There is also wasted space near the wall that could accommodate at least a couple more tabletops, four tops, if someone would consider traffic flow. The lighting is inconsistent. Some areas are too bright, while others are too dim. It creates an atmosphere that feels more like a haunted house than a welcoming establishment.

And then the customers.

Oh, the customers.

Their posture is appalling. People are slouching and hunching, practically melting into their chairs as if they have never heard of spinal alignment. One man is sitting with both elbows on the table, one on each side of his plate, and I have to physically restrain myself from going over and correcting him.

I do not restrain myself with the woman at table twelve.

She's young, maybe in her mid-twenties, sitting with her legs crossed in a way that makes her lean awkwardly to one side. That's terrible for her back and looks uncomfortable.

And before I can think better of it, I'm standing at her table.

"Excuse me," I say. "I couldn't help but notice your posture. If you uncross your legs and sit with your feet flat on the floor, you'll feel a lot more comfortable. The way you're sitting is putting unnecessary strain on your lower back."

The woman stares at me.

Her companion, a bearded man, stares at me, too.

"I'm sorry," the woman says slowly. "Who are you?"

"Eleanor Whitfield. I own this establishment."

The words are becoming commonplace for me.

"I also have extensive training in deportment and physical presentation, and I'd be happy to give you some tips if—"

"I'm good," the woman interrupts. "Thanks."

"Are you sure? Because that posture really is—"

"She said she's good." The bearded man's voice has an edge. "Maybe you could just bring us our drinks?"

I open my mouth to explain that I am not actually their server, that I was just trying to help, but something in their expression stops me. They are looking at me like I'm crazy. Like I've done something wrong.

So I walk away without another word, my face burning.

The incident with the biker happens around ten o'clock.

I have been trying to stay out of the way, mostly hanging out by the bar, watching the controlled chaos unfold. The band is on a break, and people are walking around, drinking and chatting.

And it is during this lull that I spot him.

He is large. Not as large as Boone, but substantial, with a leather vest, tattooed arms, and a beard that could house a family of small birds. He is standing at the bar waiting for his drink, and he has just been handed a beer by Presley.

And he takes that beer with his left hand and shakes her hand with his right.

Except it is not a handshake. It is that thing that men sometimes do, that limp-fingered grasp that is more of a little squeeze than a shake. The kind that suggests they don't think women deserve a real handshake.

I am moving before I can even stop myself.

"Excuse me," I say, inserting myself into the interaction. "I couldn't help but notice your handshake technique."

The biker looks at me. Up close, he is even more intimidating. Small eyes, a scar on his chin, and an expression that suggests to me that he is not used to being interrupted.

"My what?"

"Your handshake. When you greeted this young lady." I gesture at Presley, who is frozen behind the bar with an expression of horror on her face. "A real handshake, a proper one, should be firm and confident, with full palm contact. What you did was more of a finger-squeeze kind of thing, and it is dismissive and, frankly, somewhat insulting."

The bar has gone quiet around us. I am vaguely aware of people turning to watch, but I'm committed now.

"Here," I say, extending my hand. "Let me demonstrate the correct technique. You want to make sure your palms meet fully, then apply even pressure. Not too hard, not too soft. Two or three pumps, and then release."

The biker looks at my extended hand like I am offering him a live snake. Although I get the feeling he probably owns snakes or some other dangerous creature.

"Lady," he says slowly, "you're trying to tell me how to shake hands?"

"I am offering instruction, yes. A good handshake is the foundation of—"

"I don't need some prissy city princess telling me how to shake hands."

"Well, I am not prissy. I am a professional. Proper etiquette is not about being prissy, it is about showing respect for—"

"You want to talk about respect?" He steps closer, and suddenly he is very large and very angry, and I am realizing I might have made a significant tactical error. "How about you show some respect by minding your own dang business?"

"I was just trying to—"

"Trying to what? Make me look stupid in front of everyone?"

His voice is rising now, drawing more attention.

"You come in here with your fancy clothes and your fancy attitude, acting like you're better than everyone."

"That's not what I—"

"Hey!" The voice is calm, authoritative, and familiar.

Wyatt appears beside me, placing himself slightly between me and the biker. "What's going on here?"

"Your new boss lady's trying to teach me manners," the man snarls, "like I'm some kind of child."

Wyatt's expression does not change, but I see something in his eyes.

"Oh, is that so?"

"I was just explaining proper handshake technique," I say.

Even as the words leave my mouth, I hear how ridiculous they sound.

"He was— well, I mean, the way he shook Presley's hand was—"

"Eleanor." Wyatt's voice is quiet but firm. "Why don't you go wait in the office? I'll handle this."

"But—"

"Office. Now."

It is not a suggestion.

I open my mouth to argue with him, but something in his expression stops me. He's not angry, or if he is, he is hiding it really well, but he is definitely serious.

I go.

The office is very quiet, and the silence feels like judgment.

I sink into the chair behind the desk. Mavis's chair,

I suppose, though it does not feel like mine. I rest my head in my hands.

The adrenaline of the night is fading, leaving a hollow feeling of shame.

What in the world was I thinking?

Teaching a biker how to shake hands. Critiquing a stranger's posture. Getting into a public argument over menu grammar. The grammar still bothers me. I can't lie.

I was not thinking. That was the problem.

I was reacting, falling back on the only skills I really have, trying to impose order on a world that does not want or need my brand of order.

All I can hear is my mother's voice echoing in my head.

Presentation matters, Eleanor. First impressions matter. If you can't control your environment, you can't control anything.

But this is not my environment.

This is Mavis's, and Wyatt's, and Dolly's, and anyone else who has built a life here. I am the inter-loper. The outsider. The prissy city princess who does not know how to exist in a world where people do not care about grammar, posture, or the proper way to shake hands.

Tears fall down my face before I can stop them.

And I do not cry prettily. I never have. My face gets all blotchy. My nose runs like a faucet, and I make these embarrassing hiccuping sounds that I cannot seem to control.

I am in the middle of this humiliating display when the office door opens.

"Hey, so the biker situation is—" Wyatt stops mid-sentence. "Oh."

I try to pull myself together, wiping frantically at my face with the back of my sleeve. Lovely.

"I'm fine. I'm just, it's been a long night and I—"

"You're crying."

"I'm not crying. I'm just—" A hiccup escapes me, undermining my denial. "Okay, so I'm crying. A little. It's fine. You can go back to the bar."

But he doesn't go.

Instead, he closes the door behind him, moves to the filing cabinet in the corner, and pulls out a bottle of bourbon and two glasses.

"Mavis kept this here for emergencies," he says, pouring a measure into each glass. "I'd say this qualifies."

He hands me a glass and settles into the worn armchair across from the desk, the same chair he sat in the other night when he told me about Mavis and her cheating at poker.

"The biker is fine," he says. "His name is Dave. He's actually a pretty nice guy once you get past his tough exterior. I bought him a beer, told him that you're new and still adjusting to the place, and he agreed to just let it go."

"I made a fool of myself."

"A little bit, yeah."

I take a sip of bourbon. It burns going down, but it's a good burn. Warm and grounding.

"I don't know what I was thinking. I was just, I just saw things were wrong, things I know how to fix, and I couldn't stop myself for some reason."

"Things that were wrong by *your* standards," he says gently, "not by ours."

"Wyatt, the grammar on the menus is objectively wrong."

"Maybe, but nobody here cares. They come here for food and drinks and company, not grammatically correct descriptions of mozzarella sticks."

I know he's right, of course. I have known it all along, really. But admitting it feels like everything I've built my life on, the rules, the standards, the careful cultivation of proper behavior, is just meaningless.

"I don't know how to be here," I say, my voice small. "I don't know how to exist in a place where all the things that I know don't even matter."

He's quiet for a moment, swirling the bourbon in his glass.

"Can I tell you something?"

"Always."

"When I came back from overseas, I didn't know how to exist anywhere. Everything I'd learned in the army, all the hypervigilance, the constant threat assessments, the need to control every variable, well, it didn't translate very well into civilian life. I'd walk into a room and immediately identify all the exits. I'd hear a car backfire and hit the deck. I couldn't turn it off."

"That sounds awful."

"It was, but here's the thing. Mavis didn't try to fix me. She didn't tell me I was doing it wrong, that I needed to adjust, or that my skills were useless. She just made space for me. She let me be who I was while I figured out who I wanted to become." He meets my eyes, and there's no judgment, just understanding. "The things you know aren't useless, Eleanor. They're just not the right tools for this particular job. And that doesn't mean they're worthless. It just means you have to learn some new tools."

"I don't know how."

"Well, nobody does at first." He takes a sip of his drink. "But Mavis didn't leave you this bar because she thought you were perfect. She left it because she believed you could grow."

I think about Mavis's letter. *A chance to figure out who you are when you're not performing for anyone.*

"What if I can't?" The fear is real, pressing against my chest. "What if I'm just too set in my ways, too rigid, just like my mother?"

"Then you'll spend six months being miserable and go back to Atlanta," he says, shrugging. "But I don't think that's going to happen."

"Why not?"

"Well, because you're sitting here crying over a

mistake instead of defending it. Because you asked me to tell you about Mavis instead of just reading about her. And because you're trying, even when you're failing." He sets his glass down and leans forward. "Rigid people don't try, Eleanor. They dig in and insist they're right. You're not doing that."

I consider this. It's not how I would have described myself, but maybe that's the point. Maybe I don't know myself as well as I thought I did.

"Dolly's going to want to talk to you," Wyatt says, standing. "She's not mad, but, you know, she's going to have some, shall we say, *suggestions* about how to approach things differently."

"Oh, I'm sure she will."

"Take them. She's been doing this for thirty years. She knows what she's talking about."

I nod and finish the last of my bourbon.

"Wyatt," I say as he reaches for the door.

He turns back. "Yeah?"

"Thank you. For this."

I gesture vaguely at the bourbon, the conversation, and the kindness I didn't expect.

"Mavis wouldn't have left you this place without a reason, and I'm starting to think maybe she knew what she was doing."

He leaves before I can respond, closing the door behind him.

I sit in the quiet office, surrounded by Mavis's chaotic files and the lingering scent of bourbon, and think about tools, about growing, about the possibility that the woman I've been isn't the one I have to stay just because my mother said so.

It's terrifying.

It's also, I realize for the first time in years, that I feel something might actually change.

Later, after the bar is closed and the staff has gone home, I climb the stairs to the apartment and stand in front of Mavis's photo wall again. I find the picture of me as a child.

"I messed up today," I tell her. "Badly. I made a fool of myself in front of everybody."

Of course, the photo doesn't answer, but I swear I can almost hear Mavis's voice.

"So what? Get up and try again."

"I don't know if I can do this."

"Only one way to find out."

I touch the edge of the photo, feeling the curl of the aged paper.

"Okay," I whisper. "I'll try."

Then I go to bed, and for the first time since I arrived in Copper Creek, I sleep without dreaming of my mother's disappointed face.

CHAPTER 7

The church potluck is at noon.

I learn this information at approximately 11:47 a.m., when Dolly appears at the top of my apartment stairs, slightly out of breath and holding a casserole dish that smells like heaven.

"You're coming, right?" she asks, as if we've already had this conversation. "To the potluck?"

I'm standing in my kitchen in my silk pajamas, holding a cup of coffee, with my hair doing something that can only be described as being "ambitious."

"I have not been informed of any potluck. What potluck?"

"The First Baptist monthly potluck. Everybody goes. Mavis never missed a single one." Dolly sets the casserole dish on my counter and looks me up and down, her expression telling me that my current state of dress is not acceptable."You've got about ten minutes to make yourself look presentable. I'll wait."

"Dolly, I can't just… I don't have anything to bring. I'm not even Baptist—"

"Honey, half the people there aren't Baptists. It's not about religion; it's about community."

She's already moving toward my closet, which feels like a huge invasion of privacy. I should protest, but I don't.

"And don't worry about bringing something. You're new. First time's a freebie."

"I really don't think—"

"Wear this," she says, holding up a dress that I don't remember packing. A navy sheath with tasteful white piping. "This is church-appropriate, but not too fancy. And for heaven's sake, you've got to do something with that hair."

Thirteen minutes later, because Dolly's definition of ten minutes is apparently flexible, I'm in the passenger seat of her ancient Buick, speeding toward the First Baptist Church of Copper Creek as she fills me in on everything I need to know.

"Now, Pastor Dale's a sweetheart. Don't let the title intimidate you. His wife, Ruthie, makes the best banana pudding in three counties, so be sure to compliment it. Mayor Birdie will corner you within five minutes of your arrival. Just smile and nod, and don't commit to anything. And whatever you do, don't mention the new stoplight. It's a sore subject."

"The new stoplight?"

"Long story. Just don't mention it."

I'm trying to process this flood of information when we pull into the church parking lot, which is already packed with vehicles, pickup trucks mostly, but also a surprising number of sedans and a few minivans.

"Remember," Dolly says as we get out. "These are good people. They loved Mavis, and they wanna love you too. Just let them."

I'm not sure how to let people love me, but I follow Dolly through the front doors anyway, clutching my purse like a lifeline.

The fellowship hall is chaos. It's organized chaos, I suppose, but chaos nonetheless. Long folding tables are covered with food, more than I've ever seen in one place. Casseroles, salads, and desserts in endless variety. People stand in groups, talking and laughing, while children weave between the adults like small, sugar-fueled torpedoes. The noise level is equivalent to that of a small stadium.

"Eleanor."

A woman stands in front of me with the sudden intensity of a heat-seeking missile. She's small, maybe five foot three, with a honey-blonde bob that's shellacked into architectural perfection. She's wearing a coral pantsuit with a big flag pin on the lapel.

"I'm Birdie Parsons, mayor of this fine town. I've just been dying to meet you properly."

She takes my hand in both of hers, and I notice her manicure is flawless. Finally, something I understand.

"It's lovely to meet you, Mayor Parsons. What a charming town you have."

"Isn't it just?" She's still holding my hand, her eyes scanning my face with an intensity that suggests she is cataloging every pore, mole, and freckle. "Now, I understand you're from Atlanta. Buckhead specifically. Very nice area. Very refined."

The way she says refined makes it sound like a communicable disease.

"Yes, I've lived there most of my life."

"And you run an etiquette school, is that right? Teaching young ladies how to behave properly?" Her smile never wavers, but something in her eyes sharpens. "How interesting. You know, we don't have much call for that sort of thing around here. Our young people learn manners at home."

I'm not sure if this is an insult or not, but it feels like an insult, even if it's wrapped in so much sweetness I can't be certain.

"Well, different communities have different needs," I say carefully. "I'm sure your young people are wonderfully well-mannered."

"Oh, they are. Mostly." She finally releases my hand. "Now, you simply must come to our next town council meeting. We have some concerns about The Rusty

Spur that we'd love to talk to you about. Nothing serious, just, you know, neighborly conversation."

"Concerns?"

"The noise ordinance, mainly. And the parking situation on Friday nights. There was an incident last
month with the—well, we can discuss all that later."
She pats my arm. "Now, you go get yourself some food.
Ruthie's banana pudding is not to be missed."

She's gone before I can ask what incident she's
referring to, swept away by someone else who needs
her attention.

"She does that," Dolly says, walking closer. "She
drops little bombs and then disappears. Don't let her
rattle you."

"Oh, I'm not rattled."

"Honey, you look like a deer caught in the headlights. Come on, let's get you some food."

The food line is where things start to go wrong.
It begins innocently enough. A woman I
don't know hands me a plate and points toward the
spread of dishes.

"Help yourself, sweetheart. There's plenty."

I look at the options. Casseroles of all different
origins. Salads drowning in what looks like mayon-
naise. Something called a "congealed salad" that
appears to be Jello with fruit suspended in it. An entire

table is dedicated to desserts, including what I think is the famous banana pudding.

I take small portions of things that look safe. Some green beans. A roll. A scoop of what looks like chicken salad, although I'm not totally sure.

The woman behind me watches my selections with horror.

"Honey, that's all you're having? You need to eat more than that. You're skin and bones."

"I'm not really that hungry."

"Nonsense."

She starts adding things to my plate without asking me. A heap of something called hash brown casserole. A square of cornbread. And a mysterious brown substance that she identifies as "Aunt Myrtle's famous beef tips."

By the time I escape the line, my plate is piled so high I can hardly see over it.

I find a seat at one of the tables between Dolly and an elderly man who introduces himself as Earl. The same Earl whose wife passed, I realize, remembering what Wyatt told me. He looks tired but grateful for the company, and I make a mental note to be especially kind to him.

"So you're Mavis's girl," he says, looking at me. "You don't look much like her."

"I'm told I have the same cheekbones."

"Well, maybe, but Mavis had a way about her. A

spark." He shakes his head slowly. "You seem a little too contained."

I'm not sure how to respond to this, but it definitely does not feel like a compliment.

"Eleanor is still settling in," Dolly says. "Give her time."

"Well, time's all any of us have," Earl agrees. "Well, that and Ruthie's banana pudding. You tried it yet?"

"Not yet. I was saving room for dessert."

"Smart girl."

The conversation swirls around me as I pick at my overloaded plate. People stop by to introduce themselves, but the names and faces blur together. I meet the hardware store owner, the librarian, and the woman who runs the hair salon. Everyone has a connection to Mavis, a story about something she did, or a memory they want to share.

And then everyone has questions about me.

"So you're single?"

"No husband waiting for you back in Atlanta?"

"What exactly is an etiquette school? Like, you're teaching people what fork to use?"

"How long are you staying here?"

I answer as best I can, trying to be polite without giving away too much information. I feel myself tensing up with each question, each curious glance, each well-meaning but invasive inquiry into my life.

～

Pastor Dale is definitely not what I expected.

He's younger than I imagined, maybe in his mid-fifties, with kind eyes and a gentle manner that immediately puts me at ease. But he's also, I remember, the person who would have inherited the bar if I hadn't accepted the terms of the will.

"Ms. Whitfield," he says, extending his hand. "I'm so glad you could join us. Mavis would have been so pleased."

"Thank you, Pastor, and please call me Eleanor."

"Eleanor, then."

He takes a seat across from me, and I notice that his plate is as overloaded as mine.

"I wanted to say, I hope there aren't any hard feelings about the will."

"Mavis and I talked about it at length, and she was very clear about her wishes. No hard feelings at all. I understand she wanted the bar to go to someone who would appreciate it. She wanted it to go to you specifically." His eyes are warm. "She spoke about you often, you know, wondered about what kind of woman you'd become."

"I wish I'd known her."

"She wished that too." He pauses, choosing his words carefully. "Mavis had a gift for seeing potential in people, and she saw something in you that made her believe you were meant to be here. So I hope that you'll trust that instinct, even when things are difficult."

Before I can respond, a woman appears at his side,

his wife Ruthie, I assume, based on the way she touches his shoulder.

"Dale, stop monopolizing the new girl. Let her eat." She turns to me with a smile. "I'm Ruthie. Has anyone told you to try the banana pudding yet?"

"Yes, everyone has told me to try the banana pudding."

"Well, good. It's my grandma's recipe. I'd be offended if you left without having some."

She's gone before I can respond, off to manage some other aspect of the potluck.

Pastor Dale watches her go.

"Thirty-two years," he says, "and she still keeps me on my toes."

"That's wonderful."

"It is." He stands up, picking up his plate. "Listen, don't be a stranger, Eleanor. Our doors are always open for worship, conversation, or just banana pudding."

He moves away, and I'm feeling strangely touched by the encounter. Whatever I expected from the man who was supposed to inherit my bar, it wasn't his kindness.

The banana pudding incident happens about twenty minutes later.

I've made my way over to the dessert table, determined to fulfill my obligation to try Ruthie's famous dessert. The pudding is in a large glass dish, layered with vanilla custard, bananas, and what look like vanilla wafers, topped with a cloud of meringue. I take a modest portion because I'm still full from the mountain of food I was forced to consume, and return to my seat.

The first bite is wonderful. It's sweet, but not too much, with a perfect balance of textures. Creamy custard, soft banana, a slight crunch of the wafers. And I understand immediately why everyone insisted I try it. But I'm so stuffed already that I can't possibly finish it.

"What do you think?" Ruthie says as she materializes beside me like an apparition.

"It's delicious," I say. "The texture is perfect. Surprisingly better than the banana pudding I've had in Atlanta."

I mean this, of course, as a compliment. I'm comparing her creation favorably to every other banana pudding I've ever tasted.

But something in Ruthie's expression shifts. Her smile freezes, becomes fixed, and slightly brittle.

"Better than Atlanta banana pudding," she repeats. "Well, that's *something*, I suppose."

She moves away before I can clarify, and I'm left wondering what I did wrong.

Dolly leans over, her voice low. "Honey, you just implied that you were surprised her pudding was any good. Like you expected it to be worse than what you're used to."

"Oh, that's not what I meant at all. I was saying it's better."

"I know that. I understand what you meant. But the way you said it," she shakes her head, "around here, a compliment that sounds like it's grading someone just doesn't land well. You don't compare. You just appreciate."

I think about this, replaying my words in my head. "It's delicious" would have been enough. Adding the comparison, even a favorable one, implied I was judging her against some external standard and was surprised she even measured up.

Yikes.

"I should apologize."

"Yeah, you should, but maybe wait a bit. Let her cool down."

I spend the rest of the potluck aware of every word that comes out of my mouth, second-guessing every interaction. When someone asks what I think of Copper Creek, I say, "It's lovely," and nothing else. When someone compliments my dress, I say, "Thank you," without adding that I got it at Neiman Marcus. When someone offers me more food, I accept even though I'm full, so full I might burst.

By the time the potluck winds down, I'm exhausted in a way that has nothing to do with phys-ical exertion.

I later find Ruthie in the church kitchen washing dishes.

"Ruthie, I wanted to apologize."

She doesn't stop washing, but she does glance up at me. "For what?" Her voice is high-pitched like she's trying to sound unbothered.

"For what I said about the banana pudding. I didn't mean to imply I wasn't…" I trail off, then try again. "I wasn't trying to suggest that I was surprised it was good. I just meant that it's the best I ever had, period. And there was no comparison necessary."

She's quiet for a moment, her hands still moving in the soapy water. Then she sighs.

"I knew you didn't mean anything by it. Dolly explained you're still learning how things work around here."

She sets down the dish she's washing and turns to face me.

"But I'm gonna tell you something, Eleanor. When you come from a place like Atlanta, with its fancy restaurants and fancy people, and you say something is better than you're used to, it sounds like you're giving us a grade. Like we're supposed to be grateful we passed your test."

"That wasn't my intention at all."

"I know. But intention isn't everything." She picks up another dish. "Mavis understood that. I mean, she came from the same world you did, but she learned to leave it behind. She didn't compare. She just joined in."

I think about Mavis, who left Atlanta all those years ago and never looked back. Who built her life here and became part of this community, earned the kind of love that fills a wall with photographs.

"How do I do that?" I ask. "How do I learn to just join in?"

Ruthie's expression softens.

"You start by just showing up. Not as an observer, not as a judge, but just as a person. You make mistakes. You apologize. You try again. And you let people see the real you, not the polished version."

"Well, I'm not sure I know who the real me is."

"That's honest at least." She turns back to her dishes. "Keep coming to the potlucks. We're patient people, most of us. We'll give you time. And if you ask, God will always give you opportunities to see who you really are. Question is, are you brave enough to ask?"

I walk back to The Rusty Spur because I need the air and time to think about what happened at the potluck.

The afternoon is warm, a perfect spring day, like a postcard. I pass the town square with its white gazebo and towering oak trees, the storefronts with their cheerful awnings, and the people who wave at me even though they do not have any clue who I am. Or maybe they do know. In a town this size, everybody probably knows everything about everyone.

I am almost to the bar when I spot Wyatt's truck sitting in the parking lot. He is sitting on the tailgate, drinking root beer from a bottle and watching me approach with an expression I cannot quite read.

"Heard you went to the potluck," he says as I get closer.

"Wow. Word travels fast around here."

"Well, it's Copper Creek. It travels at the speed of gossip, which is faster than light." He pats the tailgate beside him. "How'd it go?"

I consider lying, telling him that it was fine and I handled it perfectly, that I am adapting to small-town life. Instead, I climb up beside him and say, "I accidentally insulted Ruthie's banana pudding."

"Uh-oh." He takes a sip of his drink. "That's a serious offense."

"I didn't mean to. I was trying to compliment her by saying it was better than the banana pudding I've had in Atlanta. Well, actually, I said it was *surprisingly* better."

"Oh." He nods slowly. "Sounds like you were surprised she could compete with Atlanta."

"Yeah. Well, that's what Dolly said. And Ruthie."

I lean back on my hands, staring at the mountains in the distance. "I don't understand the rules here. I've spent my entire life learning etiquette and how to navigate social situations, and it seems like none of that applies. I'm speaking a different language here."

Wyatt is quiet for a moment. "You are speaking a different language. The language you learned, the Atlanta society language, is about hierarchy. About establishing where you fit. You know, who's above you, who's below. Every compliment, every comment, it's positioning."

"Well, that's not—" I start to protest.

He's not wrong.

"Up here, it's different," he continues. "It's not about hierarchy. It's about connection. When someone asks you what you think of their banana pudding, they're not asking for an evaluation. They're asking you to share a moment with them. To appreciate what they made."

"So what would you have said?"

"Just, 'This is delicious,' would've been fine. Or, 'I love it.' Or, 'Ruthie, this is the best thing I've ever tasted. Can I have the recipe?'" He grins. "That last one would've made you her best friend for life."

I think about all the interactions I have had since arriving in Copper Creek. All the times I have said the wrong thing, made the wrong impression, and failed to connect with people.

"How do I learn this?" I ask. "Like, the real rules, not the ones I was taught."

"You watch. You listen. You stop trying to impress people and start trying to know them. You show up as

Eleanor Whitfield, not the etiquette instructor. Just Eleanor. The person who's trying to figure things out."

"Well, that's terrifying." I realize I've been walking around my whole life wearing the mask my mother put on me the day I was born.

"Most real things are."

We sit in silence for a moment, watching the late afternoon paint the mountains gold.

"Manners matter," he says. "That part you've got. But so does showing up as a real person. That's the part you need to learn."

"Showing up as a real person," I repeat. "What does that even mean?"

"It means being honest about who you are, even when who you are is messy and confused and doesn't have all the answers. It means letting people see you struggle. It means asking for help when you need it and accepting it when it's offered."

"Yeah. Well, I'm not good at any of those things." I think about how my mother always instructed me to never let anyone see me sweat. Always stay in control.

"I know."

He hops off the tailgate and extends a hand to help me down. "But you're trying, and that counts for something."

"Why weren't you at the potluck anyway?"

"My grandmother needed me today." He doesn't say more, and I don't press.

I take his hand, feeling the warmth of his palm against mine. He helps me down with easy strength.

"Tomorrow's Sunday," he says, not letting go of my hand immediately. "The bar's closed. Dolly's having a few people over for dinner. You should come."

"Is this a pity invitation?"

"No. It's a 'you need to practice being a real person and Dolly's house is a safe place to do it' invitation." He finally releases my hand. "Also, she's making fried chicken, and you haven't lived until you've had Dolly's fried chicken."

"I thought Ruthie's banana pudding was the thing I hadn't lived without."

"Well, that too. Copper Creek's full of food you haven't lived without."

He heads toward the bar.

"Six o'clock," he calls over his shoulder. "Dolly's place is the yellow house with all the wind chimes near the post office. You can't miss it."

"Wyatt?"

He turns back.

"Thank you. For explaining things. And for not making me feel stupid. I realize being a human being should come naturally for me, but…" I shrug my shoulders.

"You're not stupid, Eleanor. You're just learning a new language. It takes time."

He disappears into the bar, and I am left standing in

the parking lot, thinking about languages and rules and the terrifying possibility of being a real person.

~

That night, I sit in Mavis's apartment and write a list.

It isn't a to-do list, and it's not a business plan, but a list of things I've learned since arriving in Copper Creek.

Number one, compliments should appreciate, not compare.

Number two, showing up matters more than being impressive.

Number three, the rules I know don't apply here.

Number four, Wyatt Rivers has very blue eyes and very warm hands, and I should probably stop noticing that.

I cross out number four, then write it again, then cross it out again.

Then I add number five, *Mavis believed I could learn to be a real person. Maybe she was right.*

I pin the list to the wall next to my childhood photo.

Then I go to bed, already nervous about tomorrow's dinner, already wondering what new mistakes I'll make and what lessons I'll learn. But for the first time since arriving, the nervousness feels a little less like dread and more like anticipation.

Maybe that's progress.

CHAPTER 8

The memory of Dolly's dinner still warms me three days later when I think about it.

I had arrived at the yellow house with the wind chimes at exactly six o'clock because punctuality is one habit I can't break. I clutched a bottle of wine I'd driven forty-five minutes to find because the Copper Creek grocery store selection consisted entirely of something called Arbor Mist and a suspicious-looking Merlot with a screw cap.

Dolly had taken one look at my expensive Cabernet and laughed.

"Honey, we're having sweet tea and fried chicken, but I appreciate the effort."

The house was small but immaculate, every surface covered with photographs and knick-knacks and the accumulated treasures of a life well lived. The dining room was set for six: Dolly, me, Presley, Boone, and, to my surprise, Wyatt with his grandmother, Meredith.

Meredith was a tiny woman with silver hair and the exact same eyes in the exact same shade of blue as her grandson's. She studied me with frank curiosity when we were introduced, her handshake firm despite the fact that she had obvious arthritis.

"Oh, so you're the one who's got my Wyatt all tied up in knots," she'd said.

My face felt like it was on fire, and Wyatt made a strangled sound of protest.

"Grandma!"

"Hush. I'm old. I'm allowed to say what I see." She patted my hand. "Don't worry, dear. He needed some knots. He's been too settled for too long."

I didn't know what she meant by any of that. Wyatt wasn't interested in me. I'm the woman who drives him crazy, picking apart menu grammar and insulting pudding all over town. Why was I tying him up in knots? I decide that Meredith is mistaken and just ribbing her grandson at my expense.

The dinner itself had been a revelation. Not the food, although Dolly's fried chicken was transcendent. The conversation. The easy flow of it. The way everyone talked over each other, laughed at inside jokes, and included me without making me feel like an outsider.

Presley told a story about a customer who tried to pay his tab with a live chicken.

"He was completely serious," she said. "Said it was worth at least forty dollars. And that chicken was as ugly as homemade sin, I'm telling ya!"

Boone shared, in his quiet way, that he'd finally finished the rocking chair he'd been building for months.

Meredith regaled us with tales of teaching elementary school for forty years.

"Oh, the children never change," she said. "The parents just get worse every generation."

And Wyatt watched me across the table with an expression I couldn't quite read. He jumped in to explain references I didn't understand, made sure my sweet tea glass stayed full, and caught my eye during funny moments to check if I was enjoying myself.

And I was.

That was the strangest part. I was genuinely, uncomplicatedly enjoying myself.

At one point, Dolly brought out a photo album with pictures of The Rusty Spur through the years, of Mavis at different ages, of the staff and regulars who had become family. I found myself leaning in, hungry for glimpses of the aunt I never knew. Dolly narrated each image with the kind of love that made my throat tight.

"Now this one was her sixtieth birthday. We surprised her with a mariachi band. I don't even know where Wyatt found them, but they drove three hours to get here. Mavis cried for twenty minutes straight and then made them teach her to play the trumpet."

"Did she actually learn?"

"Oh Lord, no. She was as tone deaf as a post, but she had fun trying."

By the time I left that night, I felt something I hadn't in years, maybe ever.

I felt like I belonged somewhere.

Now it is Tuesday night, and The Rusty Spur is hosting what the hand-painted sign outside calls the "Two-Step Tuesday - Line Dancing for Everyone."

The "everyone" part is apparently literal because the bar is packed with people of all ages - teenagers awkwardly shuffling around next to their grandparents, couples holding hands, groups of friends laughing at their own mistakes. The band is a three-piece outfit playing country songs I do not recognize, but everyone here seems to know by heart.

I am the epitome of "fish out of water".

I'm perched on my usual stool at the end of the bar, nursing a glass of boxed Chardonnay I have reluctantly come to accept as my signature drink, while watching the chaos happen on the dance floor. I've officially turned into Norm from that old TV show, "Cheers." I have my own stool, and I fully expect people to start yelling "Eleanor!" when I walk into the bar the next time.

"You should try it."

I turn to see Presley beside me, her auburn hair loose tonight instead of in its usual braid.

"Try what?"

"Line dancing. It's fun!"

"Oh, I don't know the steps."

"Nobody knows the steps at first. That's the whole point. You learn as you go."

"My feet hurt."

"You liar!" She grabs my hand and tugs me off the stool."Come on. I'll teach you."

"Presley, I really do not think—"

"Listen, you've been sitting on that stool for two weeks watching everybody else have fun. I can literally see the imprint of your butt cheeks on the fake leather. Mavis would be horrified." She is still pulling me toward the dance floor."Besides, you're supposed to be learning to be a real person, right? Real people dance badly and then laugh about it."

I want to protest that I can dance. I took ballroom dance lessons for years. I can waltz and foxtrot with the best of them. Maybe even salsa if my life depended on it and there was enough good wine involved. But something tells me that particular skill set won't help me here.

Before I can formulate a proper objection, I am standing at the edge of the dance floor, surrounded by people in cowboy boots and jeans, feeling spectacularly out of place in my slacks and silk blouse.

"Okay," Presley says, standing beside me. "This one is easy. It is called the electric slide. Surely you've heard of it and danced this at weddings. If not, just follow along."

I want to tell her that people in my neck of the woods don't do the electric slide at weddings. My mother would've had a heart attack and died right in front of me just to avoid something like that.

The music shifts to something with a driving beat, and suddenly everybody around me is moving in unison, stepping to the right, stepping to the left, forward, backward, in a pattern that looks simple but is absolutely not simple when you are trying to do it for the first time.

I step where I am not supposed to step. I go left when I should go right. I turn the wrong direction and almost collide with a woman who is at least seventy and executing all these moves with the precision of a drill sergeant. I lose the rhythm entirely and stand frozen while everybody grapevines right on past me.

"You know, you're thinking too hard," Presley calls over the music. "Stop counting and just feel it."

I try to feel it. I fail to feel it. All I feel is out of place.

I step on someone's foot, a man who laughs good-naturedly, and then consider fleeing back to my stool and planting my butt cheeks right into their allotted slots.

But then something strange happens.

The woman I nearly collided with, that seventy-year-old drill sergeant, takes my hand and physically guides me through the next sequence.

"Step, step, step, turn," she says, her voice cutting through the music. "There you go! Now again."

I do it again and again. And somewhere around the fourth repetition, it finally clicks.

I am *not* good. I would not even say I am competent. But I am moving, and my feet are in a pattern that is starting to feel almost natural, while my body is responding to the music in a way that has nothing to do with the careful, controlled movements of ballroom dancing.

And I'm *laughing*.

I do not even know when it started. Somewhere between the third wrong turn and the fifth stepped-on foot. But I'm laughing, like really laughing, the kind that comes from somewhere deep in your chest and doesn't care who is watching.

When the song ends, I'm breathless. My hair is coming loose, and my silk blouse is probably ruined by sweat, but I feel amazing.

"See?" Presley is grinning at me. "That wasn't so bad."

"That was terrible. I was terrible."

"You were having fun, though. That is the whole point."

The band launches into another song, something even faster and more complicated, and Presley is pulled away by a young man who has clearly been waiting for his chance.

So I start to retreat to my stool, but the drill sergeant woman grabs my arm.

"Oh no, you don't. You're staying for the boot scootin' boogie. It is a classic."

"I don't know—"

"You didn't know the electric slide either. Look at how that turned out."

She has a point. A terrifying point, but a point nonetheless.

The boot scootin' boogie is definitely harder than the electric slide. There are kicks involved, and this heel movement, and something called a scoot that I cannot, for the life of me, execute correctly. I look like a marionette being operated by somebody who has never seen a human being move before.

But this drill sergeant, whose name I learn between songs is Betty, and who taught high school gym for thirty-five years, refuses to let me give up. She corrects my posture, adjusts my arm position, and at one point actually physically moves my hips in the right direction.

"You've got good bones," she tells me. "Good foundation. You just need to loosen up."

"Yeah, well, I have never been very good at loosening up."

"I can tell. But you're getting there."

By the third song, I've stopped caring how I look. I

am sweating, my hair is a disaster, and I think I have developed a blister on my left heel, but I am also smiling. Genuinely smiling.

And that is when I notice Wyatt watching me.

He's behind the bar where he has been all evening, but he has stopped what he's doing, and he is just looking at me with an expression that makes something flutter in my stomach. I miss a step, stumble slightly, and have to grab Betty's arm.

"Eyes on the floor, not the bartender," Betty says, smiling knowingly. "Plenty of time for that later."

The line dancing portion of the evening winds down around nine o'clock and transitions into what Presley calls "couples time."

The music slows down, the lights dim slightly, and people pair off to two-step across the floor. I've retreated to my stool, of course, nursing a fresh glass of wine and trying to catch my breath. My feet ache, my blouse is definitely ruined, and I'm pretty sure I look like I've been through some kind of natural disaster. But I've also never felt more alive.

"You did good out there."

Wyatt appears beside me, leaning against the bar with an easy confidence. That seems to be his default state. He's wearing a blue flannel tonight that makes his eyes look even more striking, and he's looking at me with something that might be admiration. Or pity. I can't tell.

"I was terrible."

"Well, you were trying. That's more than most people do their first time."

He tilts his head toward the dance floor, where couples are swaying to a slow country song.

"You know how to two-step?"

"I know how to waltz, and I'm guessing that's not the same thing."

"Not exactly." He sticks out his hand. "Wanna learn?"

I look at his hand, calloused, strong, steady. Then I look at the dance floor, at the couples moving together in easy synchronization. I look back at him.

"I'll probably just step on your feet."

"I'll survive."

I take his hand.

Wyatt leads me onto the floor, finding a spot near the edge where we won't be in anyone's way. His left hand settles on my waist, warm and sure, while his right hand holds mine at shoulder height. We're close, closer than I've been to anyone in months, and I can smell his cologne, something woodsy and clean.

"The two-step is simple," he says, his voice low enough that I have to lean in to hear him over the music. "Quick, quick, slow, slow. Quick, quick, slow, slow. Just follow my lead."

He starts to move, and I follow, or I try to at least.

My ballroom training kicks in, making me want to take larger steps, to move in these sweeping patterns I learned in dance class. But Wyatt keeps me close, his hand on my waist, guiding me into smaller, more intimate movements.

"Relax," he mumbles. "You're too stiff." I can feel his breath against my cheek, and I try really hard to ignore it.

"I'm always too stiff."

"Yeah, I've noticed." He's smiling as he says it. "Stop thinking about the steps. Just feel where I'm going and go with me."

I try. I fail. I try again.

And then, somehow, it clicks.

We're moving together, his body guiding mine in a way that feels natural and effortless. The music wraps around us, and I stop counting my steps. I stop analyzing my posture. I stop thinking about anything except the warmth of his hand on my waist and the steadiness of his gaze.

"There you go," he says softly. "You're getting it."

"It's different from what I learned."

"Most things are around here."

We dance in silence for a moment, the music carrying us in slow circles around the floor. And I'm acutely aware of every point where our bodies connect. His hand in mine. His palm on my waist. The occasional brush of his chest against mine.

"Can I ask you something?" I say.

"Shoot."

"Why do you stay here?"

He looks at me, surprised.

"What do you mean?"

"Well, you're obviously good at this stuff. You know, running the bar, managing people, handling difficult situations. But you could probably get a job anywhere. A bigger city, maybe a bigger establishment. Why stay in Copper Creek?"

He's quiet for a long moment, guiding me through another turn, before answering.

"I grew up here. Left when I was eighteen. Joined the army. Saw the world. Did things I'm not always proud of. When I came back, I was so broken. When Mavis gave me a chance to start again, I couldn't leave her."

"But that was five years ago. You could leave now."

"I could." He pulls me slightly closer as another couple passes. "But why would I want to? Everything I care about is here. My grandmother. The bar. The people who have become family." His eyes meet mine. "Why would I trade that for a bigger city and a fancier job? Some things are more important to me."

I think about my life in Atlanta, the studio I inherited from my mother, the apartment I can barely afford, the social circles I moved in where success was measured in square footage and net worth.

"I don't understand that," I admit. "Staying somewhere for love instead of advancement. It's, I guess, foreign to me."

"Yeah, I know," his voice is gentle, but not judgmental. "Maybe that's part of why Mavis left you this place. Maybe she thought you needed to learn there's more to life than climbing ladders."

The song ends and transitions into something faster. Around us, all the couples separate, some heading to the bar, others staying for another dance.

But Wyatt doesn't let go of my hand.

"One more?" he asks.

I should say no. I should. I should retreat to my stool, maintain professional distance, and remember that he works for me. Any romantic entanglement would be complicated at best.

"One more," I hear myself say.

We dance three more songs before the band finally takes a break.

By the end, I've learned that Wyatt's grandmother taught him how to dance when he was twelve years old. She said every gentleman should know how to lead a lady around a dance floor. I now know that his favorite song is something by George Strait that I've never heard of because I've never listened to George Strait. I also know that he has a small scar on his left hand from a bar fight he broke up a couple of years ago. The guy had a broken bottle.

"I have quick reflexes," he told me, "but not that quick."

I've also learned that dancing with Wyatt Rivers makes me feel things I haven't felt in a very long time, maybe ever.

When the music stops, we stand on the edge of the dance floor, still holding hands. Neither of us is quite ready to take a break from the connection.

"I guess I should get back to work," he says.

He doesn't move.

"And I should sit down, rest my feet," I say, pointing downward. "Betty gave me a workout earlier."

"Betty is a force of nature," he laughs, a warm, unguarded, real laugh, and finally releases my hands. "She taught gym for many years. She's broken stronger people than you."

"Well, that's not comforting."

"Wasn't meant to be."

He turns toward the bar and then pauses.

"Eleanor?"

"Yes?"

"You looked good out there on the dance floor." He grins. "I mean, not the steps, because those were pretty rough. But the laughing, the letting go, that looked good on you."

He's gone before I can respond, disappearing

behind the bar to help Presley with a rush of customers looking for drinks during the break.

I make my way back to my stool on legs that feel slightly unsteady, though I'm not sure if that's from all the dancing or something else entirely.

Later, the bar has closed, and the staff has gone home, and I sit in Mavis's apartment and think about motivations.

My whole life, I've been driven by these external measures of success. Good grades because I wanted to please my teachers. Perfect posture because I wanted to please my mother. The right clothes, the right address, the right fiancé to please who? Society? It just feels like there have been imaginary judges that I've always felt were watching me and evaluating my every move, and I never even questioned it. Didn't even ask myself what I actually wanted, separate from what I was supposed to want.

Wyatt stays in Copper Creek because he loves it here. Because the people matter to him more than the opportunities he could find somewhere else. Because he's built a life based on connections rather than achievement. Because he's content not chasing the next thing or worrying about what other people think of his choices. I don't think I've ever felt content in my life.

I came straight out of my mother's womb with a

book on my head, trying not to knock it off while I walked across the delivery room.

And Mavis, well, she left Atlanta. Walked away from everything she was supposed to want and found something real. Something that filled a wall with photographs and a community with love. Something that is still alive after she's gone, so much so that people still talk about her like she's here.

I think Mavis is still living more than I am.

What would it be like to make choices based on love instead of advancement? What would it be like to stay somewhere just because it made you happy and not because it looked good on paper?

I pull out the list I started after the potluck disaster and add to it.

Number six: Wyatt stays for love, not money. I don't know how to do that.

Number seven: Dancing badly and laughing is better than sitting on a stool and being miserable.

Number eight: The way Wyatt's hand felt on my waist is not something I should be thinking about.

I cross out number eight, then I write it again. Then I leave it, because maybe part of being a real person is admitting what you feel, even when it's inconvenient.

I look at Mavis's photo wall. At the picture of me as a gap-toothed child. At all the images of a life lived fully and authentically.

"I'm starting to understand," I tell the empty room,

"what you were trying to show me. Why you left me this place."

Of course, the room doesn't answer, but I swear I feel something. An approval. A sense that I'm heading in the right direction.

I go to bed with aching feet, sore cheeks from laughing, and a full heart.

For the first time since I arrived in Copper Creek, I start to dream about staying. And not because I have to. Not because of the will. But because maybe this is where I'm supposed to be.

The next morning, I wake up early and do something I've never done before. I go outside for a walk with no destination in mind. I have no idea where I'm going. Hopefully, I don't get lost in the mountains because that would be very bad.

The mountain air is crisp and clean, and the sun is just starting to warm the valley. I walk past the bar, past the church, past the town square with its beautiful white gazebo. I walk until I reach a spot where the road curves, and suddenly and unexpectedly, I can see the whole valley spread out below me. Copper Creek in miniature, surrounded by mountains, the gleaming gold and green in the morning light.

It's beautiful. Genuinely, achingly beautiful.

I used to think that the view of downtown Atlanta

from a high-rise was quite lovely, but it doesn't even come close to this. Standing there and looking at the town I never even knew existed a month ago, I feel something shifting around inside of me.

I've spent my whole life trying to live up to what I thought other people wanted. Trying to meet standards that I didn't even set. Achieve goals that I didn't choose for myself. Become a person I'm not even sure I ever wanted to be.

But here, in this tiny town with its potlucks and pickup trucks and line dancing nights, I'm starting to see something very different. A life where success isn't measured in client lists or social standing. A life where showing up matters more than being impressive. A life where love for the community, for a place, for people who become like your family, and maybe even more than your family, is reason enough to stay.

I don't know if I can become that person. I don't even know if I can unlearn thirty-four years of conditioning and shed this armor that I've built up around myself.

But once I start watching the sunrise over the Blue Ridge Mountains, I know one thing for sure.

I think I want to try.

CHAPTER 9

The call comes on a Thursday afternoon while I'm in my office still trying to make sense of the way Mavis filed things. I don't know that I can ever accomplish that task, but I'm going to give it my best shot.

I've been at this for about three hours, sorting the receipts into piles that I think make logical sense, creating spreadsheets to replace the chaos of sticky notes, and making very little progress. It's tedious work, but it's comforting. A task I understand. A problem I hopefully know how to solve.

And that's when my phone buzzes with a familiar Atlanta code, area code, so I answer without thinking.

"Hello? Eleanor Whitfield."

"Ellie." The voice is smooth, polished, and instantly recognizable. It's Archie.

My stomach does some sort of complicated flip. I feel dread. I feel nostalgia. I feel something I can't quite name.

"Archie, this is unexpected."

"I know, I know. I should have called you sooner." He sounds the same - confident, charming, utterly certain of himself. "I heard about your inheritance. Cynthia mentioned it at the Hendersons' cocktail party last week. A bar in the mountains? I have to admit, I chuckled."

"It's a honky tonk, actually."

"A honky tonk," he repeats, laughing. It's a cultured chuckle I used to find sophisticated, and now I find it slightly grating. "Eleanor Whitfield, owner of a honky tonk. Your mother would have had a stroke."

"That's what Cynthia said."

"Great minds." I can picture him sitting in his corner office, his feet propped up on his mahogany desk, looking out over the Atlanta skyline like he owns the place. "Listen, I've been thinking about your situation, and I want to help."

"My situation?"

"The inheritance, the bar, whatever it is that you're dealing with up there in, um…" I hear papers rustling. "Copper Creek? Dear Lord, is that really the name of the town?"

"Yes, it is really the name of the town."

"Oh, charming. Very, um, rustic." The way he says

rustic makes it sound like a communicable disease. "Anyway, I've done some research, and property values in that area are actually pretty promising, especially with the development interest in the Blue Ridge region. So if you play your cards right, you could walk away with a significant return."

I lean back in my chair, staring at the ceiling.

"Archie, I haven't even decided what I'm doing with the place yet."

"What's to decide? You're not actually planning to stay there, are you?" He laughs again, as if the very idea is absurd. "Ellie, come on. You're not a bar owner. You're not even a small-town person. You belong in the city, in civilization, doing what you do best."

"And what exactly is that?"

"Being Eleanor Whitfield." He says it like it's obvious. "Elegant, sophisticated, refined. Not serving beer to hillbillies in the middle of nowhere."

The word hillbillies lands like a slap to my face.

I think about Dolly, with her big hair and bigger heart. About Boone, who reads poetry and builds furniture and carries peppermints for nervous children. And Presley, with her dreams of music and her fierce loyalty. And about Wyatt, who stayed in the middle of nowhere because love mattered more than ambition.

"They are not hillbillies," I say quietly.

"What?"

"The people here, they're not hillbillies. They're just people. Good people."

Archie is silent for a moment, and when he speaks again, his voice has shifted to what I recognize as being his "handling a difficult client" tone.

"Of course, I didn't mean to offend. I'm just saying this isn't your world, Ellie. You don't belong there."

"Well, maybe I don't know where I belong anymore."

"That's exactly my point," his voice warns. "You've been through a lot these past couple of years: your mother's death, our breakup, the business struggles, and it's natural that you'd feel lost and grasp at anything that feels different. But running away to the mountains isn't the answer."

"I'm not running away. I inherited a bar. There are conditions."

"Conditions can be negotiated. Laws can be interpreted. I know some great attorneys who specialize in estate disputes. We could probably find a way to break a will or at least modify the terms so you're not trapped up there for six months."

For a moment, just a flicker of a moment, I'm tempted.

The familiar pull of Atlanta. Of my old life. Of the world I understand.

His voice is like a siren song calling me back to everything I used to be.

The etiquette studio. The social circles. The endless

performance of being Eleanor Whitfield, acceptable, appropriate, and utterly hollow.

"I don't know if I want to break the will," I hear myself saying slowly.

"Oh my gosh, of course you do. Think about it logically. What does a honky tonk in Copper Creek offer you? I mean, six months of your life wasted in a town with no culture, no future, no opportunity. You can come back to Atlanta use that money to revitalize the studio. I can help you. We could…" He pauses for a moment. "We could talk about things. About us."

"There is no us, Archie. We broke up."

"We took a break. There's a difference." His voice drops. "I've missed you, Ellie. These past six months, I've realized what I let go. I was too focused on my lifestyle, on appearances. I should have seen what really mattered."

I want to believe him. Part of me, the part that's spent over two years planning a future with this man, wants to desperately believe that he's changed, that he sees me now, and that going back to Atlanta would mean going back to something real.

But another part of me, a new part that's been growing since I arrived in Copper Creek, knows better.

"What really mattered?" I ask. "What do you think really mattered?"

"You. Us. The life we were building."

"Archie, the life we were building was exhausting. The constant networking, the social climbing, the pressure to be perfect all the time. I literally felt like I couldn't breathe."

"But that's just how things are in our world. You have to play the game."

"Well, maybe I don't want to play the game anymore."

Silence.

He finally speaks. "You're obviously not thinking clearly. That place is affecting your judgment. Let me come up there and talk to you in person. I can help you see."

"I don't need you to help me see anything." The words come out sharper than I intended, but I don't take them back. "I appreciate the call, Archie. I do. But I need to figure this out on my own."

"Ellie—"

"I'll call you if I need legal advice. Goodbye, Archie."

I hang up before he can respond, with my heart pounding in my chest and my hands shaking slightly.

And that's when I notice Wyatt has been standing in the doorway.

I don't know how long Wyatt has been standing there. Long enough to hear Archie call the people of Copper Creek hillbillies? Long enough to hear me defend them, or maybe I didn't defend them forcefully enough? Long enough to know that someone in Atlanta is trying to convince me to leave?

His expression, of course, gives nothing away. That's what I'm learning about Wyatt Rivers. He's all easy smiles and gentle jokes until he's not, and then his face becomes an unreadable mask that reminds me of what he's survived, things I probably can't imagine.

"Didn't mean to interrupt," he says. "Dolly sent me back to let you know the beer distributor is here for our weekly order."

"Right, of course." I stand up quickly, and my chair scrapes loudly against the floor. "I'll be right there." He nods and turns to leave. "Wyatt, wait." He pauses in the doorway but doesn't turn around. I can tell his shoulders are tense. "That was my ex-fiancé, Archie. He heard about the inheritance, and he was just, well, I suppose he was offering me unsolicited advice about what I should do with the bar."

"Seems like he had strong opinions about it."

Wyatt's voice is still neutral, but there's definitely an edge underneath it.

"He has strong opinions on everything. It's one of the reasons we're not together anymore."

Wyatt finally turns around. "Are you planning to sell?"

The question is direct. No judgment. Just a man asking for information that affects his livelihood and his life.

"I don't know what I'm planning," I say. "I'm still trying to figure that out."

He nods slowly. "Fair enough. I mean, of course you don't owe me or anyone else an explanation about what to do with your own property."

The way he says it lets me know that even though I don't owe him an explanation, the choice will have consequences for him, for Dolly, for Presley, for everyone who depends on this place.

"The distributor," I prompt, trying to move us past the awkward moment.

"Right. I'll tell him you'll be out in a minute."

He disappears down the hallway, and I'm left standing in Mavis's office—my office now, I guess—with my heart beating too fast and my hands shaking slightly from the adrenaline of back-to-back difficult conversations.

I take a moment to breathe and smooth my hair, even though it's already falling out of its twist, and then I head out to deal with the beer distributor.

The next few hours pass in a blur of inventory checks and signature scrawls, with Dolly teaching me the difference between various craft IPAs like it's vital information for my survival.

Wyatt is there helping unload cases, but he's not his usual self. He's not cold, exactly, but he's distant and professional, as if I'm his boss rather than someone he's been teaching how to make decent coffee and teasing about my complete lack of knowledge of country music, and definitely not someone he taught to two-step not long ago.

It shouldn't bother me this much. I mean, I've known this man for a very short amount of time, but it does bother me more than I want to admit.

By the time the distributor leaves and the inventory is sorted, it's late afternoon, and the bar is preparing for the evening crowd. I'm about to go back to my office when Dolly corners me by the ice machine.

"Sugar, can we talk for a minute?"

Her tone is gentle but serious. This isn't just a casual chat.

"Of course."

She glances around to make sure we're alone, then leans against the counter with her arms crossed. She's still wearing her signature rhinestone-studded denim vest, but her sparkle seems dimmed.

"I don't mean to stick my nose where it doesn't belong," she starts, which is usually how people begin talking right before they stick their nose exactly where it doesn't belong. "But I've been working here for a long time, and I care about this place. I care about the people who count on it."

"I understand that."

"Do you?" She's not being confrontational, just honest. "Because from where I'm standing, you've got one foot in Atlanta and one foot here, and eventually you're gonna have to choose which way you're gonna fall."

I want to defend myself, to explain that it's not that simple, but she's not wrong.

"Archie called me," I say quietly. "I didn't reach out to him. He heard about my inheritance and called with his opinions about what I should do."

"What did you tell him?"

"I told him I needed to figure it out on my own."

She studies me for a long moment. "Eleanor, I like you. You're trying real hard, and you're a lot tougher than you look. But this town, these people… well, we've been burned by folks who treated us like a cute little experiment. People who showed up, bought properties, made promises, and then disappeared when things got hard or when something better came along."

"I'm not—"

"Let me finish." Her voice is kind but firm. "Five years ago, a development company bought up half of Main Street. Promised they were gonna bring in boutique shops and upscale restaurants. Said it would be a boon to the local economy. And you know what happened?"

I shake my head.

"They gutted the buildings, made them too expensive for any local businesses to afford. And then the whole project fell apart when the investors pulled out. Now we've got three empty storefronts on Main Street that used to be a bakery, a bookstore, and a hardware store that had been family-owned for sixty years. Those families who ran those businesses… well, most of them moved away because they couldn't afford to start over here."

The story settles over me like a weight. I think about Archie's confident assertions that I could sell the property for a profit and how easy he made it sound.

"I'm not a developer," I say. "I'm just somebody who inherited a bar I didn't even know existed a few weeks ago."

"I know that. But the question is, are you somebody who's gonna stay and make a go of it, or are you somebody who's just gonna cash out when it gets tough?"

"I don't know yet, Dolly. I truly don't know. This was all supposed to be temporary, just six months to fulfill the conditions of a will, and then I could go back to my life. But now it's starting to feel…" I'm not sure how to finish the sentence.

"Like home?" Dolly supplies gently.

"I don't know. Maybe. Is that crazy? I've only been here a few weeks."

"Well, sometimes you know faster than that." She reaches out and pats my arm. "I'm not trying to pressure you, honey. I just want you to understand what's at stake. This isn't just about business. It's about people's livelihoods, their gathering place, and the heart of the community."

"I understand."

"And Wyatt?" She chooses her words carefully. "Wyatt's been through a lot, and he came back here to heal. This place helped him do that. He's very protective of it—and of all of us."

"Someone left him before, didn't they?"

Dolly nods. "That's his story to tell, not mine. But yes. And it just about broke him. So when he hears somebody talking about selling this place or about leaving it, it hits him in a vulnerable spot. Not that he'd ever admit it."

"I wasn't planning to sell," I say. "Archie was just offering his opinion."

"Well, Archie sounds like a piece of work."

Despite everything, I laugh. "He is. But he's not a bad person. He just lives in a very different world."

"And honey," Dolly says softly, "which world do you want to live in?"

That's the question I've been avoiding since I got here. The question I'm still not ready to answer.

"I should get back to work," I say instead.

Dolly lets me off the hook with a nod, but her words follow me all the way back to the office.

That evening, the bar is packed. There's a group celebrating a birthday, a few couples on dates, and the regulars who treat this place like their second living room. I'm starting to recognize faces, remember names, and understand the rhythms of the space. Presley's working the floor with me, teaching me her system for remembering orders without writing them down. I'm terrible at it, but she's patient with me.

"Table six wants another round," she tells me. "Two Bud Lights, one Michelob Ultra, and a Coke. Table eight needs fresh napkins. Boone just came in. He always sits at the end of the bar and drinks Yuengling before his shift."

I glance over, and sure enough, Boone is settling onto his usual stool. Wyatt is already putting his beer in front of him before he even asks for it.

"How does everyone know what everyone drinks?" I ask, feeling overwhelmed.

"You just pay attention," Presley says, smiling. "Give it time. You'll get there."

I'm not sure I will get there, but I appreciate that she has confidence in me.

I deliver the round to table six, only messing up once and having to come back for the Coke I forgot. I bring napkins to table eight, then drift toward the bar, where Boone and Wyatt are talking.

"Eleanor," Boone greets me warmly. "Heard you held your own with the beer distributor today. Dolly said you asked some good questions."

"Yeah, I asked a lot of questions because I'm lost. I'm not sure how good they were."

"Well, questions are how you learn." He takes a sip of his drink. "Settling in okay?"

"I think so. It's a lot to take in."

"Well, Mavis would be glad to see you here. She always said the place needed some fresh eyes."

The rest of the evening passes in a blur of drink orders, small talk, and learning how to run the credit card machine without Dolly helping me. By the time we close at midnight, my feet are aching, and I smell like a combination of beer and barbecue sauce, but I feel good. Tired, but good.

Dolly leaves with a wave and says, "See you tomorrow, sugar."

Presley leaves with a group of friends who are going to the Waffle House.

And then it's just me and Wyatt, closing up the bar like we've done every night this week.

There's a routine to it now that feels comfortable. He counts the register, and I wipe down the tables. I sweep while he locks up the cooler. We move around each other in an easy rhythm that shouldn't feel as natural as it does.

"Eleanor," he says as I'm putting away the broom.

I turn to find him standing by the back door, keys in his hand. "Yeah?"

He seems to be struggling with something, like he's choosing his words carefully.

"Earlier, when I heard that phone call, I wasn't trying to eavesdrop. I heard just enough to know that someone was trying to convince you to leave and sell this place."

"Archie doesn't understand what this place means to people."

"Do you?"

The question isn't accusatory. It seems genuine.

"I think I'm starting to," I say. "I mean, I'm starting to understand a lot of things."

He nods slowly. "The people here, we're protective of what's ours. Maybe we're too protective sometimes. We've been let down by outsiders who didn't get it, who saw dollar signs instead of people." He pauses. "I guess what I'm trying to say is if you're not planning to stay, if you're just gonna go through the motions to fulfill the will and then you're gonna cash out, it would really be easier for everyone if you just said so now. So people can make plans."

His words sting, even though I understand where they're coming from.

"And what if I don't know what I'm going to do yet?"

"Well, then I guess we're all gonna have to trust you'll figure it out and do the right thing."

"The right thing for whom?"

"For yourself," he says quietly. "Because if you stay for the wrong reasons, you'll just end up resenting this place and all of us. And that won't do any good for anyone."

"Wyatt, I'm not Archie. I'm not my mother. I'm just somebody trying to figure out where I belong."

Something flickers across his face. Understanding, maybe, or empathy.

"Fair enough. Good night, Eleanor."

"Good night."

He leaves through the back door, and I hear his truck start up a minute later.

I stand in the empty bar, surrounded by the smell of beer and floor cleaner, and wonder what in the heck I'm doing.

CHAPTER 10

The next morning, I wake up to somebody knocking on my apartment door.

I stumble out of bed, still wearing my oversized T-shirt I sleep in, and look through the peephole. It's Wyatt, holding two coffee cups from what I am learning is the only decent coffee place in Copper Creek.

My heart does a complicated little flip.

I open the door, suddenly very aware of my bedhead, my complete lack of makeup, and the fact that my T-shirt says, *Ain't no hood like motherhood.* It was free with purchase at Target, and I've never actually been a mother, but it is comfortable.

"Hi."

"Morning."

He holds out the two coffee cups. "Peace offering for being a jerk last night."

"You weren't a jerk."

"I was a little bit of a jerk." His mouth quirks into a small smile. "I made assumptions. Got in my head about a few things. Anyway, I brought coffee. Figured you might need it."

I take the cup, and our fingers brush. Just for a second. Just long enough for me to feel the warmth of his hand and something electric that makes me very grateful I'm holding hot coffee, so I suddenly have an excuse for my pink cheeks.

"Thank you. You didn't have to do this."

"I know." He shifts his weight, looking almost nervous, which is not an expression I've seen on him before. "But I wanted to. I wanted to tell you I'm also sorry for putting pressure on you about your decision. It's not fair. I mean, it's your inheritance, your choice. I just…"

"I know," I finish for him. "You care about this place. And the people who depend on it. Trust me, I totally get it."

"Yeah." He lets out a breath. "I do."

We stand there in my doorway, me in my ridiculous T-shirt and him in his work boots and flannel shirt, holding our coffee cups and looking at each other like we're trying to figure out what to do next.

He nods, then looks down at my shirt and smiles. "Nice shirt."

I look down and remember what I'm wearing and want to die.

"It was free," I say defensively.

"I'm not judging. It's very maternal."

"Yeah. I'm gonna close the door now."

He laughs. Really laughs. "Drink your coffee. I'll see you downstairs in an hour."

"I'll be there."

He turns to leave, then pauses and looks back.

"For what it's worth, Eleanor, I'm actually glad you're here. Even if it's temporary. And even if you leave in a few months. I'm glad you got to know this place. Got to know…"

He doesn't finish his sentence. He just gives me one of those looks that makes my stomach flutter, and then he's gone.

I close the door and lean against it, holding my coffee, trying to calm my racing heart.

This is bad.

This is very bad.

Because somewhere in the last few weeks, somewhere between learning to pour beer and organizing inventory and listening to Dolly's stories and watching Wyatt move through the bar like he belongs here, I've started to care.

Not just care about the bar.

Not about the business.

But about the place and the people.

And maybe possibly, or actually definitely, about the man who just brought me coffee and looked at me like I might be worth the risk of hoping.

I take a sip of my coffee.

He remembered that I like it with cream and two sugars.

I think about Dolly's question from yesterday.

Which world do I want to live in?

I'm still not one hundred percent sure of the answer.

But I'm starting to think I know which one feels more like home.

An hour later, I've showered and dressed in jeans and a cotton blouse that feels almost too casual for me. I head downstairs to the bar. My hair is still up in its usual twist, although I've left a few strands loose. Baby steps.

Wyatt is already there, moving around the bar, restocking glasses. I watch him for a moment before he notices me.

"Hey," he says, looking up with a smile. "Feeling more human now?"

"Marginally. The coffee helped."

"Good. Listen, I was thinking we could go over the supply order for next week, you know, make sure we're—"

Before he can finish, the front door opens.

A woman in her fifties walks in wearing sensible shoes and carrying a clipboard. She looks far more businesslike than anyone else I've seen in this town. She has short gray hair and an expression that suggests she is already unimpressed by what she sees.

My stomach drops.

"We're not open yet," I start to say, but she's already pulling out a badge.

"Gloria Patterson. Health inspector. I'm here for your routine inspection."

"Routine inspection?" My voice comes out higher than I intended. "But we weren't scheduled until—"

"Surprise inspection," she says. "Standard procedure. Are you the owner?"

"I'm Eleanor Whitfield. I inherited the bar from my great-aunt a few weeks ago."

"I see. Well, Ms. Whitfield, let's take a look at your operations, shall we?" I look over at Wyatt, panic rising in my chest. He gives me a small nod that I think is meant to be reassuring, but all I can think is that I've only been here a few weeks, I have no idea whether we're up to code, and what if she shuts us down. "Ms. Whitfield," Gloria says, already heading toward the kitchen, "this way, please."

I follow her on shaky legs, Wyatt close behind me.

The inspection takes about forty-five minutes. Forty-five minutes of Gloria opening every cabinet, checking every temperature, and examining every surface with the thoroughness of a crime scene investigator. She runs her finger along the edge of a shelf and studies it. She peers into the walk-in cooler, frowning at the thermometer. She opens the storage area and looks up at the water-stained ceiling tile.

With each note she makes on her clipboard, my anxiety ratchets up another level.

"Your cooler is reading forty-two degrees," she says, tapping the thermometer. "It needs to be at forty or below for food safety."

"Yeah, it's been acting up," Wyatt explains calmly. "We're scheduling a repair."

Gloria makes a note. "When?"

I open my mouth to answer and realize I don't actually know, so I close it again.

Wyatt steps in. "We're getting quotes this week. Should have someone out before next Monday."

Another note.

"Let's see the storage area."

We move through the kitchen, and with each space Gloria examines, I notice new problems I hadn't seen before. The leak in the ceiling. The bucket under the stain. The dry goods aren't organized properly because I haven't had time to implement a real system yet. The handwashing sink is fine, but the soap dispenser is nearly empty.

By the time we finish, I feel like I failed a test I didn't even know I was taking.

Gloria flips through her notes, her expression unreadable.

"Overall, you're not in terrible shape," she says finally. "But there are issues that need to be addressed.

The cooler temperature is a concern. The roof leak needs to be fixed before it causes mold or structural damage. Your storage organization needs improvement. I'd like to see a clear system for stock rotation and cross-contamination prevention. And your soap dispensers must be kept full at all times."

She tears a sheet from her clipboard and hands it to me.

It's a list of violations. None serious enough to shut us down immediately, but all of them urgent.

"You have thirty days to correct these issues," she says. "I'll return for a follow-up inspection. If things haven't improved, we'll discuss potential fines or a temporary closure."

Temporary closure.

The words hit me like ice water.

"I understand," I say. "We'll take care of everything."

"I'm sure you will," Gloria says. "Mavis ran a tight ship here for years. I know this is new for you, but this place is important to the community. Don't let it fall apart."

"Oh, I won't."

After she leaves, I stand in the middle of the bar, clutching the violation report like it's a death sentence.

Wyatt gently takes it from my hands. "This isn't bad, Eleanor. We can fix all of this."

"In thirty days?" I ask. "While also running the bar and dealing with everything else?"

"Yes," he says easily. "The cooler repair was already

on our radar. I can fix the roof this weekend. The organization just takes time and a plan. And soap
dispensers are easy."

I sink onto one of the barstools, suddenly
exhausted.

"I don't know what I'm doing," I admit. "I spent
weeks thinking I was getting the hang of things, and
then someone shows up with a clipboard, and I realize
I'm completely in over my head."

"You're not in over your head," Wyatt says.

He moves behind the bar and starts making coffee.
He doesn't ask if I want any. He already knows.

"You're just learning," he continues. "You think
Mavis knew how to run a bar when she first bought
this place? She was a society woman from Atlanta
who'd never poured a beer in her life. Just like you." He
sets a mug in front of me. "She figured it out," he says
gently. "And you will too."

The comparison to Mavis hits harder than it
should. I've been reading some journals of hers that I
found, learning about her life, but I hadn't really
thought about the fact that she probably started out
just as lost as I am now. How long did it take her to
figure it out?

And how do I miss a woman I never met?

"From what she told me, a while," Wyatt says. "She
had help. That's what we do here. We help each other.
And before you say you can't ask for help, I'm going to

remind you that you're not asking. I'm offering. And so is half the town, probably."

He pulls out his phone and starts texting someone.

"What are you doing?"

"Texting Boone. He's going to want to know about this."

"Why would Boone care about the health inspector?"

Wyatt looks at me like I've said something especially naive. "Because this is his bar, too. I mean, not legally, but in every other way that matters. Boone's been coming here for decades. Dolly's worked here a long time. This place is part of the town's fabric. When it has a problem, we all have a problem."

His phone buzzes almost immediately.

"Boone says we need to organize a workday. Get a group together, tackle all the little repairs ourselves, save you money on labor."

"I can't ask people to give up their weekend to fix my bar."

"You're not asking. We're offering."

He's already typing another message.

"I'm texting Dolly and Presley too. We'll plan it for Sunday. That'll give us some time to get supplies."

I want to argue, to insist that I can handle this myself by hiring people, but the truth is, I can't. I don't know how to fix a roof, repair a cooler, or organize a commercial storage area to meet health code standards. And I really don't have the extra money to do it.

"Thank you," I whisper.

"Don't thank me yet. Wait till you see what happens when I let Boone organize a workday."

Despite everything, I laugh.

The rest of the day passes in a blur of worry and planning. Wyatt gets quotes from three companies for the cooler repair in case he and Boone can't fix it. The cheapest is $3,500, which makes my stomach hurt. He insists he can patch the roof himself for about $500 in materials.

$4,000. Four thousand dollars I barely have.

I'm in the office after closing, staring at the bar's bank account on my laptop, when there's a knock on the door frame. It's Dolly, wearing her favorite pink vest with the little hearts on it. She looks concerned.

"Sugar, Wyatt told me about the inspection. You doing okay?"

"I'm fine."

"Well, that's bull, and we both know it. You've got that look you get when you're trying to hold it together."

I close my laptop and rub my eyes. "I don't… I just… I don't know how I'm gonna pay for all this. The bar account has about $3,000 right now, and I need $4,000 just for the repairs. Plus, I have to pay all the normal bills, and I'm not really paying myself anything, and my personal credit cards are maxed out from Atlanta," I stop myself before I completely spiral.

Dolly sits down across from me. "First of all, the work day on Sunday is gonna save you a lot of money. Wyatt can do the roof, Presley can help reorganize the storage, and Boone knows a guy who might be able to look at the cooler for cheaper. The point is, we'll figure it out."

"Why are you all doing this?"

"Because Mavis would have done the same for any of us. And honestly, she did, many a time. And because you're trying, Eleanor. You're showing up every day, working hard, caring about this place, and that matters."

"Does it? Or am I just fumbling around pretending I know what I'm doing?"

"Honey, we're all just fumbling around. That's called life." She pats my hand. "You're doing better than you think, and you're not alone, so stop trying to carry this all by yourself."

After she leaves, I sit in the quiet office, surrounded by Mavis's notebooks and the weight of the responsibility I've been given. I pull out my phone and look at my bank account.

$347 in checking.

That's it. That's all I have in the world, besides the bar account, which needs to cover payroll, supplies, utilities, and everything else.

I could put the cooler repair on my credit card, but

I'm already close to maxed out, and if something else goes wrong, or *when* something else goes wrong, I'll have nothing.

For a moment, I let myself imagine what it would be like to just walk away. To sell this place to someone who actually knows what they're doing. To go back to Atlanta and start over with whatever I can salvage.

But then I think about how kind Dolly is, and the dreams Presley has, and Wyatt's steady presence, and the community that's starting to feel like home.

I can't walk away. Not yet. Not when people are willing to fight for this place, and not when I'm starting to think I might want to fight for it, too.

S unday morning arrives quickly. I'm awake at 6 a.m., nervous and grateful, but completely unsure of what to expect. Wyatt told me people would start showing up around 8, but the first truck pulls up at 7:30. It's Boone, and he's brought three other people with him, all holding thermoses of coffee and wearing work clothes.

By 8 o'clock, there are twelve people in the bar. Twelve people who showed up on a Sunday morning to help me fix a place I've barely begun to figure out.

I stand there, overwhelmed and not sure what to say. I've never had a community around me. I always basically worked alone or with my mother.

Wyatt puts a hand on my shoulder. "Just say thank you and point us toward the coffee maker. We've got work to do."

He takes charge with the easy authority of someone who's done this before. He assigns tasks, explains what to do and what needs to happen, and makes sure everyone has the tools they need. I watch him work the crowd and understand, maybe for the first time, what a wonderful leader he must have been in the military.

"Eleanor," he calls, waving me over. "You're with me. We're caulking the windows in the main room. They need to be sealed before winter."

I follow him to the first window, where he's already laid out the supplies. Caulk guns, tubes of sealant, rags, and painter's tape.

"Okay," he says, "first lesson in home repair. Have you ever caulked anything before?"

"I once paid a very nice man $300 to caulk my bathroom."

He laughs. "Well, today you're learning to do it yourself. Here, watch me."

He loads a tube of caulk into the gun like a professional, cuts the tip at an angle, and then demonstrates on a small section of the window frame. His movements are smooth and precise, laying down a perfect bead of white sealant.

"See? Not that hard. Your turn."

He hands me the caulk gun, his first mistake. It's heavier than I expect, and the trigger is stiff. I position it against the window frame as he showed me and squeeze.

And then a giant glob of caulk erupts from the tip, completely missing the seam and landing on the windowsill in an ugly blob.

"Okay," Wyatt says, trying not to laugh. "That's a start, I suppose."

"I'm terrible at this."

"You're learning. Try again. Slower this time, and keep steady pressure."

I attempt it again. This time, I overcorrect, and barely anything comes out.

"Here," Wyatt says, stepping behind me. "Like this."

He puts his hands over mine on the caulk gun, guiding my movements. His chest is pressed against my back, and I can feel the warmth of him and smell a combination of cologne, coffee, and some other scent that is just Wyatt.

"Steady pressure," he murmurs, his voice close to my ear. "Move at a consistent speed. There you go. You've got it."

The caulk comes out in a perfect bead this time, smooth and even.

But I'm not paying a bit of attention to the caulk, because I'm acutely aware of every point at which his body is touching mine. His hands over mine, his breath on my neck, the solid presence of him behind me. This is very, very bad.

"See?" he says. "You're a natural."

He steps back, and I feel the loss immediately. I clear my throat, trying to focus on the window instead of the way my heart is racing.

"Okay. I can do this."

"I know you can."

We work side by side for the next hour, caulking windows. I do get better as I go, though I still make a mess more often than not. At one point, I get caulk in my hair, and Wyatt has to help me get it out with a rag and mineral spirits.

"How did you even do that?" he asks, carefully working caulk out of a strand of my hair. "The window is three feet away from your head."

"I guess I'm just really unique."

"Well, that's one word for it."

He's smiling, and his fingers are gentle in my hair, and I think maybe unique isn't the worst thing someone could call me.

By noon, we've made real progress. The windows are done. The storage area is looking more organized, thanks to Presley's expertise. And a group of people I don't even know are cleaning the kitchen, which didn't really need to be done, but I'm thankful for it nonetheless.

Someone shouts that lunch is ready, and we all migrate outside, where a spread of food has materialized on folding tables. Casseroles and fried chicken and potato salad and biscuits and sweet tea, and about seventeen different kinds of dessert.

"Is there a potluck rule in Copper Creek that I don't know about?" I ask Dolly, taking in the abundance of food.

"Honey, in the South, we don't do anything without food. It's basically a law."

I fill a plate and find a spot on the ground, sitting cross-legged in the grass like I haven't done since I was a child. Wyatt settles beside me, close enough that our shoulders are touching.

"You did good today," he says.

"I got caulk everywhere and almost fell off a chair trying to clean a top shelf."

"Well, you tried. That's what matters."

Across the way, Boone is telling a story that has everyone laughing. Presley is sitting with two other women her age, animated and happy. Dolly is moving through the groups like a queen holding court, making sure everyone has enough food and drink, and whatever else they need. I guess she really is a server at heart.

And I'm sitting in the grass in my jeans that now have paint on them, eating potato salad with a plastic fork, surrounded by people I didn't even know a month ago.

And I feel something I'm not sure I've ever felt before.

I feel like I belong.

For the first time in my life, I don't care which side

the fork is on. It's plastic anyway, so my mother definitely wouldn't approve.

"Can I ask you something?" a woman named Carol
says, sitting down near us. I recognize her from the bar.
She comes in on Fridays with her husband.

"Of course."

"What do you think of Copper Creek so far?"

The question catches me off guard. Everyone stops
talking and is looking at me, waiting for an answer.

"Well, it's definitely different than anywhere I've been
before, but I like it. The people have been very nice to me."

"Your great-aunt was a smart woman," Boone says.
"She knew what she was doing when she left you this
place."

"Did you know her well?"

"Well enough. She was a straight shooter, didn't
suffer fools, and worked harder than anyone I ever
met. But she also knew how to have fun. That was what
she was best at. She knew how to make people feel
welcome. And she knew the bar isn't just about the
drinks; it's about the community."

He takes a sip of his sweet tea.

"And she saw something in you, Eleanor. Something worth investing in. And Mavis didn't invest in
people she didn't believe in."

"I'm not sure I've lived up to that yet."

"Well, you're here, aren't you? That's a start."

The conversation drifts to other topics. Town

gossip, upcoming events, somebody's daughter who just had a baby, and has big ears, apparently. I mostly listen, soaking up the warmth of community and the easy way these people just exist together.

At one point, Dolly shares a story about her first marriage, how she left an abusive situation with nothing but a suitcase and $37.

"Came to Copper Creek because it was where the bus stopped when I ran out of money," she says. "Thought I'd stay a few days, figure out my next move. Well, that was over thirty years ago."

"What made you stay?" I ask.

"People gave me a chance when I didn't deserve one. Mavis hired me, even though I had no experience. Gave me a place to live when I didn't have anywhere to go. This town saved my life." She looks at me directly. "Sometimes you're meant to be in a place you hadn't planned on. Sometimes it's just the place where people see you for who you are and decide that's enough."

The words settle over me like a blanket.

Presley shares next, talking about her mother's addiction, about being raised by her grandmother, and the constant fear that her mom would show up and disrupt her life.

"My grandmother died two years ago," she says quietly. "And I thought about leaving. Maybe I'd go to Nashville and try to make it as a singer. But this town, well, the people here are my family. Blood doesn't always make a family. Sometimes family is just who shows up."

By the time we finish eating, I've heard at least a dozen stories of heartbreak and resilience. People who came to Copper Creek lost and then found themselves here.

It's like the town is a magnet for broken people, and somehow, by being broken together, everyone becomes whole.

I think about my own brokenness, about the mother I could never please and the fiancé I never really loved, and the life I was living that felt like a performance.

And maybe Copper Creek is exactly where I needed to be.

CHAPTER 11

The afternoon passes quickly. We tackle the rest of Gloria's list with methodical efficiency. The storage area gets completely reorganized. The soap dispensers are filled to the brim. The kitchen gets a deep clean, and someone even washes all the windows inside and out until they sparkle like brand new.

A man named Rick, who apparently knows his way around HVAC systems, takes a look at the cooler and decides that it just needs a new compressor and some refrigerant.

"I can do it for parts. Costs probably run you about $1,500 instead of three grand. I'll come by tomorrow."

$1,500 instead of $3,500. I could cry with relief.

By five o'clock, we're done, and the bar looks better than since I arrived, maybe better than it has looked in years.

"We did it," I say, looking around in wonder.

"*You* did it," Wyatt corrects. "We just helped."

People start packing up, loading tools into their trucks, and saying goodbye. Everyone refuses my offers of payment, reimbursement for supplies, or anything.

"Just keep the bar open," a woman says. "That's payment enough."

When it's finally just me and Wyatt standing in the cleaned and repaired bar, I feel tears threatening my eyes.

"Hey," he says softly. "You okay?"

"I don't know why they did this, why they helped me."

"Because you're one of us now, whether you realize it or not."

"But I've only been here for a few weeks."

"Doesn't matter. You showed up, you tried, and you let people help. That's all it takes."

I look down at my hands. They're dirty, stained, and blistered from a day's work. I don't think I've ever had a time in my life when my hands looked like this.

"Come on," Wyatt says. "Let's take care of those blisters before they get worse."

He leads me to the office, where he pulls out the first-aid kit from one of the desk drawers. Of course, he has a first aid kit, and he knows exactly where it is, even though I've been in the office for weeks and never saw it.

"Sit," he instructs.

I settle into the desk chair. He kneels in front of me

and takes one of my hands. His touch is gentle as he examines the blisters on my palm, his fingers surprisingly soft.

"These aren't too bad," he says, "but we should bandage them so they don't get infected."

He cleans the blisters with antiseptic, and I wince slightly at the sting. Then he carefully applies the bandages, his movements precise and practiced.

"You're good at this," I observe.

"Had to be. Combat medic training. Plus, you spend enough time building things, and you learn how to patch yourself up."

He finishes one hand and moves to the other, his head bent over my palm. I watch him work, noticing details I haven't allowed myself to notice before. The way his hair falls across his forehead, the concentration in his expression, the competence of his hands.

"There," he says, finishing the second bandage. "Good as new. Well, almost."

But he doesn't let go of my hand. He just holds it, his thumb brushing across my wrist. He looks up at me, and there's something in his eyes that makes my breath catch.

"Eleanor…"

His phone rings, shattering the moment. He pulls back, checks the screen, and sighs.

"It's Boone. Probably forgot something." He answers. "Hey, what's up?" I can hear Boone's voice, but not the words."Yeah, no problem. I'll bring it by tomorrow."

Wyatt hangs up and looks at me apologetically.

"He left his good hammer. Did you know that men have a good hammer? Anyway," he says, "he needs it first thing in the morning."

"A good hammer is important."

My voice sounds normal, which is impressive because my heart is racing.

Wyatt stands, offering me his hand to help me up. When I take it, he pulls me to my feet, and for a moment, we're standing very close, neither one of us moving.

"Today was good," he says quietly.

"It was."

"You're good at this, you know. The community thing. Making people feel welcome."

"I'm just trying not to mess it up."

"You're not messing anything up."

He reaches up, unexpectedly, and tucks a stray strand of hair behind my ear, his fingers lingering for just a second longer than necessary.

"You're doing exactly what Mavis hoped you'd do."

"What's that?"

"Becoming yourself."

The words echo what Harlan said weeks ago, and they hit me just as hard now.

Before I can respond, he steps back, breaking the spell.

"I should go. Early start tomorrow."

"Right. Of course."

He heads for the door and then pauses and looks back.

"I know I've said it before, Eleanor, but I'm really glad you're here. Even if it's just for six months. Even if you leave in October. I'm glad I got to know you. You're getting to know this place and…"

He doesn't finish the sentence, just gives me one of those looks that makes my stomach flip. And then he's gone.

I stand in the office, surrounded by Mavis's notebooks and the smell of paint and cleaning supplies, touching the spot behind my ear where his fingers were.

Oh, this is dangerous, I think. This feeling growing between us. This pull I feel whenever he's near. The sense that I'm exactly where I'm supposed to be.

In less than six months, I have to make a choice. Stay or go. Build a life here, in this place I never expected, or return to Atlanta and figure out what comes next.

And the longer I stay, the harder that choice is going to be.

I sink into my desk chair and let myself sit with it for a moment.

Tomorrow I'll worry about the follow-up inspection, whether that Rick guy can really fix the cooler for

$1,500, and all the other million things that need my attention.

But for tonight, I'm going to let myself feel grateful. Grateful for this new community that showed up. Grateful to be in a place that's starting to feel like home. Mostly grateful for a man with kind eyes and gentle hands.

The week after the workday, everything feels different. Maybe it's because I'm not constantly panicking about the health inspection anymore. A guy named Rick, Boone's friend and an HVAC pro, came on Tuesday, fixed the cooler for $1,500, and had it running perfectly by the end of the day.

Then Gloria came back Thursday for her follow-up inspection, walked through the place, and finally said the words I desperately needed to hear, "You're in compliance."

I might have cried a little bit after she left. Just a little.

But passing the inspection doesn't mean my problems are solved.

Thursday evening, I'm in my office trying to make sense of Mavis's files again, which feels like a full-time job, when an email notification pings on my laptop. The sender's name makes me pause.

Gary Allen, Ashby and Associates.

I stare at it for a moment before clicking it open.

Dear Ms. Whitfield,

My name is Gary Allen, and I represent Ashby and Associates, a development firm specializing in mountain resort properties. We've been watching the Copper Creek area with great interest, and we believe your property, The Rusty Spur, would be an ideal acquisition for our clients.

We understand you recently inherited the property and may be weighing your options for the future. We'd like to discuss a potential purchase that would be mutually beneficial. Our clients are prepared to offer significantly above market value for the right location.

As you know, the Copper Creek region is poised for significant growth and development, and we believe this property has great potential as a part of a larger resort and hospitality project. The location on Mountain Road is ideal, with excellent visibility, ample space for expansion, and the kind of authentic mountain atmosphere that attracts high-end tourism.

We envision transforming the area into a destination experience: boutique accommodations, upscale dining, event venues, and spa facilities. Your property would serve as an anchor for this development, and we are prepared to make it worth your while. I'm talking about a number significantly higher than your current inheritance evaluation.

I'd welcome the opportunity to discuss this with you in more detail. Would you be available for a call this week? If you prefer, I'm happy to drive to Copper Creek to meet in person and present our full vision.

Best regards,

Gary Allen

Senior Acquisitions Manager

Ashby & Associates

I read it twice, then a third time.

A development firm wants to buy The Rusty Spur. Wanting to turn this weathered honky-tonk with its neon cowboy boot and string lights into some part of some upscale resort project.

My inheritance appraisal valued the property at two and a half million. If they're offering "significantly above" that…

I close the laptop and lean back in Mavis's office chair and stare at the wood-paneled walls covered with photos of smiling people, of community gatherings, and forty years of memories.

This should feel like good news. Like a solution. A way out if I need one.

But all I feel is sick.

I think about Dolly's story from our workday when she talked about the developers who bought up Main Street five years ago with big promises, and then about the businesses that closed and the families who had to leave. I think about the community that showed up last Sunday to help fix a bar they don't even own. And I think about what The Rusty Spur would become in the hands of developers. Probably torn down. Replaced with something sleek, modern, and expensive. Something that doesn't belong here.

I should delete the email. I should respond with a firm "not interested."

But I don't.

I just close the laptop and try not to think about why I'm keeping it.

"Y ou okay in here?"

Wyatt appears in the doorway, leaning against the frame in that casual way he does. He's in his usual jeans and flannel, his hair slightly mussed, like he's been running his hands through it.

"You know, just finishing up some paperwork."

He looks at me carefully. "You sure? You got that look."

"What look?"

"The one where you're overthinking something and trying to convince yourself that you're not."

I laugh. "I don't have a look."

"You absolutely have a look." He comes in and sits on the edge of the desk, close enough that I can smell his cologne. "Want to talk about it?"

Yes. No. Maybe.

"It's nothing. Just thinking about money, the bar, and what happens at the end of the six months."

"Wow, that's a lot of thinking for a Thursday night."

"I'm good at overthinking."

"I've noticed."

"You know you don't have to figure it all out today, right?"

"I know, but my brain doesn't work that way."

"Well, then maybe we need to get your brain to shut up for a while." He grins. "Tomorrow night, be prepared."

"Wait, prepared for what?"

"Well, if I told you, it wouldn't be a surprise."

"Wyatt."

"Trust me. You'll like it, or you'll hate it, but either way, you'll stop overthinking for a few hours."

Friday night arrives, and The Rusty Spur is packed. I'm starting to understand the rhythm now. Fridays are always busy, but the last Friday of the month is really crowded.

"Payday," Dolly explains.

I'm behind the bar helping pour drinks when Presley bounces over, her eyes glimmering with excitement she can barely contain.

"What?" I ask suspiciously.

"Nothing. Just excited about tonight."

"Why? What's tonight?"

"You'll see." She looks at Wyatt across the bar, and they both grin.

I don't like this at all.

"Oh, you'll like it," Presley says, "or you'll hate it, but it'll be memorable."

Around eight o'clock, I understand what they mean.

A truck pulls up outside, and through the window, I

watch two big guys start unloading something large and mechanical-looking.

"What is that?" I ask as they maneuver it toward the door.

Dolly appears beside me, grinning too. "Well, that, sugar, is Tommy's mechanical bull."

"And before you ask, yes," Wyatt says, appearing on my other side, "I arranged this."

"Why would you arrange for a mechanical bull?"

"Well, because," Wyatt says, "you need to have more fun."

"I have plenty of fun. Without a bull involved."

"When's the last time you did something completely ridiculous?"

I open my mouth to answer and realize that I can't. When was the last time?

In Atlanta, everything I did was calculated, controlled, and appropriate. Even my fun was carefully curated. Tasteful gallery openings, charity events, and brunches at the right restaurants.

"Exactly," Wyatt says, reading my silence. "So tonight, you're going to do something totally ridiculous."

"I am *not* getting on that thing."

"We'll see."

The mechanical bull gets set up in the corner where they've pushed back tables and laid down thick padding. Tommy, the operator, is a guy who looks to be in his forties and has a handlebar mustache and the kind of enthusiasm usually reserved for rodeo announcers.

"Who's first?" he calls out.

Immediately, three guys volunteer.

I watch from the safety of the bar as customer after customer climbs on. Most last less than thirty seconds. A few make it to forty-five, and everyone ends up on the mat, laughing.

It actually looks a little fun, in a terrifying, potentially humiliating kind of way.

"Your turn," Presley says.

"Absolutely not."

"Come on!"

"Presley, I'm thirty-four years old. I'm not riding a mechanical bull in front of half of Copper Creek."

"Why not?"

"Because I have dignity."

"Boring," someone yells from the crowd, and I realize half the bar is now listening to this conversation.

"Eleanor, Eleanor, Eleanor!" The chant starts somewhere and spreads like wildfire through The Rusty Spur.

I look at Wyatt, who's watching me with an expression of pure challenge.

"Scared," he mouths.

That does it.

"Fine," I announce loudly. "Fine. But when I break

something, you're all witnesses." I point my finger at everyone.

The bar erupts in cheers and applause.

I make my way to the bull on shaky legs. This is absolutely insane. I'm wearing dark jeans and a black fitted T-shirt I bought at the local clothing store that seemed professional enough for bar work, but definitely was not designed for mechanical bull riding.

Tommy helps me climb on. Up close, the thing is much bigger and more menacing.

"First time, I assume?" he asks.

"That obvious?"

"You've got the look. Don't worry. I'll start easy. Just grip tight with your thighs, hold on with one or both hands, your choice, and try to move with it instead of fighting it."

"I've never ridden anything in my life. Like, not even a horse."

"Well, then today's your lucky day," he grins. "Ready?"

I grip the handle with both hands, and I don't care if it's proper technique. I just want to survive. I'm not ready to die yet.

The bull starts moving, slowly at first, a gentle rocking motion.

Okay. I can do this. This isn't that hard.

Then it speeds up.

I try to move with it, as Tommy said, but the bull has other ideas. It rocks back and forth, then starts to spin. My grip is so tight that my knuckles are white, and I can hear people cheering, but it sounds far away because my focus is on not being thrown off this thing.

The bull bucks harder.

My grip slips.

I'm weightless.

For one terrifying split second, I'm airborne—and then I'm being caught mid-fall by a pair of strong arms.

Wyatt.

He's holding me against his chest, one arm under my knees, one behind my back, and he's looking down at me with an intensity that makes the rest of the bar fade into background noise.

This man somehow made it across the room and over a barricade to catch me in midair.

"I've got you," he says, his voice low and rough.

"You always do," I reply breathlessly, immediately regretting the words that fell out of my mouth.

I don't know why I said that.

The Rusty Spur is cheering and whistling, but I barely hear it. Wyatt's arms are solid around me. His face is inches from mine, and time seems to have slowed down to a crawl.

"That was maybe the bravest thing I've ever seen," he says, and there's something in his expression that makes my stomach twist.

"I lasted, what, ten seconds?"

"Fifteen. I counted."

"Still pathetic."

"Still brave." His thumb brushes against my ribs where he's holding me, and I feel the touch everywhere. "You could have said no," he adds. "But you didn't."

"I'm starting to think saying no to you is impossible."

Something flashes in his eyes. Someone whistles, loud and pointed, and reality crashes back.

Wyatt sets me down carefully, but his hands linger on my waist for a beat longer than necessary.

Dolly shows up beside us with two shot glasses.

"You earned this."

"I don't drink whiskey."

"Well, you do tonight. You just rode a mechanical bull in a honky-tonk. That requires whiskey."

She hands one to Wyatt, too.

"For both of you. For courage."

We take the shots together. Mine burns going down, and I cough, which makes everyone laugh, but Wyatt's hand finds the small of my back, steadying me.

And somehow, that feels like it burns more.

The silver Audi pulls into the parking lot of The Rusty Spur on a Tuesday afternoon, looking as out of place as I did two months ago.

I'm behind the bar, restocking glasses, when I see it through the window. And when the doors open and

Cynthia steps out, followed by Archie, my stomach drops to my boots.

Thank goodness Wyatt isn't here. I don't think he'd like either one of them very much.

They pick their way across the gravel as if it might damage their shoes. Cynthia wears a cream silk blouse and tailored pants, her blonde hair blown out to perfection. Archie wears the navy blazer he always wears on weekends, the one that costs more than most people's rent.

They look like an advertisement for the life I used to live.

The door swings open, and Cynthia's face cycles through about four expressions—confusion, horror, amusement, and something that settles into pitying concern.

"Oh, Eleanor." She rushes toward me, arms outstretched. "Oh, honey. It's worse than I thought."

"What are you doing here?"

"We came to rescue you, of course." She pulls back and holds me at arm's length, examining me like I'm a patient. "Look at you. You're wearing flannel. And are those cowboy boots?"

"They're comfortable," I say, looking down at my feet.

"They're tragic." She glances around the bar—at the mounted deer heads, the neon signs, the disco ball, the mechanical bull in the corner. "This place is... It's very... rustic."

"It's a honky-tonk."

"I don't even know what that means."

Archie has been standing by the door, surveying the room with the expression he usually reserves for opposing counsel's weak arguments. Now he approaches, hands in his pockets, shaking his head slowly.

"Eleanor, we need to talk."

"About what?"

"About this." He gestures vaguely at everything. "About the fact that you've been stuck in this backwater town for two months and haven't once asked me to look into breaking the will."

"Because I don't want to break the will."

He laughs as if I've made a joke. "Right. You want to spend six months running a bar in—where even are we? I couldn't find this place on GPS. I had to ask a man on a tractor for directions."

"Copper Creek. It's called Copper Creek."

"It's called nowhere." He pulls out a chair and sits without being invited, crossing his ankle over his knee. "Listen, I've done some preliminary research. The terms of this will are unusual, but they're not ironclad. We could argue undue influence or diminished capacity—your great-aunt was clearly not thinking straight when she wrote this."

"Mavis was perfectly lucid."

"She left you a bar, Eleanor. A bar in the middle of the mountains with a—" he squints at the corner "—is that a mechanical bull?"

"Yes."

"She left you a bar with a mechanical bull and expected you to run it for six months. That's not the decision of a sound mind. That's a cruel joke."

Something hot flares in my chest. "It wasn't a joke. It was a gift."

Cynthia sits down beside Archie, reaching for my hand across the table. "Sweetie, we're worried about you. You stopped answering my texts. You missed Miranda's engagement party. And when I finally got you on the phone last week, you talked for ten minutes about someone named Dolly and how she makes the best fried chicken you've ever had."

"She does make the best fried chicken I've ever had."

Cynthia and Archie exchange a look. The kind of look that says she's lost it.

"Eleanor." Archie leans forward, his voice dropping into the patient tone he uses with difficult clients. "You don't belong here. You know that, right? This isn't your world. These people—" he waves his hand dismissively, "they're perfectly nice, I'm sure, but they're not your people. You're Eleanor Whitfield. Your mother built one of the most respected etiquette schools in the Southeast. You trained diplomats' children. You belonged to the Junior League."

"I hated the Junior League."

"That's not the point."

"Then what is the point?"

"The point is that you're hiding." Cynthia squeezes my hand. "You're scared about starting over after your mother's death, so you're hiding in this little town where no one knows you and no one expects anything from you. And we understand that. We do. But you can't hide forever."

I look at her—at my best friend since college, at the woman I've shared a thousand lunches and shopping trips and gossip sessions with—and I realize I don't know what to say to her anymore.

Because she's not wrong. I was hiding, at first. I was terrified and lost and desperate to escape.

But somewhere along the way, hiding turned into something else.

"I'm not hiding," I say slowly. "I'm... figuring things out."

"Figuring what out? How to pour beer?" Archie laughs. "Come on, Eleanor. Let me make some calls. We can have you out of this by the end of the month. You can come back to Atlanta, start over properly, maybe open your own studio—"

"No."

The word comes out sharper than I intended.

They both stare at me.

"No," I say again, softer this time. "I'm not leaving. I'm staying the six months. I'm honoring Mavis's wishes."

"But why?" Cynthia's face is genuinely confused.

"What's here for you? What could you possibly want from this place?"

I think about Dolly's fried chicken and Ruthie's banana pudding. About Meredith's garden and Presley's songs. About the regulars who know my name now, who wave when they see me in town, who've started treating me like I belong.

About Wyatt, with his blue eyes and his quiet steadiness and the way he looks at me like I'm worth knowing.

"Everything," I say. "Everything is here."

Archie stands, brushing invisible dust from his blazer. "Fine. Stay. Play cowgirl for a few more months. But when you come to your senses, call me. I'll still be able to get you out."

"I won't be calling."

He shakes his head, that condescending half-smile on his face. "You know what your problem is, Eleanor? You've always been too sentimental. Your mother saw it. She spent years trying to train it out of you." He buttons his blazer. "Clearly it didn't take."

Six months ago, that would have gutted me. The invocation of my mother, the implication that I was somehow failing to live up to her standards. But now I just look at him—really look at him—and wonder what I ever saw there.

"Goodbye, Archie."

He walks out without another word.

Cynthia lingers. She's looking around the bar again,

but this time her expression is less horrified and more... searching. Like she's trying to understand something that doesn't fit into any category she knows.

"I really don't get it," she says finally. "This place. These people. What could they possibly offer you that Atlanta couldn't?"

I think about the question. Really think about it.

"They don't expect me to be perfect," I say. "They just expect me to show up."

"That's not—" She stops, presses her lips together. "You could show up in Atlanta. You could show up at Miranda's engagement party. You could show up to brunch."

"That's not showing up. That's performing." I shake my head. "I've spent my whole life performing, Cynthia. Saying the right things, wearing the right clothes, knowing which fork to use and how to make small talk with people I don't care about. And I was good at it. I was so good at it that I forgot there was any other way to live."

"There's nothing wrong with manners and presentation—"

"No. There isn't. But there's something wrong with thinking that's all there is." I gesture around the bar—at the worn wooden floors, the Christmas lights that stay up year-round, and the jukebox in the corner that plays only country. "These people don't care what fork I use. They don't care what I'm wearing or who my mother was. They care whether I show up when someone needs help, whether I remember their names, and whether I'm kind."

Cynthia stares at me like I'm speaking a foreign language.

And maybe I am. Maybe I've started learning a new one.

"I should go," she says. "Archie's waiting."

She hugs me at the door, and it's awkward in a way our hugs have never been before. Like we're strangers pretending to be friends. Or maybe like we were always strangers, and I'm just now realizing it.

"Call me when you're back," she says. "We'll do lunch."

"Sure."

We both know I won't call. We both know there won't be lunch.

I stand in the doorway and watch them pull away, the silver Audi kicking up dust as it turns onto Mountain Road. Cynthia doesn't wave. Archie doesn't look back.

And I feel... nothing.

No, that's not true. I feel something, but it's not loss. It's not longing for the life they represent.

It's relief.

I'm still standing there when Dolly's voice comes from behind me.

"Friends of yours?"

I turn to find her leaning against the bar, arms

crossed, one eyebrow raised. I don't know how long she's been there. Long enough, probably.

"They used to be."

"Mmm." She comes to stand beside me, looking out at the now-empty parking lot. "Fancy car."

"Fancy people."

"They wanted you to leave?"

"They wanted to rescue me. They think I'm hiding here. Running away from my real life."

Dolly is quiet for a moment. Then she says, "And what do you think?"

I watch the last of the dust settle on Mountain Road. I think about Archie's condescension, Cynthia's confusion, and the way they looked at The Rusty Spur like it was a joke. The way they looked at me like I was a puzzle they couldn't solve.

"I think," I say slowly, "that I spent thirty-four years living someone else's idea of a real life. And I think maybe it's time to figure out what mine actually looks like."

Dolly nods, satisfied. "Good answer."

She pats my shoulder and heads back inside, leaving me alone with the mountains and the quiet and the strange, fragile feeling of becoming someone new.

CHAPTER 12

The next night continues in a blur of music and laughter, and the kind of ease I didn't even know existed. Someone puts a Garth Brooks song on the jukebox. A group starts line dancing. The mechanical bull claims victim after victim, all of them laughing as they fall. Around ten o'clock, a group near the bar starts chanting for karaoke, and someone wheels out the machine that usually lives in the storage room.

"You should sing something," Presley says.

"Absolutely not. I can't carry a tune in a bucket."

"Come on, it's fun."

"I'm *not* singing karaoke."

"You're always so serious. Live a little."

"I recently rode a mechanical bull. I've lived plenty for one week."

But then Wyatt's name starts being chanted, and he good-naturedly climbs up on the small stage area we've cleared out. He picks some country song I don't know, but that everyone else apparently does, because the whole bar is singing along. He's not a great singer. His pitch is questionable at best, but he's confident and fun and completely unselfconscious. Watching him, I feel something shift in my chest.

This man. This place. This life.

When did it become so easy to imagine staying here forever?

When he finishes to a big round of applause, he comes straight to me at the bar.

"Your turn."

"Absolutely not."

"Oh, come on. You rode the bull. Compared to that, singing karaoke is nothing."

"Those are actually not equivalent challenges."

"Scared?" He says it with that small smile that means he knows exactly what he's doing.

"I'm not scared. I'm just…"

"Scared?"

I narrow my eyes at him. "Fine, but you're doing it with me."

His eyebrows rise. "A duet?"

"A duet. Take it or leave it."

He grins. "I'll take it."

We end up choosing *Islands in the Stream*. It's the only duet in the karaoke catalog that I know most of the words to. Presley cues it up, and Wyatt takes one microphone while I take the other. The opening music starts, and I immediately regret every decision that has led me to this moment.

But then Wyatt starts singing Dolly Parton's part in this ridiculous falsetto, and I can't help but laugh.

Suddenly, we're doing it.

Singing to each other, hamming it up for the crowd, being completely ridiculous and completely free. I'm terrible, and Wyatt is not much better. We're off-key and laughing through half the lyrics, and neither of us can remember the bridge. But The Rusty Spur loves it. They clap along and cheer us on.

When we get to the chorus, Wyatt pulls me closer, and we're singing into each other's faces. His eyes are bright with laughter, and I think this might be the most fun I've ever had in my entire life.

The song ends, and the crowd goes wild. Wyatt's arm is around my waist, and we're both breathless and grinning like two idiots. And for a moment, we just stand there in the middle of The Rusty Spur looking at each other.

"That was…" I start.

"Amazing?" he suggests.

"I was gonna say humiliating, but sure. Amazing."

He laughs. "You had fun, though."

"Unfortunately, yes."

"Then my work here is done."

But his arm stays around my waist, and mine somehow ends up on his chest, and we're still standing very close together in the middle of a honky-tonk. The crowd has started to fade back into their own conversations, and it just seems to be us in this little bubble.

"Thank you," I say quietly.

"For what?"

"For this, for making me do ridiculous things and reminding me what fun feels like."

His hand comes up to tuck a strand of hair behind my ear, his fingers lingering against my cheek.

"Last call!" Dolly shouts from behind the bar, and just like that, the moment shatters.

Wyatt drops his hand and steps back, and I feel the loss of his touch.

"I should help close up," he says.

"Yeah, me too."

But as he walks away, he looks back at me, and the expression on his face makes my heart skip.

After we close, we fall into our normal routine. I wipe down the tables while he counts out the register. We move around each other in silence, but there's something different tonight, a charge in the air that wasn't there before, or maybe it was always there and tonight just made it impossible for us to ignore.

"Back deck?" he asks when we're done.

"Always."

We grab our drinks, sweet tea for both of us tonight, and head out to the deck behind The Rusty

Spur. Out here, the mountains are dark against the night sky, and the stars are so bright they look like someone spilled diamonds across black velvet. I've never seen stars like these before. In the city, it was impossible to see stars.

I settle into what's become my usual spot, and Wyatt sits beside me, close enough that our arms brush. For a while, we sit in silence, but I'm hyper-aware of every point of contact, the warmth of him beside me, and the way the crickets and tree frogs create a symphony in the darkness.

"Can I ask you something?" Wyatt says finally.

"Of course."

"This week, the bull, the karaoke, all of it, that's not who you were in Atlanta, is it?"

It's not really a question, but I go ahead and answer anyway.

"Nope. In Atlanta, I was controlled. Everything was calculated and appropriate. I never did anything spon-taneous, crazy, ridiculous, or just for the pure fun of it."

"Why not?"

I think about the question. I really think about it.

"Because fun wasn't part of the plan. My mother had this vision of who I should be. Elegant, refined, accomplished, appropriate at all times. I spent a long time trying to be that person that I forgot how to just… Well, be. And now, while I rode a mechanical bull in front of a bunch of people, sang karaoke badly, and laughed until my face hurt, I can't remember the last time I actually felt this alive."

He's quiet for a moment, and when I glance at him, he's looking at me with such tenderness that it makes my breath catch in my throat.

"I'm glad you're here," he says softly. "I know I've said that before, but I really mean it. You're different here, more yourself."

"Or maybe this is the first time I've actually been myself anywhere."

"Maybe."

He reaches over and takes my hand, lacing his fingers through mine, like it's the most natural thing in the world. My heart starts racing, but I don't pull away.

"Eleanor," he says, his voice more serious now. "I need to tell you something."

"Okay."

"I'm trying really hard not to, and I don't want to complicate things for you. I know you're only here for six months, and we're almost halfway through that. I know you have a decision to make in October, and I don't want to make this decision harder. But, well, it's getting harder for me to pretend that I don't—" He stops and shakes his head. "I'm not good at this talking about feelings thing."

"Try," I say softly, squeezing his hand.

He looks at me fully, and in the dim light spilling over The Rusty Spur's windows, I can see a conflict in his expression.

"I like you, Eleanor, more than I should. More than is smart, considering you're probably leaving soon. And I'm trying to be okay with that, with just enjoying whatever time we have, but tonight I'm watching you laugh and let go and just be yourself." He swallows. "It's getting really hard to keep my distance."

My heart is pounding so hard I'm sure he can hear it. And I'm sure I should probably make an appointment for an EKG.

"What if I don't want you to keep your distance?"

He looks me in the eye.

"You don't know what you're saying."

"Don't I? Wyatt, I haven't decided anything about this place, but I know that right now, right here with you, I'm happier than I've been in years, maybe ever. And I'm tired of overthinking everything. I'm tired of being careful and controlled and afraid of feeling too much."

"Eleanor—"

"I'm not asking for promises. I'm not asking you to plan a future with me. I'm just asking you to stop pulling away every single time we get close."

For a long moment, he doesn't say anything. He just looks at me with those eyes, those big blue eyes, like he's trying to read some answer on my face.

Then slowly, he reaches up and cups my cheek, his thumb brushing across my bottom lip.

"And you're sure?" he asks.

"I'm sure."

He leans in, and my eyes start to close. This is it. It's finally happening.

His phone erupts in his pocket, a sound impossibly loud in the quiet night.

We both freeze.

He closes his eyes, clearly debating whether he should answer it.

"You should get that," I say, even though every part of me is screaming at him not to.

He reluctantly pulls back and takes his phone out of his pocket, looking at the screen. "It's a text from my grandmother," he sighs. "Her toilet's leaking again. She's got water all over the bathroom floor."

"Then you have to go."

"I really don't want to." But he's already standing. "But yes, I have to go. She's in her eighties and shouldn't be trying to fix plumbing at midnight."

"Of course. Go."

He pauses at the door and looks back at me. "Eleanor—"

"Go take care of your grandmother. We'll finish this conversation later."

"Promise?"

"Promise."

He disappears inside, and a minute later, I hear his truck start up and pull out of the parking lot. I sigh and fall back into my chair, staring up at the stars.

I sit alone on the deck behind The Rusty Spur, my lips still tingling from the kiss we almost shared and my hands still warm where he held them, or maybe still warm from where I held his. What am I doing? I'm falling for him. That's what I'm doing. Falling hard and fast for a man who lives in a small town and has a plan to stay there, building a life I could never have imagined wanting.

I pull out my phone, and before I can overthink it, I open my email and find Gary Allen's message. I stare at it for a long moment, at the promise of money and security and an easy out, and then I hit delete. I don't need an escape hatch. I don't need a backup plan. I just need to figure out what I actually want.

After riding a mechanical bull and singing karaoke and almost kissing Wyatt Rivers on the deck of a honky-tonk bar under a sky full of stars, I'm starting to think I might already know. But the question is whether I'm brave enough to choose it.

I finish my sweet tea and head back inside to lock up. The Rusty Spur looks different in the quiet, with neon signs casting colored shadows across the worn wooden floor and string lights still glowing warmly. I can almost hear tonight's laughter, music, and cheers. This place is starting to feel like mine, like Mavis knew what she was talking about, like she knew exactly what she was doing.

That should terrify me. Instead, it feels right.

I lock the front door, make sure everything is secure, and climb the stairs to my apartment above the bar. It's small, but comfortable, more so than my pristine Atlanta condo ever was. I get ready for bed, and sleep doesn't come easily. I keep replaying the moment on the deck, the way Wyatt looked at me, the feel of his hand cupping my cheek, and how time seemed to stop just before his phone rang.

What would have happened if his grandmother's toilet hadn't started leaking?

I know what would have happened. He would have kissed me, and I would have kissed him back. And then what?

I roll over, punching my pillow into a better shape. This is why I can't sleep. I keep asking "and then what" about everything. It's exhausting.

Finally, sometime after 2 a.m., I drift off.

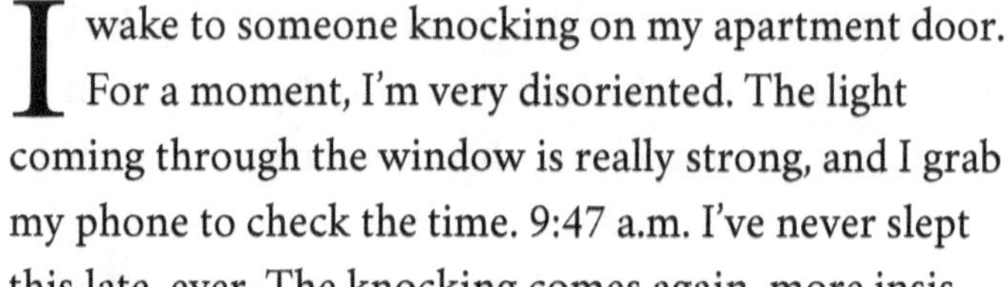

I wake to someone knocking on my apartment door. For a moment, I'm very disoriented. The light coming through the window is really strong, and I grab my phone to check the time. 9:47 a.m. I've never slept this late, ever. The knocking comes again, more insistent this time.

I stumble out of bed wearing my oversized T-shirt and peer through the peephole. It's Wyatt, of course. My heart does that flip it does when I see him, but this time there's an extra layer of nervousness. After last night and our conversation and the almost kiss on the deck, what do I even say?

I open the door. He's holding two cups of coffee, as usual, and a white paper bag that smells like heaven.

"Morning," he says, his eyes taking in my appearance, bedhead and sleep-wrinkled shirt, with obvious amusement. "I brought breakfast and an apology."

"An apology for what?"

"For last night. For leaving right when—" He stops and shifts his weight. "Can I come in? We should probably talk."

The words "we should probably talk" have never, in the history of the world, preceded anything good. But I step back and let him pass, suddenly very aware that I'm braless and that my hair probably looks like a disaster zone.

"Give me just one second," I say, darting into the bathroom.

I splash a little water on my face, try to tame my hair into something that looks normal, and grab a cardigan to throw over my T-shirt. When I come back out, Wyatt has set the coffee mugs and bag on my small kitchen table and is standing by the window, looking out over the mountains.

"What's in that bag?" I ask, trying to keep my voice light and airy.

"Biscuits from the diner. Dolly told me they're your favorite."

I sit down at the table and take the coffee he offers. He's made it exactly how I like it. Wyatt sits down across from me, but he doesn't reach for his own coffee. He just looks at me with an expression I can't quite read.

"So," I say, wrapping my hands around the warm cup, "your grandmother's toilet?"

He lets out a laugh. "The timing was unbelievable. The flapper valve was stuck. Water was pouring all over her bathroom floor. Took me an hour to fix it and then clean up the mess. But she's okay. Mostly annoyed that I wouldn't let her help clean up. You know, she's very independent." He pauses. "She also asked exactly who I was in such a hurry to get back to."

"And what did you tell her?"

"I told her I was closing the bar. She didn't believe me for a second. You know, my grandmother has a built-in lie detector."

I smile. "So you're a terrible liar."

"The worst." He finally picks up his coffee and takes a sip. "Eleanor, we need to talk about last night, okay?" He takes a breath, like he's gathering up his courage. "You said you wanted me to stop pulling away, and I heard you. But I need you to understand why I've been keeping my distance. It's not because I don't—" He stops for a moment. "Look, there's something I need to tell you about why I'm so careful, why I'm so not good at this. Okay?"

"Okay."

"There was someone before. Her name was Laney." He says the name like it still leaves a bitter taste on his tongue. "We were together for over two years. Got engaged right before my second deployment."

My stomach tightens. I feel a strange sense of jealousy. "What happened?"

"Well, she said she'd wait. Promised, actually, that she'd wait. I believed her." He's looking down at his coffee now, not meeting my eyes. "Eight months into that tour, I got an email. She'd met someone else. Someone who was there and not halfway around the world getting shot at. Someone who could give her a normal life."

"Oh, Wyatt, I'm so sorry."

"The worst part wasn't even that she left. It was… it was that I understood it. I mean, on some level, I really got it. Being with someone in the military is hard. The deployments, the uncertainty, the fear. And I was different when I came home. Quieter. Harder to reach. I don't blame her for not wanting to deal with that. But it still hurt."

He finally looks at me.

"When I came back here after I got out, I tried dating. Tried keeping things light and casual. Told myself it was better that way. No promises. No expectations. Nobody gets hurt. But it turns out I'm not built for casual. When I care about someone, I'm all in. Which means I get hurt all in, too."

I set my coffee down, my hands suddenly shaking a bit. "And you're telling me this because…"

"Because last night on that deck, I almost kissed

you. And I wanted to. Gosh, Eleanor, I really wanted to. But then I went home, and I couldn't sleep because all I could think about was October and the fact that in a few months, you have to decide whether you're staying or going back to Atlanta. And if you're going to leave, I'm trying to protect myself. I'm not doing a great job of it, clearly, since I'm sitting at your kitchen table right now bringing you coffee and biscuits and telling you things that I don't tell people."

He runs a hand through his hair.

"The thing is, I already care about you more than I should after such a short time. And I know that if we keep going down this road, if we keep having these moments and almost kisses and late-night conversations, I'm going to fall for you completely. And then when October comes, and you decide Atlanta is where you belong…"

"It'll break your heart."

"Yeah."

His honesty is devastating, but it deserves equal honesty in return.

"I don't know what I'm going to do in October," I say quietly. "A few weeks ago, I couldn't wait to leave. Two weeks ago, I was counting down the days, even. But now…" I look around the tiny apartment, thinking about The Rusty Spur downstairs, about riding mechanical bulls and singing karaoke, and feeling like more of myself than I ever have. "Now I'm not sure I want to leave. But, Wyatt, it's not the same thing as being sure that I'm staying."

"I know."

"And it's not fair to ask you to wait around while I figure that out, to risk your heart on a maybe."

"No, it's not fair," he agrees. "But here's the thing. I don't think I can stay away from you. Even knowing how this might end, even knowing I should be way smarter about this, I don't want to keep my distance. I just don't know if I can handle going all in when I don't know if you're staying."

We sit in silence for a moment.

"So what do we do?" I ask finally.

He thinks about it, really thinks about it.

"What if we just take it slow? Like, actually slow. Not 'saying we're taking it slow while having intense moments on the back deck' slow."

Despite everything, I smile. "Well, what does that actually look like?"

"We date. For real. Like normal people. I take you to dinner, we go to the movies, and we spend time together without the pressure of figuring out the rest of our lives. We get to know each other without this intense, all-consuming thing we're doing. And we don't…" He gestures vaguely between us. "We don't complicate it until you know what you want, until you've decided about October. Because, Eleanor, if we cross that line and kiss each other and then you leave…" He shakes his head. "I don't think I'd even recover from that."

The honesty in his voice breaks my heart a little, but he's right. He's protecting himself, and I can't blame him for that.

"Okay," I say. "We'll take it slow. We'll go on dates. We'll get to know each other. Maybe we'll hate each other. Who knows?"

He laughs.

"And you're okay with all that?"

"No. Yes. I don't know." I laugh. "Last night I was ready to jump in with both feet, but this morning, I think I want to protect you from me, which is a very weird feeling. But I think you're right. We need to know. We need to be smart about this."

"Well, smart isn't nearly as fun as reckless," he says with a small smile.

"No, but it's probably better in the long run."

He reaches across the table and takes my hand. His thumb brushes against my knuckles. Even that small touch makes my heart race.

"For what it's worth," he says quietly, "I really do hope you stay. And I'm going to do everything I can to show you why Copper Creek is worth choosing, why this life right here is worth choosing."

"That's a lot of pressure."

"I know, but I'm willing to take the risk if you are."

I squeeze his hand. "I'm willing."

"Okay then." He stands, pulling me up with him.

"So, dinner tonight. Seven o'clock. I'll pick you up, take you somewhere nice, and we'll have an actual first date like normal people."

"I don't think either of us has probably ever been normal."

"Well, then we'll fake it."

He's standing close now, close enough that I can see flecks of gold in the middle of his blue eyes. For a moment, I think he's going to kiss me anyway, but he doesn't. He just reaches out and tucks a strand of hair behind my ear, his fingers lingering for a second. It's becoming a pattern, and I love it.

"Seven o'clock," he repeats.

"I'll be ready."

After he leaves, I lean against the closed door, touching the spot behind my ear where his fingers were. This is torture, sweet, exquisite torture. But he's right. If we're going to do this, we need to do it right. I need to figure out what I want before I risk his heart along with mine.

I just hope I can figure that out before it's too late.

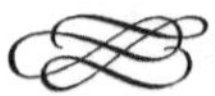

CHAPTER 13

I spend the rest of the day in a weird haze of nervous energy. I try to do my paperwork, but I just can't focus. I fiddle around in the storage area, even though Presley already organized it perfectly. I polish the bar top until it gleams. Dolly arrives for her shift around three and takes a look at me.

"Well, you're fidgety today."

"I am not fidgety."

"Sugar, you've wiped down that same section of the bar four times in the last five minutes. What in the world is going on?"

"Wyatt and I are going on a date tonight."

Her face lights up. "Finally. About time you two stopped dancing around each other."

"We're taking it slow."

"Uh-huh." She doesn't seem convinced.

"We are. We had a whole conversation about it.

About how we're gonna be smart and not rush into anything and make sure we know what we want before we complicate things."

"And how do you think that's working out for you?"

"Terrible so far. I'm a nervous wreck."

She laughs. "Well, that's because you like him. Really, really like him. And that's scary when you don't know what's coming next."

"So how did you get so wise?"

"Honey, I've been watching people fall in love in this bar for many, many years. You pick up a few things." She starts slicing lemons. "Can I give you some advice?"

"Please."

"Stop trying to figure out what you're gonna do in October right now. You've still got months. That's a lot of time. You just focus on tonight, on getting to know him, on seeing if this thing between you is real or if it's just proximity and loneliness."

"Proximity? You think it could just be proximity?"

"Oh, no. I think it's real, for sure. But you have to figure that out for yourself." She points the knife at me. "Now go on upstairs and get ready for your date. Wear something nice, but not too nice. Remember, this is Copper Creek, not Atlanta."

At 6:45, I'm standing in front of my closet, having a minor crisis. Everything I brought from Atlanta is just way too formal. The dresses are cocktail appropriate, the blouses need statement jewelry, and the shoes require valet parking. I finally settle on a pair of dark jeans, my nice ones without any paint stains, and a soft blue sweater that Dolly convinced me to buy at a boutique in town last week. It's casual, but pretty, and it makes my eyes look brighter. I leave my hair down, just a little bit of wave to it. Minimal makeup, simple silver earrings. I look like someone who might belong in Copper Creek, definitely not like the Eleanor Whitfield from Atlanta. Like Eleanor, just Eleanor.

At exactly seven, there's a knock on my door. I take a deep breath, check myself in the mirror one more time, and open it. Wyatt is standing there, also in dark jeans and wearing a button-down shirt, navy blue, rolled up at the sleeves. And he looks just so good, it should be illegal.

"Hi," I say, suddenly feeling very shy.

"Hi." He's looking at me like I'm the only thing in the world worth looking at. "You look beautiful."

"Thank you. You clean up pretty nice yourself."

"Well, I tried."

He offers his arm. "Ready?"

I take his arm, lock my apartment door, and let him lead me down the stairs. This is our first real date, the first step toward figuring out whether this thing between us is real, whether it's worth the risk. As we walk out into the warm evening, his hand finds mine as if it belongs there, and I think maybe it could be.

So I say, "Are you gonna tell me where we're going, or is this a surprise?"

"It's a surprise. Well, sort of." We walk toward his truck. "I'm cooking."

"You're cooking?"

"Yeah, at my place. I mean, that's okay, right?"

To me, it's more than okay. It's unexpected in a way that makes my stomach do something interesting. "That's perfect. That sounds perfect," I say.

Wyatt's truck rumbles down Mountain Road and then turns onto a narrow street I haven't noticed before, one that cuts away from the main road and disappears back into the trees. We follow it for at least half a mile, the forest pressing close on both sides, before the trees open up and his cabin comes into view.

It's small, a single-story building made from dark wood with a stone chimney and a wide front porch that stretches the full length of the house. String lights are wound around the porch posts, not the kind you put up for a party, but the kind that have been there long enough to just become part of the place. A rocking chair sits near the front door, and beside it, a small table with a mason jar of wildflowers that someone clearly just picked.

Behind the cabin, the mountains stretch out in an endless ridge, the last light of evening turning them that particular shade of blue and gold that makes your breath catch.

"Oh," I say softly as he kills the engine.

"Yeah." He looks at me, and there's something about his expression. "It's not much."

"Wyatt, it's beautiful."

He nods, pleased but trying not to show it, and then hops out of the truck to come around and open my door.

Inside, the cabin is exactly what the outside promised, a single open room that serves as the living space and kitchen, with old wood floors worn smooth by years of use. A stone fireplace takes up most of one wall, and even though it's too warm to use tonight, I can tell from the stack of seasoned logs that it gets plenty of use during the colder months.

A simple sofa in dark leather, a couple of wooden chairs, and a table that looks handmade, sturdy, and beautiful. The kitchen is small but well organized. It has a gas range, a butcher-block counter, and copper pots hanging from a rack. Everything has a place, and everything is clean, but not sterile clean, not trying to impress clean like I used to see in the city, just a quiet tidiness of someone who takes care of what they have.

What catches my eye is the windowsill above the kitchen sink. It's lined with small carved wooden figures: a deer, a bear, an owl, a fish, a little horse, no bigger than my thumb. Each one is different, clearly handmade.

"Did you make these?" I ask, picking up the little bear and turning it over in my fingers.

"Yeah, it's something I do, mostly in the mornings when things are quiet." He's already moving around the kitchen, pulling things from the refrigerator. "Started when I came back from the service, needed something to do with my hands."

"They're gorgeous, Wyatt."

"It's just whittling."

"It's not just whittling." I set the bear down carefully. "They're art."

He glances at me over his shoulder, surprised. "Well, thank you."

I settle onto one of the tall stools at the kitchen counter and watch him cook. Of course, I offer to help him, even though I'm probably one of the world's worst cooks, but he declines.

He moves through the kitchen with the same confidence he shows behind the bar. I realize he's making trout as he unwraps two fillets from butcher paper. They're golden brown and fresh-looking, and he handles them with care.

"Where'd you get those?" I ask.

"Caught them this morning. Off the creek, about a mile up the mountain." He sets them on a plate and reaches for a cast-iron skillet. "My grandmother taught me how. Said if you're going to live in the mountains, you might as well learn how to eat what the mountains give you."

"Well, that sounds exactly like something she'd say." I smile, thinking about having dinner at Dolly's, about Meredith's eyes and the way she'd squeezed my hand and told me not to worry. "She's something else."

"She is." He sets the skillet on the stove and drizzles oil into it. "She liked you, by the way. Told me so afterward, which, trust me, is not something she does easily."

"Oh yeah? Well, she told me that I'd gotten you all tied up in knots."

Wyatt lets out a groan. "Yes, I remember."

"I didn't know what she meant at the time," I pause, "but maybe I think I'm starting to figure it out."

He goes very still for a moment, the oil shimmering in the skillet, and then looks at me with something in those blue eyes. He clears his throat and turns back to the stove, laying the fillets in the pan with a satisfying sizzle.

"She also said I needed some knots," he adds. "Said I'd been too settled for too long."

"Do you think she's right?"

He doesn't answer right away, just watches the trout cooking.

"Yeah," he says finally. "I think maybe she was."

He seasons the trout simply with salt, pepper, and a little squeeze of lemon. The smell that rises from the skillet is incredible: butter, lemon, and something earthy.

"What else are we having?" I ask, leaning forward on my stool, feeling my stomach start to rumble a bit.

"Roasted potatoes. They're already in the oven. Collard greens with bacon and a little apple cider vinegar. And my family recipe for cornbread, of course."

"Wow, you really had this planned out."

"I did." He flips the trout, golden and crispy on the first side. "Wanted it to be good."

There's something in the way he says it, simple and honest, with no performance, that makes my chest ache a little. This man, who could have taken me somewhere impressive, instead chose to stand in his own kitchen and cook me a meal from scratch. He caught the fish himself this morning and took the time to plan it out.

It's the most romantic thing anyone has ever done for me, and it doesn't look anything like romance the way I was taught to recognize it.

We eat at a small table by the window. He has set it simply: forks, plates, and cloth napkins that have been washed many times and are soft and worn from use. There's a mason jar of sweet tea that sits between us, and he pours mine before his own.

The food is extraordinary. The trout is perfectly cooked, crispy on the outside and tender and flaky within. The lemon and butter brighten against the richness of the fish. The potatoes are golden and caramelized, and the collard greens are wonderful, with just enough tang from the vinegar to cut through the richness of the bacon.

I close my eyes on the first bite of fish. I can't help it.

"That good, huh?" Wyatt asks. I can hear a smile in his voice.

"I'm not going to dignify that with a response," I say, opening my eyes. "But yes, that good."

He grins, and I see the crinkles at the corners of his blue eyes.

We talk while we eat, the way we've been learning to talk, not about the bar, not about me possibly leaving in October, not about anything heavy. Just each other, small things, real things.

He tells me about growing up in Copper Creek, about fishing with his grandfather before he passed away, about getting into trouble with Boone as teenagers, about the summer he was fourteen and tried to build a canoe in his grandfather's garage, but flooded the whole thing.

"My grandmother was so mad at me. She didn't speak for an hour." He shakes his head. "Then she handed me a mop and said, 'Well, are you going to learn from this or not?'"

"That is exactly how she handled it at Dolly's dinner when Boone knocked over the sweet tea pitcher. Same look and everything."

"Oh, you saw the look?" Wyatt laughs.

"Yeah, that's the one."

"Forty years of elementary school kids. She's definitely perfected it."

I tell him about the secret garden I had as a kid. About sneaking out back as a young child to dig in the dirt when my mother thought I was practicing piano. About the tomatoes that were too small and too lopsided to eat, but I was prouder than anything I had ever accomplished in etiquette school.

"I used to talk to them," I admit.

It sounds absurd to say that out loud, but Wyatt just nods, completely serious.

"Plants respond to that. I've seen some scientific studies about it, and my grandmother swears by it. She talks to her roses every single morning."

"And does it actually work?"

"Well, her roses are the best on the mountain, so I'd say yes."

"You know, you should start a garden here," he says, leaning back in his chair. "There's a sunny patch on the south side of the building. It's just sitting there doing nothing. I think it's pretty good soil, too."

I picture it, a garden behind The Rusty Spur, with herbs and maybe tomatoes tucked against the weathered wood of the building, the mountains rising in the background. Mine. Something that grows or doesn't grow, with no one grading me on it.

"You know," I say slowly, "I might actually do that."

After dinner, Wyatt clears the table and waves off my offer to help, saying, "You're my guest. No helping. Come on, there's something I want to show you."

I follow him out to the front porch, and the evening air hits me like cool water. The sun has almost set now, with just a thin line of gold along the ridge of the mountains. The sky above it is deepening from blue to indigo, and the first stars are beginning to appear.

He pulls the rocking chair into the center of the porch and sets it facing the view, then drags one of the wooden kitchen chairs beside it.

"Best seat in the house," he says, pointing to the rocker. "Ladies first."

I settle into the old rocking chair, and it creaks softly beneath me. It's well-worn and perfectly balanced, far better than any brand-new rocking chair could be. Wyatt sits in the wooden chair beside me, his long legs stretched out in front of him, a mason jar of sweet tea in his hand.

And for a while, we just sit there.

The mountains darken by degrees, the last of the light bleeding out of them until they're silhouettes against the stars. We can hear the creek murmuring somewhere below us, and the crickets have begun an evening symphony. Somewhere in the distance, an owl calls out, and another answers.

It's the quietest I've ever been.

Not the forced quiet of an empty studio with too many bills or a too-big apartment, but the real quiet. The kind that doesn't feel empty but full. Full of sound and life and the simple, steady presence of another person beside me.

"Thank you," I say after a long while. "For cooking, for tonight, for all of it."

He looks at me. "I enjoyed it. More than I expected, actually."

"Why do you say that?"

"Because I was a little nervous," he laughs. "I don't do this. I haven't done this in a long time. I wanted it to be right."

"It was definitely right," I say quietly. "It was exactly right."

He holds my gaze for a moment, and that charged, electrical thing happens again between us. My breath goes shallow. I can see it in his eyes, the pull of it, the wanting. But he doesn't lean in, and I don't either.

Instead, he reaches over and takes my hand, lacing his fingers through mine the way he did this morning at the kitchen table. His palm is warm and rough, and his thumb traces a slow, steady circle on the back of my hand.

We sit like that for a long time, watching the stars come out over the Blue Ridge Mountains.

And it's enough.

~

He drives me home through the dark with the windows down, the warm night air rushing through the truck's cab. We don't speak much, but it's not an awkward silence. It's the silence of two people comfortable enough with each other to let the quiet breathe.

When we pull into The Rusty Spur's parking lot, he turns off the engine but doesn't move to get out right away.

"So," he says, turning to look at me. "Same time next week?"

"I'd like that very much."

He nods, then gets out and walks me to the side entrance. We stand on the small porch for a moment, as we did this morning. This morning, we were setting ground rules, and now we're standing in the aftermath of something that felt effortless.

"Good night, Eleanor," he says softly.

"Good night, Wyatt."

He reaches out and tucks a strand of hair behind my ear, gently, the way you'd want to touch something you're careful with, and then he steps back. It's our thing.

I watch him walk to his truck. He raises his hand in a small wave before climbing in, and I wave back.

Then I go inside, climb the stairs, and sit on the sofa in the dark.

I think about the little carved bear on his windowsill and how he caught fish himself this morning, planned a whole meal, and set the table with worn cloth napkins because that's what you do when someone matters to you. About how he held my hand on the porch and didn't ask for anything more than that.

I think about how, for the first time in my life, I sat across from someone and didn't once wonder if I was impressive enough.

I just felt seen.

CHAPTER 14

Monday morning starts the way most Mondays do at The Rusty Spur, with me still trying to figure out Mavis's filing system and failing spectacularly. I'm not sure who was crazier, me or her. I'm in the office, surrounded by folders labeled with things like *This Is Important Stuff* and *That Thing I'm Supposed to Remember From 2019*, when my phone buzzes with an email notification.

I almost ignore it, but the sender's name catches my eye.

Gary Allen.

I thought I'd deleted his last email, put it out of my mind, but apparently, he's not taking my silence as an answer, so I open it.

Ms. Whitfield,

I wanted to follow up on my previous message regarding our interest in The Rusty Spur property. I understand you may need time to consider such a significant decision, so I want to present our formal offer in person.

Our clients are prepared to offer you $3.5 million for the property, with flexible closing terms to accommodate your timeline. This is significantly above the current market evaluation and is a unique opportunity for you.

I'll be in Copper Creek this Wednesday and would welcome a chance to meet with you. I believe once you see the full scope of what we're proposing, not just for your property, but the entire Copper Creek community, you'll understand why this partnership makes sense for everyone.

I plan to be at your establishment on Wednesday at 2 p.m. and look forward to our conversation.

Best regards,

Gary Allen

I read it three times.

$3.5 million.

I paid off the last of my mother's medical bills six months ago and sold everything I could to keep the studio afloat. My credit cards are maxed out, and my savings account currently has $1,247.

And last week, without telling anyone, I closed the studio. Didn't renew the lease. Hired a company to remove my personal belongings and put them in storage.

Why? Because I have decided that even if I don't stay in Copper Creek long-term, I know now that I don't want to teach etiquette again. That much I have learned about myself.

Still, three and a half million dollars would solve every single financial problem I have. It would let me start over, give me options I haven't had in years, and probably never would have.

I close my laptop and lean back in the chair, staring at the wood-paneled walls covered with photos of people who loved this place.

Wednesday at 2 p.m.

That's in two days.

I don't tell anyone about the email. Not on Monday night when Wyatt and I close up the bar together and he walks me to the stairs, his hand lingering on the small of my back. Not on Tuesday when Dolly asks me how the date went and I just smile like an idiot and say, *It was perfect.* Not on Tuesday night when Wyatt texts me, *thinking about you,* and I stare at my phone for five full minutes before texting him back, *thinking about you, too.* We have a conversation entirely in emojis that makes me laugh until my face hurts.

I don't tell anyone because saying it out loud would make it real, and I don't know what to do with it all yet.

Wednesday arrives too fast.

At 1:55 p.m., a black Mercedes pulls into The Rusty Spur's parking lot. It's so out of place among the pickup trucks and sensible sedans that people actually stop and stare. A man gets out, 50-ish, wearing an expensive suit, perfectly styled silver hair, and the kind of confident posture that comes from never having been told no. He surveys the building with an expression of someone mentally calculating property values.

I watch from the office window as he approaches the front door.

I've changed three times, settled on dark jeans and a white blouse, professional but not trying too hard. Not the pencil skirt and pearls version of Eleanor, but not the paint-stained work clothes version either. I land somewhere in between.

The bell over the door chimes, and I hear Presley's cheerful voice.

"Hey there, welcome to The Rusty Spur. What can I get ya?"

"I'm here to see Eleanor Whitfield. I have an appointment."

Gary Allen is everything I expected and worse. He's charming in that practiced way that wealthy people are charming, with all their big white teeth and firm handshakes and compliments that feel calculated rather than genuine. He orders a beer he never drinks and spreads papers across the table like he owns the place.

"Ms. Whitfield, thank you for taking the time to

meet with me." He gestures to the seat across from him. "I promise this will be worth your while."

I sit, keeping my expression neutral. "You mentioned an offer."

"Direct. I appreciate that."

He slides a folder across the table. "Three and a half million dollars for the property, the building, and the land. We'd give you sixty days to vacate, though, of course, we'd be flexible on timing if needed in your situation."

"My situation?"

"The inheritance stipulation. The requirement." He leans back, completely at ease. "We've done our research, Ms. Whitfield. We know you inherited the property with some conditions attached. We also know you had a successful business in Atlanta that unfortunately had to close, and that can't be an easy transition for you."

The way he says it, sympathetic but with an edge, makes something cold slide down my spine. He's done his homework. Probably knows exactly how much debt I'm carrying and exactly how desperate I should be.

"Well, I'm managing," I say coolly.

"Oh, I'm sure you are, but managing isn't thriving, is it?" He taps the folder with one of his well-manicured fingers. "This is life-changing money, Ms. Whitfield. The kind of money that gives you options, the freedom to start over on your own terms."

I don't open the folder. I don't look at the number printed on the page, because if I look at it, if I actually see it written out with all those zeros, I might find it impossible to say no.

"And what do you want to do with the property?" I ask.

"Transform it." His eyes light up with the kind of enthusiasm typically reserved for a kid in a candy store. "The Copper Creek area is on the verge of significant growth. Mountain tourism is booming. People are looking for the authentic experience combined with modern luxury. We envision a boutique resort, upscale accommodations, fine dining, spa facilities, event spaces, and this property would be the cornerstone."

"And what happens to The Rusty Spur?"

"Well, it would be incorporated into the vision, reimagined as an upscale restaurant and event venue. We would probably keep the name, of course, maintain local flavor, but elevate the experience."

Everything he's saying sounds reasonable, like progress. Sounds like exactly what somebody in my position should want to hear.

So why does it feel like he's describing the death of something instead of its evolution?

"This isn't just about you, Ms. Whitfield." He leans forward. "This is about Copper Creek, about bringing jobs and economic growth to a community that desperately needs it, about putting this town on the map."

"Copper Creek seems to be doing just fine without being on a map."

"Well, for now." His expression shifts. He's still friendly, but there's an edge now. "But small towns like this don't survive without growth, without investment. In ten years, fifteen years, places like Copper Creek will be a ghost town unless someone does something to save them."

"You mean by buying local businesses and then turning them into luxury resorts?"

"By giving them a future." He sits back. Now he's very pointed. "Ms. Whitfield, I'm offering you three and a half million dollars. That's not just generous, it's extraordinary. Most properties like this sell for a million, maybe a million five. I'm giving you more than double market value."

"Yeah, and why is that?"

The question catches him off guard. "Excuse me?"

"Why are you offering me so much? I mean, if the property's only worth a million five, why pay more than double?"

He recovers quickly and smooths back into his professional warmth mode. "Because we believe in the project. Because your property is key to making that work. And because we're prepared to make it worth your while to say yes."

"And if I say no?"

Something flickers across his face. It's gone too fast to read. "Then we'll be disappointed, but we'll respect your decision. Of course."

He doesn't sound like he'll respect my decision at all.

"I need time to think about it."

"Okay. But I do need an answer by Friday. We have other properties we're considering and other opportunities. I certainly can't hold this offer open indefinitely."

"Forty-eight hours?"

"Less, actually, since it's already Wednesday afternoon."

He stands, extending his hand. I shake it automatically, years of etiquette training kicking in even as every instinct tells me to run.

"I think you'll find this is the right decision, Ms. Whitfield. For you and for Copper Creek."

He picks up his untouched beer and sets it on the bar with a crisp twenty-dollar bill. "Think about it. I mean, really think about it. Three and a half million dollars. Freedom. Options. A fresh start."

He walks out, and the bell over the door chimes behind him.

I sit at the table, staring at the folder he left, and my hands are shaking.

～

"Who was that?"

I look up and find Wyatt standing behind the bar, wiping down glasses as usual. His expression is neutral, but there's something behind his beautiful blue eyes.

"That was a developer." The words come out more defensive than I intended. "Gary Allen, from Ashby and Associates."

"And what did he want?"

"He wants to buy the bar."

Wyatt's hands stop moving. "What?"

"He made me an offer, a formal offer for the property."

"How much?"

I shouldn't tell him, but the number is so big, so impossible, that it just pops out anyway. "Three and a half million."

The glass in Wyatt's hand hits the top of the bar harder than necessary.

"And what did you tell him?"

"I told him I needed time to think about it."

"To think about it." He's not even looking at me now, just staring down at the glass. "So you're actually considering this? You've only been here a few weeks, and you're already looking for the exit door?"

"Well, now that's not fair, is it?"

He finally looks up, and his expression is harder than I've ever seen. "You said you were trying. You wanted to figure out what you wanted for once in your life. But the second someone waves money in your face, you're ready to bail."

"I didn't say I was ready to bail. I said I needed time to think about it."

"What is there to think about? This is people's lives, Eleanor. Their jobs. Their community. This place," he gestures around, and his voice cracks, "this place is more than real estate. It's our home."

"I know that."

"Well, do you? Because from where I'm standing, it looks like you're still thinking it's a business transaction. Like everything that's happened here—" He stops himself, his jaw tightening.

"Like everything that's happened here, what?" I stand up, anger rising to match his. "Say it, Wyatt."

"Like everything that's happened between us is just something you're willing to walk away from as long as the price is right."

The words hang in the air between us, sharp and painful.

"That's not fair," I say again, my voice shaking. "You don't get to make this about us. This is about my future, my financial survival. You have no idea what it's like to—"

"To what? To need money? To make hard choices?" His laugh is bitter. "I came back from Afghanistan with PTSD and medical bills I'm still paying off. I moved back in with my grandmother because I couldn't afford rent. I worked three jobs before Mavis gave me this one, so don't you tell me what I don't understand."

"Well then, you should understand why I'm considering it."

"I understand that you're scared. I understand that it is life-changing money. But I also understand there are things worth more than money. And if you can't see that, if you can't see what you'd actually be giving up—" He stops, shaking his head.

"What? What would I be giving up?"

He looks at me for a long moment. And suddenly he's resigned, like he's lost everything. He says quietly, "You'd be giving up everything."

He turns and walks away, disappearing into the back of the bar, leaving me standing alone at the table with Gary Allen's folder and the weight of the offer pressing down on my chest like a boulder.

I don't see Wyatt for the rest of the afternoon. Presley works the bar, looking at me, concerned but not asking questions. Dolly arrives for her evening shift and immediately knows something is wrong.

"What happened?" she asks, cornering me in the office.

"A developer made an offer on the bar."

"Gary Allen?"

I blink. "You know him?"

"I know *of* him." Her expression darkens. "He's been sniffing around Copper Creek for months. He's made offers on the hardware store, the bakery, and Grits and Grind. He's been turned down every single time."

"Why didn't anyone tell me?"

"Because we didn't think you'd be foolish enough to even listen to him." She crosses her arms. "What did he offer you?"

"Three and a half million."

She lets out a low whistle. "Wow. That is a lot of money. But not enough."

"What do you mean, not enough?"

Dolly looks at me with sharp eyes. "Sugar, I told you that developers came through here promising the moon. Jobs, growth, prosperity. They bought up half of Main Street, turned the old hotel into luxury condos, and opened fancy shops that no one here could afford to shop in. Locals got priced out. Rents went up. Property taxes went up. Small businesses that had been here for generations had to close because they couldn't compete anymore. And those developers? They made their money, and then they moved on to the next town. Left Copper Creek with empty storefronts and people who couldn't even afford to live in their own community anymore."

"Gary says he wants to help the town bring economic growth."

"Oh, I'm sure he did say that. And I'm sure he believes it in his own way. But men like Gary Allen don't see places like The Rusty Spur as homes. They see them just as investments. And when the investments stop paying off, they move on." She moves toward the door and then pauses. "Mavis got offers, too, you know. Every year or so, someone would come through wanting to buy the bar, turn it into something 'better.' She always said no."

"Why?"

"Because she knew the place was worth what the place was worth. Not in dollars, but in people, in memories, in the kind of community that can't be bought or sold. The question is, do you know that?"

She leaves me alone in the office with that question echoing in my mind.

Friday comes too fast. I haven't slept more than a few hours each night. I've read Gary Allen's proposal a dozen times and looked at my bank account. I've made lists of pros and cons till my hand cramped. I haven't talked to Wyatt. He's been avoiding me, working different shifts, leaving before I can corner him, responding to my texts with one-word answers that tell me everything I need to know about where we stand now.

During my process of making a decision, I decided that I can't worry about what Wyatt thinks. I have to make this decision for myself. I've never had the chance to make a decision without someone else being involved, namely my mother. This time, I decide, the decision needs to come from me. No outside pressure. No guilt. Wyatt was right about one thing - I have to figure out what I really want.

Friday afternoon at 1:45 p.m., Gary Allen's Mercedes pulls into the parking lot yet again. I watch from the office window as he gets out, looks at his expensive watch, and adjusts his expensive tie. He looks confident, like he knows he's about to close a deal.

I think about the folder on my desk with all the zeros. I think about my maxed-out credit cards and my failed business, and the life I left behind in Atlanta, I can never get back.

But I don't want it back anyway.

I think about Wyatt's face when he said I would be giving up *everything*. I think about Dolly's story about the developers who turned part of Copper Creek into something unrecognizable. And then I think about Mavis, who said no every single time.

I take a deep breath, and then I walk out to meet him.

Gary Allen is sitting at the same table as before, looking relaxed and confident. He seems to think he's got this whole thing sewn up already. He stands when he sees me approach, his fake smile already in place.

"Ms. Whitfield, I was hoping we'd have good news to celebrate today."

"Mr. Allen," I don't even sit down. "I've made my decision."

"Excellent. I've already drawn up the preliminary paperwork."

"I'm declining your offer."

His smile doesn't falter, but I see something shift behind his eyes. "I'm sorry, could you repeat that?"

"I'm saying no. I will not be selling The Rusty Spur."

He laughs, but it's a short, disbelieving sound. "Ms. Whitfield, I don't think you understand what you're turning down. Three and a half million dollars for a bar that probably brings in, what, two hundred thousand a year? Three hundred? This is a once-in-a-life-time offer."

"I understand perfectly, and my answer is still no."

"May I ask why?" His tone is pleasant, but there's an edge. "Surely you can see the benefits."

"I can see what you're offering, and I can see what it would cost, and the answer is no."

He sits back and studies me. His pleasant mask slips just slightly. "You've been here, what, a few weeks? A couple of months? You think you understand this place, but you don't. You're playing at being a small-town bar owner, but we both know you don't belong here."

"You don't know anything about me."

"Well, I know you're broke. I know your business failed. I know you're one emergency away from financial disaster." He leans forward. "And I'm offering you a way out. Security. Stability. The kind of money that means you never have to worry again. And you're throwing it away for what? For these people who aren't even your family? For a building that's falling apart?"

"This conversation is over."

"Think about October," he says, the pleasant tone now completely gone. "You're gonna have to decide whether to keep this place or walk away. If you walk away, it goes to the church, and you get nothing. So you can take my offer now and set yourself up for life, or you can gamble that you'll actually want to stay in this backwater town. Because let me tell you something, people like you don't stay in places like this. You'll get bored. You'll miss the life you had. And when you realize you want out, I won't be here with this offer anymore."

"Good."

"Excuse me?"

"I said good. Because I don't want your offer now, and I won't want it in the future." I lean forward, matching his posture. "You say you want to help Copper Creek, but you don't. You want to turn it into something else entirely. Something that pushes out people who actually live here. And I won't be a part of that."

He stands abruptly, his chair scraping against the floor. "You're making a mistake."

"And that's my right."

"You think these people are your friends? You think they care about you?" He gestures around the empty bar. "They care about what you can do for them. The minute you stop being useful, and this bar stops being theirs, they'll turn on you. I'm trying to help you."

"Get out."

We stare at each other for a moment, and then Gary picks up his briefcase and adjusts his tie. "Fine. But when you change your mind, and you will change your mind, don't expect me to be so generous." He starts toward the door, then turns back. "Oh, and Ms. Whitfield, Ashby and Associates doesn't give up easily. We wanted The Rusty Spur to be the centerpiece of our project, but there are other properties, other ways to make this work. You might want to keep that in mind."

The bell over the door chimes as he leaves.

I stand there shaking, adrenaline coursing through me. I just turned down three and a half million dollars. I just told off a developer in my own bar. I just chose The Rusty Spur, and I have no idea if I just made the best decision of my life or the worst.

CHAPTER 15

"That was something."

I turn around to find Dolly standing in the doorway of the kitchen with her arms crossed, a small smile on her face.

"How long were you listening?"

"Long enough." She walks over and squeezes my shoulder. "You did good, sugar."

"Did I? Because I feel like I might throw up."

"Well, that's how you know you made the right choice, because the wrong ones always feel easy." She heads behind the bar and pours me a glass of water. "Now, sit down before you fall down."

I collapse onto the stool, my legs suddenly weak. "Three point five million," I say to no one in particular. "I just turned down three point five million."

"You turned down a lot more than that. You turned

down the easy way out, the path that would have let you run from everything messy and complicated." Dolly sets the water in front of me. "Mavis would be so proud."

"Mavis never had to choose between financial ruin and doing the right thing."

"Well, actually, she did. Several times. First time was when she left Atlanta, walked away from the family money, from her inheritance, from everything she was supposed to be, and came here with nothing but what she could fit in her car." Dolly leans against the bar. "She told me once it was the scariest thing she ever did, but also the best."

I take a sip of water, trying to calm my racing heart. "Gary said they're not giving up, that they'll find other ways."

"Oh, I'm sure they will. Men like him always do." Dolly shrugs. "But that's a problem for another day. Today, you stood up for this place, for all of us, and that matters."

"I just hope I didn't make everything worse."

"Honey, you can't make the right choice and have it turn out wrong. It just doesn't work that way."

I'm still standing in the bar an hour later, staring at my water glass and second-guessing every decision I've ever made, when the front door opens.

Wyatt.

He stops when he sees me, his hand still on the

door. We haven't been alone in a room since our fight, and the tension is immediate and suffocating.

"I heard what happened," he finally says.

Of course he did, because this is Copper Creek. Word probably spread before Gary's Mercedes even left the parking lot.

"From Dolly?"

"From half the town." He lets the door close behind him and takes a few steps closer, but still keeps his distance. "So it's true? You told him no?"

"I told him no."

Something in his expression shifts, maybe relief or surprise. He runs a hand through his hair, a gesture I've come to recognize as his way of buying time to figure out what to say next.

"Why?"

"Why what?"

"Why did you say no? Three and a half million dollars, Eleanor. That's big money."

"I know what it is."

"So why?"

I look at him, standing there in his worn jeans and flannel shirt, guarded and careful, trying not to hope. And I realize he needs to hear this. Not for the bar, not for Copper Creek, but for him.

"Because he was wrong," I say, "about all of it. He said I don't belong here, that I'm playing at being a small-town bar owner, and that people like me don't stay in places like this. And I realized something. He's right that I'm not who I was in Atlanta anymore, but he's wrong that I don't belong here." I stand up, needing to move to get the nervous energy out of my body. "I belong here more than I ever belonged there. And yes, this place is messy and complicated, and I have no idea what I'm doing half the time, but it's real, and the people are real. This," I gesture around The Rusty Spur, "is real."

Wyatt takes another step closer. "And what about us?"

The question hangs in the air like a thick fog.

"That's real too," I say quietly, "and I wasn't willing to sell that for any amount of money. But I don't appreciate the pressure you put on me. It was very hard to pull my feelings for you… for us… out of the equation so I could make a decision. The whole point of all of this is to make my own decisions, Wyatt. To stop living the life other people want for me."

He closes the distance between us in three long strides, and suddenly his hands are cupping my face, and he's looking at me with those blue eyes full of something that makes my breath hitch in my throat.

"I'm sorry," he says, "for what I said the other day about you looking for an exit. It wasn't fair."

"You were scared."

"I was *terrified* because I'm…" he stops and swallows hard. "I'm falling for you, Eleanor. Have been since you rode that mechanical bull like you never had fun in your whole life. And the thought of you leaving and of selling this place and going back to Atlanta—"

"I'm not going back to Atlanta."

"You're staying?"

It's the question, the one everyone's been dancing around.

"I don't know about October yet," I admit. "I don't know if I can make this work long-term or if I can actually run a bar. If I could build a life here. But I know I'm not selling, and I want to try. And I know…" I take a breath and gather courage. "I know I'm falling for you, too. That scares me more than anything Gary Allen said."

A smile breaks across Wyatt's face. "Yeah?"

"Yeah."

"Good." His thumb brushes across my cheekbone. "Because I was really hoping I hadn't screwed this up completely.

"You didn't screw it up. I did. I should have told you about the offer right away."

"We both messed up." He leans his forehead against mine, and we stand there breathing the same air. "But we're okay?"

"We're okay."

"Good, because I'd really like to kiss you right now, but I'm trying to respect the whole 'taking it slow' thing we agreed on."

My heart is racing, and every nerve in my body is screaming at me to close the distance and forget about being smart and careful. But Wyatt's right. We made an agreement. We decided to wait until I was sure. And I'm not sure yet. Not about October, not about my future, not about whether I can make a life in Copper Creek like Mavis did.

But I'm sure about this moment. About him. About us.

"Just a few more months," I say. "Until October, until I have to decide."

"A few more months," he agrees.

That evening, The Rusty Spur fills up like it always does on Friday nights, but tonight feels different. People keep coming up to me, regulars I barely know, faces I recognize from the potluck, people who've said maybe ten words to me total. They're all saying some version of the same thing.

"Heard what you did."

"Thank you for standing up to that developer."

"Mavis would be proud."

By ten o'clock, I've been hugged more times than I can count, offered more drinks than I can accept, and pulled into at least three conversations about Gary Allen.

Pastor Dale shows up around ten thirty with Ruthie, which is unusual because they don't usually come out on Friday nights.

"Eleanor," he says, extending his hand. When I shake it, he covers my hand with his other one. "I wanted to thank you personally. What you did today, standing up to that developer, well, that took a lot of courage."

"I just said no to an offer."

"You did more than that. You chose this community over your own financial gain. That's no small thing."

Ruthie nods beside him. "If there's anything we can do to help you, anything you need, you just let us know. The church, the congregation, we're all rooting for you."

"Thank you. That means a lot."

After they leave, I stand behind the bar helping Presley pour drinks, and I watch the crowd. The regulars. The families. The couples dancing to the jukebox. A group of twenty-somethings celebrating someone's birthday.

This is what Gary Allen wanted to buy. Not just the building or the land, but this. The community. The people. The feeling of belonging. And he was willing to pay three point five million for it, but it was never his to buy.

At closing time, after everyone has gone home and the last glass has been washed and the floor swept clean, Wyatt and I are on the back deck like we always are. He's got his sweet tea. I've got mine. The stars are out in full force, and the mountains are dark silhouettes in the distance.

"Long day," he says.

"Longest of my life."

"You holding up okay?"

I think about the question, really think about it. "Actually, yeah, I am."

"No regrets?"

"Ask me tomorrow when the adrenaline wears off." I lean back in my chair and look up at the stars. "But right now, no regrets."

We sit in silence for a while, then Wyatt says, "What do you think he meant when Gary said they'd find other ways?"

"I don't know, but Dolly said something similar, that men like him don't give up easily."

"Well, we'll deal with it if it comes up."

"We?" I repeat.

He looks at me. "Yeah, we. You're not doing this alone anymore, Eleanor. Whether you stay or go in October, whether you sell or keep the place, whether Gary Allen comes back or not, you've got people here. You've got me. And we're not going anywhere, even if you do."

There's something comforting about knowing I now have "people". Even if I leave in October, my people will be here in Copper Creek.

My throat tightens. "Thank you."

"For what?"

"For not giving up on me, even when I was being an idiot and considering that stupid offer."

"You weren't being an idiot. You were being practical. There's a difference." He reaches over and takes my hand. "Besides, I kind of like it when you're human and figuring things out. It looks good on you."

I laugh. "Human. That's what you're going with?"

"Well, better than being pristine and perfect, right?"

He's right. It is better. Everything about this life, this messy, complicated, uncertain life I'm building in Copper Creek, is better than the pristine, careful, perfect, empty life I left behind.

I just hope I have the courage to choose it when October comes.

The week after I turn down Gary Allen's offer passes in a blur of routine. The bar opens. The bar closes. I learn to work the register without Presley hovering over my shoulder. I start recognizing regulars by name. Betty from line dancing teaches me the two-step, and I only mess it up about half the time. It's starting to feel like normal. Like a life.

Wednesday afternoon, I'm in the office trying to make sense of quarterly tax forms when Wyatt appears in the doorway.

"Hey, you busy Saturday?" he asks.

I look up from the spreadsheet that's been giving me a headache for the past hour. "It depends. What do you have in mind?"

"Well, there's a place I want to show you, up in the mountains. It's a little bit of a hike, but not too bad. Maybe an hour up."

"A hike?"

"Yeah. Wear good shoes. Bring water. I'll pack a lunch."

"Ooh, that's very mysterious."

"It's a surprise," he grins. "A good one, I promise. I'll pick you up at nine?"

"Okay."

He starts to leave, then turns back. "Eleanor?"

"Yeah?"

"Wear layers. It gets a little cooler up there."

Saturday morning dawns clear and perfect, the kind of spring day that makes you understand why people write poems about May in the mountains. The sky is an impossible blue that only happens at this elevation, and the air smells of pine, wildflowers, and hope.

Wyatt pulls up at exactly nine in his truck, and I climb in wearing jeans, hiking boots I bought at a local shop, and a light jacket tied around my waist.

"Morning," he says, handing me a travel mug of coffee.

"You made coffee?"

"I know how you like it. Cream, two sugars."

It's such a small thing, such a simple thing, but it means more than anything.

We drive for about twenty minutes, winding up narrow roads that get progressively more remote. The houses thin out until it's just forest on both sides, thick and green and alive with birdsong. Wyatt turns onto what is generously called a road, which is really more like two tire tracks through the trees, and we bounce along for another five minutes before he parks in a small clearing.

"This is it," he says, turning off the truck.

"This is what?"

"The trailhead." He hops out and grabs a backpack from the truck bed. "Come on. It's worth it, I promise," he says as he opens my door.

The trail starts out easy enough, with a gradual incline, towering pines and oaks, and dappled sunlight filtering through the canopy overhead. Birds call to each other in the branches, and somewhere in the distance, I hear running water. I'm just hoping I don't see a bear.

Wyatt sets an easy pace, checking every few minutes to make sure I'm okay, which I am. Barely. I know he could be going a lot faster. He's more experienced at this. I'm not exactly out of shape, but I'm not used to hiking uphill for an extended period either.

"You doing okay?" he asks after about ten minutes.

"Fine," I say, only slightly out of breath. "How much farther?"

"We're about halfway."

"Oh. Halfway. Great."

He grins. "Do you want to take a break?"

"No, I'm good. Let's keep going."

We climb higher. The trees change as we ascend, more evergreen. The air gets cooler and thinner, and my legs are burning, but in a good way.

"So what's at the top?" I ask during a relatively flat stretch.

"You'll see."

"Why are you still being mysterious?"

"Well, do you want me to ruin the surprise?"

"Yes, actually. I'd like to be prepared."

"Life doesn't work that way, Eleanor. Sometimes you have to trust the process."

I think about that as we climb. About trust. About letting go of the need to control everything, the need to know everything, and plan everything. About how terrifying and freeing that is all at once.

We reach the top, or what I assume to be the top, and the trail opens up into a clearing. But Wyatt doesn't stop. He just keeps going, following an even narrower path that cuts through the trees. Then I hear it. Water. Not the gentle murmur of a creek, but something louder.

The trees thin out, and suddenly we're standing on a flat expanse of rock at the edge of a waterfall.

I stop walking and just stare.

The waterfall isn't huge, maybe thirty feet high, but it's absolutely perfect. Water cascades over dark rocks into a clear pool below, surrounded by moss-covered boulders and ferns. It looks like something out of a children's storybook or a painting. The mist from the falls catches the sunlight, creating tiny rainbows hanging in midair. The sound is incredible, constant, and soothing.

"Oh," I manage to breathe out.

"Yeah." Wyatt comes to stand beside me. "I thought you might like this."

"Like it? Wyatt, this is…" I trail off, searching for the right word. "It's beautiful."

"Yeah. It's also a secret. Well, I mean, not a secret exactly, but not many people know about it. It's not on any of the tourist maps."

"How did you find it?"

"My grandfather brought me here when I was a little kid. It's something only the locals really know about. He said it was a special place, somewhere to come when you needed to think, be quiet, or just remember what matters in life." He sets down the backpack. "I come up here sometimes," he continues, "when things get too loud in my head."

I look at him and understand what he's telling me. This is his place. His sanctuary. And he's sharing it with me.

"Thank you," I say. "For bringing me here."

"Come on. There's a spot over here where we can eat."

He leads me to a flat rock beside the pool, far

enough from the falls that we can hear each other talk, but close enough to feel the cool mist on our faces. He unpacks the backpack. Sandwiches wrapped in wax paper, apples, a thermos of sweet tea, and cookies that look homemade.

"Did your grandmother make these?" I ask, holding up the chocolate chip cookie.

"She did. She insisted. Said I couldn't bring a lady on a hike without proper provisions."

"Your grandmother is wonderful."

"She is. She's also been asking when you're coming for dinner again."

"Tell her anytime. I loved being there. It was nice to be a part of a normal family."

We eat in comfortable silence, with the sound of the waterfall filling the space where words might other-wise go. The sandwiches are simple—turkey and cheese, lettuce, and good bread—but they taste incred-ible up here with the mountain air and the view, and of course, the company.

After we finish eating, Wyatt packs the trash away and leans back on his hands, looking out at the waterfall.

"Can I ask you something?" he asks.

"Sure."

"Why did you really turn down Gary Allen's offer?"

"Because I realized something," I say. "My whole life, I've made decisions based on what I was supposed to want. What my mother wanted, what society expected, what looked good on paper. Every single one of those decisions led me to a place where I was successful and accomplished for a while, and absolutely miserable. And, well, turning down three point five million dollars made no sense on paper. It was the opposite of what I was supposed to do. But it just felt right in a way nothing else has felt right in years."

He nods slowly. "I get that."

"Do you?"

"Yeah. When I came back from Afghanistan, everybody told me what I was supposed to do. Go get a good job. Use my military experience. Make something of myself. Try to get over what I'd been through. And I did try. I really did. I got a construction job in Asheville. Good pay, good benefits, room for advancement.

"What happened?"

"I lasted three months. I couldn't sleep. I couldn't focus. I had panic attacks in the middle of meetings. Really embarrassing." He picks up a small stone and turns it over in his fingers. "Everyone said I was wasting my potential by coming back here to Copper Creek, working at a bar of all things. But it saved my life. Mavis saved my life."

"How?"

He's quiet for a moment. I can see him deciding what to tell me, whether to trust me with whatever comes next.

"You know I have PTSD," he says. "I was in a convoy that hit an IED. I survived, and my best friend didn't."

My heart clenches.

"Oh, Wyatt, I'm so sorry."

"I had really bad survivor's guilt, and there was a time I wasn't sure I wanted to be here anymore. It's been a few years. I've learned to manage it. Therapy, medication, just trying to take care of myself. But for a long time, I couldn't. I was drowning. And Mavis, well, she didn't try to fix me. She just gave me a place to be, a reason to get up in the morning, people who needed me to show up."

He throws the stone into the pool, and we watch the ripples spread across the surface.

"This bar was never just a job for me. It was my lifeline."

I reach over and take his hand. He looks surprised for a moment, then laces his fingers through mine.

"Thank you for telling me that."

"Thank you for listening and for not…" He pauses. "Well, most people, when they find out, either treat me like I'm broken or like I'm dangerous. But you're just here."

"I'm here."

We sit like that for a while, holding hands beside the waterfall. I feel something between us deepen.

"Can I ask you something now?" I say.

"Fair is fair."

"What really happened with Laney? You said she left, but…" I trail off.

"But you wanted to know why."

I nod.

"She left because I couldn't be what she needed. When I came back from my second deployment, I was a mess. The PTSD was really bad. I mean, really bad. Like, I couldn't sleep without nightmares. I couldn't go to crowded places. I couldn't handle loud noises or sudden movements. And Laney tried. She really did. But I was so focused on just trying to survive every day that I didn't have anything left to give to her or anybody else. She needed more than I could give, and I didn't know if I'd ever be able to give it again."

"So she found someone else," I say quietly.

"Yeah. Someone who was there. Someone who could be present in a way that I wasn't sure I ever would again."

"That must have hurt."

"It did. But I understood it. That's the worst part. I couldn't even really be angry at her, because I knew she was right. I was no longer capable of being in a relationship, at least not at that time. I was barely capable of being a person."

"And now?" I ask softly.

"Now I'm better. Not perfect. I mean, I still have bad days. But I've learned how to manage it better. How to take care of myself. How to be honest about what I need." He turns to look at me. "Which is one of the reasons I wanted to wait on this, take things slow, because I need you to know what you're getting into."

"Wyatt…"

"I have nightmares sometimes. I still don't like crowds very much, except at The Rusty Spur. Sometimes even that gets a little overwhelming. Fireworks are a nightmare. July Fourth is my least favorite day of the year. Sometimes I still have panic attacks. And when that happens, I need space and quiet and time to work through it in my own way." He's looking at me now, searching my face for something. "If that's too much, if that's more than you want to sign up for… I mean, you've got your own things to deal with. I just need you to tell me now, before this, well, before we go any further."

I squeeze his hand tighter.

"Wyatt Rivers, do you really think I'm scared of you having bad days, of you needing space sometimes, of you being human and complicated and dealing with trauma?"

"Some people are."

"Well, I'm not some people, I guess." I shift closer to him. "You want to know what I think? I think you're one of the bravest people I've ever met. You went through hell, literally, and you came out the other side. You built a life for yourself. You help people every day. You take care of your grandmother and run a bar, and you carve beautiful things out of wood. You show up every day, even when it's hard."

"Eleanor—"

"I'm not done." I smile a little. "You also caught fish so you could cook me dinner on our first date, and you brought me to your secret waterfall, and you hold my hand like it matters. And yes, you have PTSD and nightmares and bad days, but that doesn't scare me." He watches me closely."But you know what does scare me?" I continue.

"What?"

"How much I'm starting to care about you. How much I want this to work. How much I want to stay in Copper Creek, even though I have no idea whether I can make this work in the long term. That's what scares me. I never knew Mavis, but I have so much respect for what she created here. She was so brave to leave her whole life behind to find the kind of peace she wanted."

He's looking at me with those blue eyes, hope and fear and care all mixed together in them.

"I want to kiss you," he says, his voice rough. "And I want you to kiss me. But we said we'd wait until you're sure."

"I know what we said."

The air between us is electric. He's so close I can see flecks of darker blue in his eyes. I can hear his breathing go shallow. His hand comes up to cup my face, not brushing across my cheekbone this time. I lean into his touch.

"Eleanor," he breathes.

And then his phone rings.

The sound shatters the moment like glass. We both freeze, foreheads nearly touching, as the phone keeps ringing in his pocket. He closes his eyes and lets out a breath.

"I should—"

"I know. Answer it."

He pulls back, digs the phone from his pocket, and looks at the screen. "It's my grandmother. Hey, Grandma. Everything okay?" I watch his face as he listens, and I see the exact moment concern turns to alarm. "I'm on my way. Thirty minutes. Don't move anything heavy. Just sit down."He's already standing, packing up the backpack. "I'll be there soon."

He hangs up and looks at me, apologetic, frustrated, and worried all at once.

"She fell in the garden. She says she's fine, but—"

"Oh, you need to go. Of course. Let's go."

We practically run down the mountain. The hike that took forty minutes going up takes maybe thirty minutes going down, both of us moving fast, Wyatt in the lead, setting a punishing pace.

When we reach the truck, he pauses with his hand on the door.

"I'm sorry," he says. "About the timing, about—"

"Don't apologize. Your grandmother needs you. That's way more important."

"Can I—" He stops and runs his hand through his hair. "Can we talk later about what almost happened up there?"

"We can talk whenever you want."

He nods, and we climb into the truck.

As we wind down the mountain road, windows down and wind rushing through the cab, I think about the waterfall and how close we came to kissing. About how, for the first time in my life, the interruption doesn't feel like the universe saying no.

It just feels like the universe is saying not yet.

Meredith's house is a small cottage-style home about five minutes from Wyatt's cabin. It's painted yellow with white trim and surrounded by the kind of garden that only comes from someone who has patiently cared for it for decades. Roses climb a trellis by the front door, and flower beds burst with late spring blooms, irises, peonies, and something purple I don't recognize.

Wyatt is out of the truck before it's even fully stopped, taking the porch two steps at a time. I follow a little more slowly, not wanting to intrude.

Inside, I find Meredith in a floral armchair in the living room, her left ankle propped on the ottoman. She looks more annoyed than hurt, but her silver hair is slightly disheveled, and there's dirt on her pants.

"I'm fine," she's saying as Wyatt kneels beside her, gently examining her ankle. "It's just a little twist. I don't know why you raced all the way down here like the house was on fire."

"Because you're eighty-three years old and you fell," Wyatt says. "And you live alone. Grandma, what were you doing out in the garden by yourself?"

"What I do every Saturday. Weeding. The peonies were getting choked out."

She spots me hovering in the doorway and smiles. "Eleanor, what a nice surprise. Well, don't just stand there, dear. Come on in."

I step into the living room, and it's exactly what I would expect from Meredith. Cozy and lived-in, with photographs covering nearly every surface and book-shelves lining the walls. A piano sits in one corner, sheet music open on a stand. The whole place smells of old books and lavender.

"I'm sorry for intruding," I say. "Wyatt and I were hiking when you called."

"Intruding? Oh, nonsense." She waves her hand dismissively. "I'm glad you're here. Maybe you can talk some sense into my grandson. He acts as if I broke my hip, when all I did was roll my ankle."

"You could have broken your hip. Can you move it?" Wyatt asks, suddenly worried about her hip.

"Of course I can move it." She demonstrates, wincing slightly. "See? Fine."

"Your ankle is swelling. We need ice." He looks at me. "Eleanor, could you—"

"Kitchen," I say, already moving.

"Through there. Ice in the freezer, dish towels in the drawer by the sink."

I find the kitchen easily. It's small and tidy, with the same yellow-painted cabinets and white tile that probably came with the house when it was built. Everything is organized with the precision of someone who's cooked in the same space for fifty years.

I wrap ice in a clean dish towel and bring it back to the living room, where Wyatt is still crouched beside his grandmother's chair.

"Here," I say, handing him the ice pack.

"Thank you."

He positions it on Meredith's ankle, and she sighs. "You're both fussing over me. I've had worse injuries gardening."

"Which is exactly why you shouldn't be gardening alone anymore," Wyatt says firmly.

"I've been gardening alone for the last few years since your grandfather died, and I managed just fine."

"You've been lucky. This time, you were lucky. You were close to the house. What if you'd been in the back garden? What if you'd fallen and couldn't get up?"

Her expression softens. "Wyatt, honey, I know you worry, but I'm not ready to be treated like an invalid."

"I'm not treating you like an invalid," he says. "I'm treating you like someone I love who scared the heck out of me."

His voice cracks slightly at the last words.

"How about this?" I say, surprising myself.

Both of them look at me.

"What if someone came and helped with the garden, not to do it for you, but with you? That way you can keep gardening, but there's somebody here if anything happens."

Meredith looks at me with interest. "You offering?"

"Well, I could. I was planning to start a garden at the bar anyway. I could use some practice."

"You know anything about gardening?"

"Well, I did grow some terrible tomatoes when I was seven, and I kept herbs alive in Atlanta for three years."

Meredith laughs. "Well, that's more experience than most people have. All right, Eleanor, you've got yourself a deal. Saturday mornings, if you're free."

Wyatt looks between us, relief washing over his face. "You don't have to."

"I want to," I say, and I realize that I mean it. Not just to help Wyatt, but because I genuinely like Meredith. The idea of spending Saturday mornings in her garden and learning from someone who's been doing it for so long sounds perfect.

We stay for about another hour. Wyatt elevates Meredith's ankle, changes the ice pack a couple of times, and makes her promise to stay off it for the rest of the day. I make tea in her kitchen and bring it out on a tray with shortbread cookies I find in a tin by the stove.

"These are good," I say, biting into one.

"Family recipe," Meredith says. "My mother taught me, her mother taught her, and I'll teach you if you'd like."

"I'd like that very much."

We sit in her living room drinking tea and eating cookies, and she tells stories about teaching elementary school for forty years, about her late husband Frank, who built the arbor in the back garden with his own hands, about Wyatt as a boy catching frogs in the creek and tracking mud through the house and reading poetry under the oak tree in the backyard.

"He was always a sensitive soul," she says, looking at him with affection. "Even as a little boy. Frank used to worry it would make life hard for him, but I told him the world needs sensitive souls, needs people who feel things deeply."

Wyatt's ears are slightly red. "Grandma."

"I'm just stating the facts, dear. You've always been tenderhearted. It's not a weakness."

I watch him squirm under her assessment because she's right. He is tenderhearted. He feels things deeply, and instead of seeing that as a weakness, she sees it as a strength.

"Did Frank ever meet Laney?" I ask.

I immediately regret it because Wyatt tenses up.

Meredith nods. "He did. She was a nice enough girl,

but not right for my Wyatt. Frank saw it before I did, actually. Told me she was afraid of feelings."

"Grandma," Wyatt says, a warning in his voice.

"Wyatt, it's true. She wanted everything neat and tidy and predictable, and you, my dear, dear boy, have never been any of those things." She takes a sip of her tea. "But Eleanor here, well, Eleanor's afraid, but not afraid of messy things. I can tell."

I laugh. "And how can you tell?"

"Because you're still here. You've been in Copper Creek for over two months, right? And you haven't run yet. Most people who come here from the city, well, they run. Can't handle the quiet, the slowness of it all. But you're still here."

"Yeah," I say quietly. "I'm starting to think I might just stay."

Wyatt's head snaps up, his blue eyes finding mine.

"Well, good," Meredith says, "because this town could use someone like you, and my grandson definitely could."

By the time we leave, it's late afternoon. Meredith's ankle is properly wrapped and elevated on pillows, and she has instructions to call if she needs anything. Wyatt has also called two of her friends from church, who promise to check on her tomorrow.

We climb into his truck, and the silence feels different than it did on the drive here, heavier, full of things unsaid.

"Thank you," Wyatt finally says as he starts the engine, "for coming, for helping, for offering to help with the garden."

"You don't need to thank me."

"Well, I do, because you didn't have to do any of that. He stops and grips the steering wheel tighter. "It means a lot."

We drive in silence for a few moments, winding down the narrow roads back toward town, and then he pulls over, not at The Rusty Spur, but at a small over-look I haven't noticed before. It's a pull-off with a view of the valley below, Copper Creek spread out like a postcard.

He turns off the engine and turns to face me.

"Earlier," he says, "at the waterfall, before my grandma called…"

"I know."

"I wanted to kiss you," he says. "I really, really wanted to kiss you. And I wanted you to kiss me. But we said we'd wait until October, until you're sure."

I take a breath, gathering up my courage. "Well, what if I told you I'm starting to feel sure?"

His eyes search mine. "Starting to feel sure?"

"I'm not ready to make promises about October yet," I say. "I still have so many questions, so many things I need to figure out. But Wyatt…" I reach over and take his hand. "I meant what I said to your grand-mother about staying. I'm starting to think I might actually do it."

"Starting to think isn't the same thing as knowing."

"I know. But it's more than I've had before. It's more than I ever thought I'd have." I squeeze his hand. "A couple of months ago, I couldn't wait to leave this place. I thought I was coming to stay for one night, maybe just a few hours. Now I'm thinking about planting a garden, learning to make shortbread cook-ies, and spending Saturday mornings with your grand-mother. That has to count for something."

A slow smile spreads across his face. "It counts for a lot, actually."

"Maybe I won't wait until October to make the decision. Maybe we can just keep doing what we're doing, you know, getting to know each other, keep building whatever this is. And if the decision comes to me sooner, all the better."

The truth is, if I went back to Atlanta, what would be waiting for me there? The failure of my mother's business. An ex-fiance. An apartment I can no longer afford.

"And if October comes and you decide to leave?"

The question hangs between us, heavy with possi-bility and fear.

"Then we'll deal with it," I say.

He leans across the center console and cups my face with one hand, his thumb brushing across my cheekbone as it always does, the way that makes my breath hitch in my throat.

"Eleanor Whitfield," he says softly, "you are the most complicated, frustrating, surprising woman I've ever met."

"Is that a compliment?" I ask, smiling.

"It's the truth."

His eyes drop to my lips. I feel the pull of it, the gravity between us.

"And I'm falling for you anyway," he says, "against my better judgment, against all common sense. I'm falling for you."

"I'm falling for you, too."

We're so close now, close enough that I can feel the warmth of his breath on my face, close enough that all I'd have to do is lean forward just a fraction, and a car drives past, honking cheerfully, and we both jump apart like teenagers caught by their parents.

Wyatt drops his hand and lets out a frustrated sigh.

"Does it seem like the universe really doesn't want us to kiss?"

"Apparently not."

"Well," he says as he starts the engine, "I guess the universe can wait because eventually—October, November, whenever you're ready—I'm going to kiss you, Eleanor Whitfield. And it's going to be worth the wait."

"Promise?"

"Promise."

He drives me back to The Rusty Spur as the sun sets over the mountains, painting them in shades of orange and pink and purple. I've never seen such beautiful sunsets as I've seen here in these mountains. There aren't words to describe the peace I feel looking at them, like I've been lost my whole life and they've been calling me home.

Wyatt and I don't talk much, but the silence is comfortable and easy, like we've just said everything we've needed to say for now.

When he pulls into the parking lot, he walks me to the side entrance, like always.

"Same time next week?" he asks.

"Actually, I have an idea. What if next Saturday we garden at your grandmother's together, and then maybe I cook for you at my place?"

He looks pleased. "You're going to cook for me?"

"Oh, don't look so surprised. I can cook. I mean, I'm not at your grandmother's level, but I'm competent."

"What are you making?"

"Well, that's a surprise."

He grins. "I like surprises."

"I know you do."

We stand there for a moment, neither wanting to move, reluctant for this beautiful day to end.

"Thank you," I say finally, "for today, for the waterfall, for sharing that with me."

"Well, thank you for being there for my grandma and me. I can't believe I'm saying this, but I'm so thankful you and your pearls appeared in my life all those weeks ago."

"I put the pearls away," I say, laughing. "I promise to only wear them for special events."

He reaches out and tucks a strand of hair behind my ear, a gesture that's become ours, and then steps back before either of us can do something stupid, like close the distance between us.

"Good night, Eleanor."

"Good night, Wyatt."

I watch him walk to his truck, and he waves before climbing in. I wave back, and I go inside and climb the stairs to my apartment and sit on the sofa.

I think about waterfalls and the almost kiss, about Meredith's ankle in the garden, about Wyatt's hands, gentle on his grandmother's ankle, the worry in his eyes. I think about what I said, *I'm starting to think I might stay*, and realize it's the first time I've said it out loud.

And it really didn't feel scary.

It felt like the truth.

My phone buzzes with a text.

> Wyatt: Thank you again for today. You're kind of amazing, you know that?

I smile and type back.

Me: Well, you're kind of amazing yourself. See you next Saturday for gardening and a mystery dinner. Not that I won't see you at work every day between then. 😊

Wyatt: Can't wait. And Eleanor?

Me: Yeah?

Wyatt: I meant what I said about falling for you.

I stare at the text for a long moment.

Me: I meant it too.

I set my phone down and look around my apartment, Mavis's apartment, with its turquoise sofa and eclectic furniture and wall of photographs, and the life she built there, and the family she chose, and the home she made.

And for the first time, I can really picture myself doing the same thing.

Building a life here.

Choosing this family.

Making this home.

The following week establishes a new rhythm. Every morning before the bar opens, I drive over to Meredith's house with something: breakfast from Dixie's Diner, fresh flowers from the grocery store, a book I found in Mavis's collection that I think she might like.

At first, she protests that I'm fussing over her, but by Wednesday she greets me at the door with coffee already brewing and a list of things she wants to show me in her garden. The tomatoes are coming along, she says Thursday, hobbling beside me on her still-tender ankle as we walk the rows of her backyard garden.

"Another few weeks and they'll be ready for pickin'."

"How do you know when they're ready?"

"Oh, you'll feel it. You just give a little squeeze. And the color, well, it deepens. It gets richer."

She points to a cluster of green tomatoes hanging on a vine. "See those? They're close. Maybe ten days out."

I crouch down to look at them, and something in my chest expands. These are nothing like the little sad tomatoes I grew as a child. These are robust and healthy and have clearly been loved.

"Mavis used to help me with my garden," Meredith says. "Every spring, she'd come over, and we'd plan out the beds together. She had a good eye for it. She knew exactly what to plant next to what. Which plants liked each other and which didn't."

"I didn't know that."

"Oh, there's a lot you don't know about her yet. But you're learning." She sits down on a wooden bench at the edge of the garden. It looks handmade. "She talked about you, you know, before she died."

"Yeah, everyone keeps telling me that."

"Well, it's true. She had a feeling about you. Said you were lost, but you didn't know it yet. That you needed something to shake you loose from whatever was holding you back."

I sit beside her on the bench and look out at the garden. Rows of vegetables, beds of flowers, fruit trees. A lifetime of growing things.

"I think she was right," I admit. "I was lost. I just didn't know how to name it."

"And now?"

"Well, I'm probably still lost," I say, laughing. "But at least I know it. I'm starting to find my way."

Meredith pats my hand with her soft, weathered, wrinkled fingers. "That's all any of us can do, dear. Find our way. One step at a time."

Friday afternoon, Dolly corners me in the office. "We need to talk," she says, closing the door behind her.

"Yikes, that sounds ominous."

"Well, it might be." She sits in the armchair across from Mavis's desk, which is my desk now, I suppose, and crosses her arms. "I've been hearing some things about Gary Allen."

My stomach tightens into a knot. "What kind of things?"

"Well, he's been busy since you turned him down. Talking to all kinds of people around town, making offers on other properties."

"Which properties?"

"The building next to Grits and Grind, the old hardware store that's been sitting empty for two years, and now there's a rumor he's sniffing around the church, too."

"The church? Why would the developer want a church?"

"Well, not the church itself, but the land behind it. The big field where they do the fall festival every year. Apparently, it's prime real estate for a hotel."

I lean back in my chair. "So he's trying to build around The Rusty Spur. If he can't have this property, he'll develop everything else and just squeeze us out."

"That's what it looks like."

"And if he does that, if he turns Copper Creek into some kind of luxury resort, property values will skyrocket, and property taxes, too. Which means people who've been here for generations won't be able to afford to stay."

"Exactly." Dolly's expression looks grim. "You know what happened before. Different developer, but same playbook. I told you they bought up half of Main

Street, raised rents, and drove out local businesses. It took years for them to recover, and some folks never did."

"Why didn't anybody stop them?"

"Because they came in with money and promises. People wanted to believe it would be different. By the time everybody realized what was happening, it was just too late." She leans forward. "I'm not saying Gary Allen is definitely going to do the same thing, but I'm saying we need to be careful. We need to pay attention."

"Well, what can we do?"

"Right now, not much. He's not breaking any laws. He's just making offers on property and making plans. But if things start moving faster, well, we just need to be ready."

"Ready how?"

"I don't know yet, to be honest. But I do know one thing. You turning him down was the first step. You showed people it was possible to say no."

CHAPTER 17

That evening, the bar fills up like it always does on Friday nights. Music plays from the jukebox, couples dance around the floor, and families crowd into booths. The mechanical bull sits in the corner. It's a permanent fixture now, since it was so successful last month, and there's a steady stream of brave souls taking their turns getting thrown into the air and onto the mat.

I work behind the bar with Presley, pouring beer and mixing drinks. I'm surprised how natural it's beginning to feel, how my hands know where everything is without thinking.

"You're getting pretty good at this," Presley says during a lull. "Almost as good as Mavis."

"Well, I had a good teacher."

"Please. You taught yourself. I just pointed you at the bottles and let you figure it out." She grins. "But seriously, Eleanor, you're different than when you first got here. More relaxed, like you actually belong."

"Do I? Belong?"

She looks around the crowded bar. "Yeah, you do. I mean, you're still a little fancy, but a good kind of fancy now. The kind that fits."

Before I can say anything, a commotion near the door draws our attention. A group of men in expensive suits has just walked in, and they look as out of place as I did a few weeks ago in my pencil skirt and pearls. They're looking around with expressions of half curiosity, half disdain, as if they've wandered into a zoo.

At the center of the group is Gary Allen.

Our eyes meet across the crowded room. He smiles that smile that I hate.

"Presley," I say quietly, "can you handle the bar for a minute?"

"Sure. Everything okay?"

"I actually don't know yet."

I walk toward the group and keep my expression neutral. Gary is already moving toward me with his hand extended like we're old friends.

"Ms. Whitfield, lovely to see you again."

I don't shake his hand.

"Mr. Allen, I wasn't expecting you."

"Oh, I'm just showing some colleagues around town. They're also interested in the area's potential." He gestures toward the men behind him. "This is David

Webb, Ronald McAllister, and Richard Patterson. Gentlemen, this is Eleanor Whitfield, owner of The Rusty Spur." They nod politely, and I nod back. Nobody smiles. "I have to say," Gary continues, "this place is really charming. Very authentic. I can see why you're attached to it."

"Can I help you with something, Mr. Allen, or did you just come to admire the décor?"

"Well, we're just having a drink. Last time I checked, this was a public establishment." He moves toward the bar, his colleagues following. "Four whiskeys neat. Whatever you've got that's top shelf."

I want him to leave. I want to throw him out like they do in the movies, with a dramatic exit, the doors swinging, and everybody cheering. But I can't. He's right. This is a public establishment. Making a scene would only give him more ammunition.

So I walk back behind the bar and pour the four whiskeys. Presley watches with wide eyes but doesn't say a word.

"Thank you," Gary says when I set the glasses down. He raises his glass in a mock toast. "To Copper Creek and its bright future."

His colleagues echo the toast, and they drink, looking around, taking mental notes.

I stand behind my bar in my honky-tonk, watching them, trying to figure out how to make it all go away.

Wyatt arrives around nine o'clock, as he usually does on Friday nights. He comes in through the back entrance, shrugs off his jacket, and I see the exact moment he spots Gary and his gang at the corner table. His whole body goes rigid.

"What's he doing here?" he asks as he crosses to me at the bar in three long strides.

"Having drinks and showing his friends around."

"His friends?"

"Investors, I assume. Or developers. I'm not sure exactly."

Wyatt's jaw is tight. "You want me to throw him out?"

"On what grounds? They're customers. They're behaving themselves. They're just…" I look over at the table, watching.

"I don't like it."

"Neither do I. But making a scene is what he wants. He's waiting for us to give him a reason to play the victim."

Wyatt takes a breath and forces himself to relax. "You're right. I know you're right. It's just…"

"I know."

He moves behind the bar and starts helping, pouring beers, wiping down the counter, doing the familiar work he doesn't need to do but that gives him something to focus on besides Gary Allen's smug face, which he desperately wants to punch.

Around ten, the group finishes their drinks and stand to leave.

Gary makes a point of walking past the bar.

"Thank you for your hospitality, Ms. Whitfield. We'll have to do this again sometime."

"Good night, Mr. Allen."

He pauses, then leans in slightly, lowering his voice so only I can hear.

"You know, this doesn't have to be adversarial. We could work together, the two of us. You could be part of what's coming instead of fighting against it."

"I don't have a clue what you're talking about."

"I think you do." His smile is cold. "Copper Creek is going to change, Eleanor, one way or another. The only question is whether you're going to change with it or get left behind."

He walks out, his colleagues trailing behind him.

Wyatt appears next to me. "What did he say?"

"Nothing important." I turn back to the bar, to the customers, to the music and laughter. "Nothing important at all."

But I can feel Wyatt watching me. I can see the worry in his eyes, and I know we're both thinking the same thing.

Gary Allen isn't going away.

Whatever it is that he's planning, we're not going to like it.

~

Saturday morning, I arrive at Meredith's house at nine o'clock with gardening gloves, a new pair of boots, and a determination to learn everything she's willing to teach me. Wyatt is already there, sitting on the porch with his grandmother, drinking coffee from mismatched mugs.

"You're early," he says, standing as I walk up the steps.

"I'm punctual. There's a difference."

"Punctual people are early people who pretend they're not."

Meredith laughs. "He's got you there, dear. Come sit and have some coffee before we start."

We drink coffee on the porch, the three of us watching the morning sun climb over the mountains. Meredith tells stories about her garden, including which plants have been there the longest, which ones she struggled with, and which ones her husband Frank planted before he died.

"The roses were his," she says, gesturing to the climbing roses on a trellis nearby. "I wanted to rip them out after he passed because it was too painful to look at them, but Wyatt talked me out of it."

"I told her Grandpa would haunt her if she touched his roses," Wyatt says.

"He probably would have. That man loved those roses more than he loved me some days."

"That's not true."

"No, it's not," she smiles. "But he did love them."

~

We work in the garden for three hours.

Meredith directs from her chair, her ankle still healing, while Wyatt and I handle the physical labor. We weed, water, check for pests, and prune dead growth. It's hard work. My back aches, and my hands are sore even through the gloves, but there's something deeply satisfying about it, about putting your hands in the dirt and watching things grow.

"You're a natural," Meredith calls to me as I carefully transplant a tomato seedling into a larger pot.

"I don't know about that."

"I do. You've got the patience and the gentleness for it. Some people treat plants like they're in a hurry, rushing through everything, and then wonder why nothing thrives. But you take your time. You pay attention."

"My mother would be horrified," I say without thinking. "She thought gardening was beneath us, something for the hired help."

"No offense to your mother, but that's ridiculous," Meredith says bluntly. "Putting your hands in the earth and growing your own food is one of the most human things a person can do. There's nothing beneath about it."

I look at the seedling in my hands, at the delicate roots and the promise of what it can become.

"I'm starting to believe that," I say.

After we clean up, Meredith insists on making lunch. Wyatt and I, of course, try to help, but she shoos us right out of the kitchen.

"Go sit on the porch. I might be old, but I can still make sandwiches without supervision."

We sit on the porch swing, the chains creaking softly as we rock back and forth.

"She's as stubborn as a mule," I say.

"Family trait." Wyatt stretches his legs out, crossing his ankles. "Thank you for doing this. She's been lonely since Grandpa died. She won't admit it, but she has been."

"I like spending time with her."

"She likes you, too. She told me this morning, before you even got here. Said you have 'good energy'." He does air quotes with his fingers. "Whatever that means."

"It means she's very polite."

He smiles. "It means she approves, which, trust me, is not something she does easily. She absolutely hated Laney."

I blink, surprised. "She told me they met, but she didn't say she hated her."

"Oh, she wouldn't. She's too polite, but I could tell. See, there's this thing she does with her mouth when she disapproves of someone, like she's trying not to frown." He demonstrates, pursing his lips slightly.

I laugh. "Does she do that with me?"

"Never. Not once. From the moment she met you at dinner, it was different. She kept looking at me during the meal, like—" He stops and shakes his head.

"Like what?"

"Like she was waiting for me to figure something out."

We rock in silence for a moment.

"Can I ask you something?" I say.

"Always."

"Last night, when Gary Allen was at the bar, you looked like you were ready to throw him through a wall."

"Because I was."

"Why?"

He's quiet for a moment, staring out at the garden.

"Because he represents everything I hate. People who come into a place and try to change it into something it's not. Who see a community like Copper Creek and think only about what value they can extract from it."

"Yeah, but it's more than that, though, isn't it?"

He sighs. "When I came home from overseas, I felt like everyone was trying to change me. The VA wanted to put me on a dozen different medications. Therapists wanted me to talk about things I wasn't ready to talk about. Everyone had an opinion about what I should do, who I should be. And I just wanted—" He stops and swallows. "I just wanted somewhere to exist. Somewhere that would let me be broken for a while without trying to fix me."

"And Copper Creek did that?"

"Well, Copper Creek and Mavis. They gave me space to figure myself out. Didn't push. Didn't judge. Just accepted." He looks back toward the garden. "And Gary Allen wants to change all that."

"Yeah. He wants to turn this place into something profitable, sleek, polished, marketable."

"If that happens, if Copper Creek just becomes another tourist destination, then the thing that saved me won't exist anymore for the next person who needs it."

I reach over and take his hand. "We won't let it happen."

"We might not be able to stop it."

"Maybe not. But we can try. And whatever happens, you won't be doing it alone."

He looks at me. "You mean that?"

"I mean it."

He squeezes my hand, and we sit there on his grandmother's porch, watching the garden grow, holding on to each other and the fragile hope that some things are worth fighting for.

That evening, as promised, I cook for Wyatt. It's nothing fancy, just roast chicken with lemon and herbs, some roasted vegetables, and a simple salad. But I put my full effort into it, paying the kind of attention Meredith talked about in the garden.

My apartment looks different when I'm preparing to host someone, smaller somehow, more intimate. I've set the tiny table by the window with Mavis's eclectic dishes and cloth napkins I found in a drawer. I even picked wildflowers from behind the bar and put them in a mason jar.

Wyatt arrives at seven, freshly showered with damp hair curling at his temples, and pauses in the doorway.

"You made it nice," he says.

"I made it mine." The words surprise me even as I say them. "Or I'm trying to make it mine, I mean."

He steps inside and looks around at the wildflowers, the table, and takes in the smells coming from the tiny kitchen. "It suits you," he says. "This place. I couldn't really see it at first, but now I can."

"What changed?"

"You did." He looks at me. "You're different than when you got here, more yourself."

"I feel more myself."

We stand there looking at each other.

"Wine," I offer, breaking the spell before I do something stupid, like cross the room and kiss him square on the lips.

"Please."

We drink wine on the sofa while the chicken finishes in the oven. We talk about nothing important, just about Meredith's garden, funny customers at the bar, and Presley's latest song. It's an easy conversation, comfortable. Underneath it, there's an awareness, a current running between us that we're both trying to ignore. Moment to moment.

When dinner is ready, we sit at the tiny table and eat. The chicken is good, better than good, actually. And Wyatt makes appropriately appreciative noises, whether sincere or merely polite. Either way, they make me smile.

"Where did you learn to cook?" he asks.

"I actually taught myself, in college, mostly. My mother thought cooking was for the housekeepers, not the Whitfields. I had a tiny apartment and no money, and takeout got expensive." I shrug. "Turns out I like it. The process, you know, the measuring, the mixing."

"Kind of like the gardening?"

"Well, yes, actually, like that. Taking ingredients and turning them into something. Watching it come together."

"Well, you're good at it."

"I would say I'm adequate."

"You're good at a lot of things, Eleanor. You should let yourself acknowledge that."

The sincerity in his voice catches me off guard. I look down at my plate, feeling very self-conscious.

"I'm working on it. The acknowledging, I mean.

That's hard. My whole life, anything I did well was expected. Anything I didn't do well was a failure. There was no middle ground."

"That sounds exhausting."

"It was. I didn't realize how exhausting until I stopped."

After dinner, we do the dishes together. I wash, he dries. And there's something so domestic about it that makes my chest ache. This is what it could be like, I think. Not just tonight, but always. This easy rhythm.

When the last dish is dry and put away, Wyatt leans against the counter.

"I should probably go," he says.

"Probably."

Neither of us moves.

"Eleanor, I know we said we'd wait. I want to wait, I do. I just…" He runs his hands through his hair. "Being here with you in this space, it's hard to remember why we made that rule."

"Because I need to be sure, because you've been hurt before, because we don't want to complicate things before we're ready."

"All good reasons. All very logical reasons."

"I hate logic." I laugh, and it breaks the tension just enough.

"Me too, right now anyway."

He pushes off the counter and crosses to me, stopping close enough that I can feel the warmth of him.

"A couple more months," he says, "until October."

"A couple of months, and then?"

"And then we'll figure it out."

He reaches up and again tucks stray hair behind my ear. He's done it over and over, and each time it feels like electricity is running through my temple.

"Good night, Eleanor."

"Good night, Wyatt."

He leaves, and I stand in my kitchen, listening to the footsteps on the stairs and his truck pulling away. A couple more months, sixty-ish days until I have to decide about the bar, about my future, about us.

I clean up the rest of the kitchen, blow out the candle on the table, and get ready for bed. But sleep is a long time coming because my head is full of Wyatt's blue eyes and the smell of his cologne. A couple of months feels like an eternity, and it also doesn't feel like nearly enough time.

CHAPTER 18

Three weeks pass.

Three weeks of gardening with Meredith every Saturday.

Three weeks of running the bar.

Three weeks of dates with Wyatt, dinners at his cabin, evenings on the back deck, long walks through town where we hold hands like teenagers and talk about everything and nothing.

Three weeks of falling deeper into a life I never thought I'd want.

It's a Tuesday morning when the email arrives.

I'm in the office, going through invoices, when my phone buzzes. I almost ignore it, probably spam or a newsletter I forgot to unsubscribe from, but something makes me look. The sender's name stops me cold.

Genevieve Ashford, Institut de Raffinement

I stare at the screen for a long moment, my heart

pounding. Genevieve Ashford. I know that name. Everyone in the etiquette world knows that name. She runs the Institut de Raffinement in Lausanne, Switzerland, the most prestigious finishing school in Europe. Royalty sends their children there. CEOs. Diplomats. The kind of people my mother spent her whole career trying to impress.

I met Genevieve once at a conference in New York five years ago. We spoke for maybe ten minutes, and I gave her my card.

Why is she emailing me now?

I open it.

Dear Ms. Whitfield,

I hope this message finds you well. We met briefly at the International Etiquette Conference in 2019, and I've followed your career with interest since then. I was sorry to hear about the closing of your mother's studio. Vivian Whitfield was a legend in our field, and I know her passing left large shoes to fill. I imagine the past year has been challenging.

I'm writing because an unexpected opportunity has arisen at the Institut. Our director of American programs has accepted a position elsewhere. Effective immediately, we find ourselves in need of someone with your background and expertise.

The position involves overseeing our programs for American students and families, teaching advanced courses in etiquette and protocol, and representing the Institute at international events. The compensation package is substan-

tial, $200,000 USD annually, plus housing in Lausanne and comprehensive benefits. The start date would be November 1st.

I realize this is rather sudden, and you may have commitments that make relocation impossible, but I wanted to extend the offer before looking elsewhere. Your mother's training, combined with your own experience, makes you very qualified for this role.

If you're interested in discussing further, please reply at your earliest convenience. I'd be happy to arrange a video call to answer any questions.

With warm regards,

Genevieve Ashford

Director, Institut de Raffinement

I read the email three times. Then I close my laptop and sit still in Mavis's chair, staring at the wall of photographs.

I don't even see any of them.

$200,000 a year.

Housing in Switzerland.

The most prestigious etiquette position in the world. Everything my mother ever wanted for me, just delivered to my inbox on a random Tuesday morning. The question is, do I want it?

My brain is in knots. I thought I knew what I wanted now. Copper Creek. The Rusty Spur. Wyatt.

So why does this email feel even slightly tempting? After all, I left the etiquette world behind, didn't I?

By Thursday, the secret is eating me alive. I've read Genevieve's email probably fifty times and drafted responses over and over.

Yes.

No.

Maybe.

Let me think about it.

And I've deleted every single one. I've Googled the Institut and looked at photos of the campus, the students, and the beautiful rooms where I would be teaching.

I've imagined myself there, in Switzerland, in that life.

I've imagined myself here, in Copper Creek, in this life.

Both of them feel real. Both of them feel possible. Neither feels like the clear answer.

Thursday night, Wyatt comes over for dinner. I make pasta, something simple, because I just can't focus enough to make anything complicated. We eat at my tiny table while the sun sets over the mountains.

"You're sure quiet tonight," he says.

"Oh, am I?"

"You barely said ten words since I got here. You keep looking at your phone like you're waiting for something."

I set my fork down. "Sorry. I'm just distracted."

"By what?"

I let the question hang in the air because I don't know what to say. This is my chance. I could tell him right now. I *should* tell him, but the words just won't come.

"Oh, work stuff," I say instead. "Nothing important."

He studies me for a long moment. His blue eyes are searching for answers. I can tell he doesn't believe me. Wyatt has always been able to read me better than I would like.

"Okay," he says finally. "But if you want to talk about it…"

"I know. I will. When I'm ready."

We finish dinner, do the dishes, and sit on the sofa to watch the last light fade from the sky. But something has shifted between us. A distance that wasn't there before. And I know it's all my fault.

Friday morning, I wake up to another email.

Ms. Whitfield,

I wanted to follow up on my previous message. I know this is a big decision, but I must be transparent. We're on a very tight timeline. If I don't hear from you by the end of next week, I'm going to need to extend the offer to other candidates. I hope to hear from you soon.

Best,

Genevieve

End of next week. Ten days. Ten days to decide whether to stay or go. Whether to choose the life I've been building for the last few months or the life I was raised for.

I close my laptop and put my head in my hands.

Saturday at Meredith's garden, I'm distracted and clumsy. I pull up a seedling that wasn't a weed. I overwater the tomatoes, and I nearly trip over the garden hose twice.

"Okay," Meredith says finally, setting down her pruning shears. "Out with it."

"Out with what?"

"Whatever's got you wound tighter than a two-dollar watch. You've been somewhere else all morning."

"I'm fine."

"Eleanor." Her voice is firm in the way that reminds me she spent decades managing classrooms of children. "I may be old, but I'm not blind. Something is definitely bothering you."

I sit down on the garden bench, my hands still dirty and my heart heavy. "I got a job offer."

Meredith goes still. "A job offer? What do you mean? What kind of job offer?"

"A good one. A really good one. In Switzerland, teaching at the most prestigious finishing school in Europe." I look down at my dirty hands. "It's everything my mother ever wanted for me. Everything I was trained for and spent my life learning. But…"

"But it would mean leaving," she says softly.

I nod. "Leaving here. Leaving everything I've…" I stop, unable to finish.

"Leaving Wyatt," she says quietly.

"Leaving everyone."

She's silent for a moment. Her expression is unreadable.

"Does he know?"

"No. I haven't told anyone. I don't know how to tell anyone. I don't even know what I want to do."

"Well, when do you have to decide?"

"Ten days. Well, less, actually, now."

Meredith nods slowly and picks up her pruning shears. She examines a rose bush, but I can tell she's not really looking at it.

"Can I tell you something?" she says.

"Of course."

"When Frank asked me to marry him, I had a choice to make. I was twenty-three years old with a teaching degree and a job offer in Atlanta. Good money, good school, everything I thought I wanted." She snips a dead branch and sets it aside. "Frank was a mountain boy with no college degree who wanted to stay in Copper Creek and build furniture. On paper, it made no sense."

"What did you do?"

"Well, I chose him. Obviously, I chose this life. And

there were times early on, especially, when I wondered if I had made a mistake. When I missed the city, the opportunities, the life I might have had."

"So do you regret it?"

She turns and looks at me. "Not for one single second. Because I learned something, Eleanor. The life that looks good on paper isn't always the life that makes you happy. And the life that makes you happy doesn't always make any sense to other people."

"So you think I should stay?"

"Oh, I think you should make your own choice. Not the choice your mother would have made, not the choice Wyatt wants you to make, not the choice that looks best on paper, but your choice." She reaches over and takes my dirty hand in hers. "But I'll tell you this. Whatever you decide, you need to tell Wyatt. He deserves to know. Keeping this secret is only going to hurt both of you."

She's right. I know she's right.

But telling Wyatt makes it real. It means having a conversation I'm just not ready to have. It means facing the possibility that whatever I decide, I'm going to lose something precious.

So I don't tell him.

Not on Saturday when he picks me up for our date. Not on Sunday when we have lunch at Dixie's Diner with Dolly and Presley. Not on Monday when he texts me good morning like he does every morning, and I type back a response that feels like a lie.

I keep the secret, and I feel it growing between us like a wall.

Tuesday night, I'm alone in my apartment staring at my laptop screen. Genevieve's email is open. My cursor hovers over the reply button.

What do I even say?

Thank you for the offer. I'm flattered, but I've fallen in love with a honky-tonk bar and a mountain town and a man with blue eyes who carves animals out of wood.

Thank you for the offer. I'm flattered, but I'm finally figuring out who I am when I'm not performing for anyone, and I'm afraid to leave. I'm afraid that if I leave, I'll lose her again.

Thank you for the offer. I'm flattered, but...

But what?

I don't know. That's the problem. I don't know.

My phone buzzes.

Wyatt: You awake?

Me: Yeah. I can't sleep.

Wyatt: Me neither. Want company?

I hesitate for a moment with my fingers hovering over the screen. I should say no. Keep my distance until I figure this thing out. I should stop digging myself deeper into this hole, I might have to climb out of.

Me: Yes.

Twenty minutes later, there's a soft knock on my door. Wyatt is standing there in sweatpants and a T-shirt, his hair rumpled like he's been running his hands through it all night. He looks worried. He looks tired.

"Hey," he says.

"Hey."

We stand there for a moment, neither of us moving, then he reaches out and pulls me into a hug. It's not romantic. It's not leading anywhere. It's just comfort, his arms around me, his chin resting on top of my head, his heart beating steady against my ear.

"Listen, I don't know what's going on with you," he says quietly. "And you don't have to tell me if you're not ready, but I need you to know that I'm here. Whatever it is, I'm here."

My eyes sting with tears, but I refuse to let them fall.

"I know," I whisper. "I know you are."

We stand there in the doorway, holding each other, and I think about that email sitting on my laptop, about the choice I have to make, about the life I could have in Switzerland and the life I'm building here. And I realize, with a clarity that suddenly terrifies me, that I'm going to have to choose not between two jobs, but between two versions of myself.

The Eleanor that I was raised to be, the polished, accomplished, impressive one, or the Eleanor I'm becoming, the messy, uncertain, and maybe real one.

We end up on the sofa, just sitting, not talking.

Wyatt's arm is around me, and my head is on his shoulder. The mountains are dark shapes against an even darker sky.

"I'm scared," I say finally.

"Of what?"

"Of making the wrong choice, of messing everything up, of…" I stop and shake my head.

"Of what, Eleanor?"

I should tell him, right now. Just say the words. Why is this so hard?

I got a job offer in Switzerland.

I have to decide in a few days.

But the words will not come, because saying them means watching his face change.

"Of not being good enough," I lie. "For any of this."

He's quiet for a moment, then he shifts and looks at me, cupping my cheek in his hand.

"You are good enough. You're more than good enough. And whatever you're scared of, whatever you're not telling me, we'll figure it out together. You just have to trust me."

Together.

The word sits in my chest like a stone.

Because if I take this job in Switzerland, there will be no "together" anymore. There'd just be me alone, in a beautiful city, doing a prestigious job that my mother would have loved. There would be no more Wyatt with his blue eyes or Dolly with her big hair. There'd be no more Saturday morning gardening or cheesy karaoke songs.

If I stay, I'm giving up everything I was raised to want for something that may not even work out. Something that has no guarantees at all. Something that requires me to trust that this life, this wildly uncertain life, is worth choosing.

"Wyatt," I say, my voice breaks on his name.

"Yeah?"

Tell him. Tell him now.

But I can't. Not yet. Not tonight.

"Thank you," I say instead. "For being here."

"Always," he says.

I hate myself for this lie growing between us.

But I'm not ready to face the truth yet.

So I lean into him and let myself have this moment, and pretend just for tonight that I don't have an impossible choice to make.

The next five days are a slow kind of torture.

I go through the motions, opening the bar, serving drinks, smiling at customers, closing up at night. I garden with Meredith on Saturday morning. She watches me with those knowing eyes, but she never pushes. I have dinner with Wyatt on Sunday and laugh at his jokes, hold his hand, and pretend everything is normal.

But it's not normal, and he knows it.

"You're pulling away," he says Sunday night, walking me to my door.

"No, I'm not."

"You are. I can feel it." He stops at the bottom of the stairs, not following me up like he usually does. "Whatever's going on, Eleanor, whatever it is that you're not telling me, it's putting up a wall between us, and I don't know how to get through it if you won't let me in."

My throat tightens like I'm being strangled.

"Wyatt—"

"I'm not asking you to tell me tonight," he says gently. "But I need you to know that I see it, and it's…" He stops for a moment. "It's hard watching you disappear somewhere I can't follow."

"I'm sorry."

"Don't be sorry. Just talk to me when you're ready. Please."

"I will."

"October is almost here, Eleanor. If you've decided to leave, please don't keep me in suspense."

He leaves without kissing my cheek, without tucking my hair behind my ear, without any of our usual rituals. I stand at the bottom of the stairs and watch his taillights disappear down Mountain Road, feeling the distance growing between us with every passing second.

～

Monday morning, I draft another reply to Genevieve.

Dear Ms. Ashford,

Thank you so much for this incredible opportunity. I'm honored to be considered for the position. After careful consideration—

After careful consideration of what?

I delete the draft and start again.

Dear Ms. Ashford, I'm writing to respectfully decline… but I can't finish that sentence either, because declining means closing the door. It means committing to this life in the mountains with absolutely no backup plan, no safety net, and no escape route. I'm just not sure I'm brave enough for that.

Tuesday is my deadline. I wake up knowing I have to make the decision today. There will be no more stalling, no more drafts, no more lying awake at three in the morning running the same arguments in my head in circles.

I sit at my tiny kitchen table with coffee I can't taste and my laptop open to Genevieve's email.

Two hundred thousand dollars, living in Switzerland, the most prestigious etiquette position in the world, or a honky-tonk bar in Georgia, a town I'd never heard of a few months ago, and a man I'm falling in love with who deserves better than someone who can't commit.

My phone buzzes.

Wyatt: Dinner tonight? I'll cook.

I stare at the message.

Tonight. I should tell him tonight. Whatever I decide, he deserves to know. He's been patient, so, so patient. And I've been lying to him through omission for almost two weeks.

Me: Yes. What time?

Wyatt: Seven. I'll pick you up.

Me: I'll drive myself. Need to run some errands first.

A pause, then—

Wyatt: Okay. See you at seven.

I can feel his confusion through the screen. I always let him pick me up. It's one of our things. But tonight I need my own car, because if this conversation goes the way I'm afraid it will, I might need to leave.

I spend the day trying to work and failing spectacularly. I mess up three drink orders, count the register wrong twice, snap at Presley for something that isn't her fault, and then have to apologize immediately.

"Okay, what is going on with you?" she finally asks at four o'clock, cornering me in the storage room.

"Oh, nothing. I'm just tired."

"You've been 'just tired' for two weeks. That's not tired, Eleanor. There's something else going on."

I lean against a shelf of liquor bottles and close my eyes. "I have to make a decision," I say, "about my future, and I don't know what to do."

"About the bar? But that's in October."

"About everything."

She's quiet for a moment. "Does this have anything to do with why you and Wyatt seem to be weird lately?"

"We haven't been weird."

"You've been super weird. He barely looks at you when he's here. You barely look at him. It's like watching two people pretend they don't know each other."

"It's complicated."

"Well, it always is." She crosses her arms. "Look, I don't know what's going on. You don't have to tell me. Whatever this decision is, make it for you, not for anyone else. Because at the end of the day, you're the one who has to live with it."

She leaves me alone in the storage room with the echoes of her words echoing in my mind.

Make it for you.

But that's the problem. I don't know who *me* is anymore. The me who was raised to want Switzerland or the me who's learned to love Copper Creek. Are they even the same person? Can they be?

At 6:45, I drive to Wyatt's cabin. The evening is warm, the kind of summer evening that makes you want to sit outside and watch the light change and look for lightning bugs. His truck is in the driveway, smoke rising from the chimney of his outdoor grill.

I sit in my car for a moment, trying to gather my courage.

Just tell him. Why is this so hard?

Whatever happens, you have to tell him the truth.

I get out and walk to the porch. Before I can knock, the door opens.

Wyatt is standing there in jeans and a soft gray T-shirt, a dish towel over his shoulder. He looks tired and worried, but beautiful.

"Hey," he says.

"Hey."

"Come in," he says finally. "Dinner's almost ready."

He's made steaks on the grill, baked potatoes, and a salad with vegetables from Meredith's garden. We eat at his table by the window, and I try to taste the food, but everything is ash in my mouth.

"You're not eating," he says.

"I'm not very hungry."

"Eleanor." He sets down his fork. "Whatever it is, just tell me. Please. The not knowing is worse than anything you could possibly say."

I look at him across the table, this man who caught me when I fell off a mechanical bull, showed me a secret waterfall, carved little animals out of wood because he needed something to do with his hands. This man who has been patient and kind and honest with me from the very beginning.

And I've been lying to him.

"I got a job offer," I say.

He goes very still. "What kind of job offer?"

"A really good one." I take a breath. "In Switzerland. Teaching at an etiquette school. It's the most prestigious finishing school in Europe. Salary is two hundred thousand a year plus housing. It's… everything I thought I wanted and everything my mother ever wanted for me."

The silence stretches between us, like a wire pulled too tight.

"When?" His voice is flat.

"The email came two weeks ago."

Something in his expression cracks. "Wait. Two weeks? You've known about this for two weeks, and you didn't tell me?"

"I didn't know how to tell you. I didn't know what I was going to do."

"So you just kept it to yourself every time we had dinner together, every time we talked about the future, while I—" He stops and pushes up from the table so abruptly that his chair scrapes against the floor. "While I sat here falling in love with you, you were planning to leave."

"I wasn't planning to leave. I wasn't planning anything. If I wanted to leave, I could've taken Gary Allen's offer. I haven't even decided anything about this job."

"Haven't you?" He's pacing now. "Two weeks, Eleanor. Two weeks of you lying to my face. Two weeks of me knowing something was wrong and you telling me you were just tired. Two weeks of—" He lets out a harsh laugh. "Gosh, I am so stupid."

"Wyatt—"

"I told myself it was different this time," he says. "That you weren't going to do what Laney did. That you actually wanted to be here, wanted this life, wanted —" He turns to face me, and the pain in his eyes makes my chest cave in. "But you've had one foot out the door the whole time, haven't you? You were just waiting for something better to come along."

"That's not fair."

"From where I'm standing, it looks exactly like that. It looks like you were keeping your options open, stringing me along while you decided if Copper Creek was good enough for you. If I was good enough for you."

"That's not what I was doing."

"Then what *were* you doing?" he demands. "Because I'd really love to understand how someone who supposedly cares about me could hide something this big for two weeks."

"I was scared," I blurt. "I was terrified, Wyatt. Because this job offer is everything I was raised to want. Everything my mother spent her whole life preparing me for. And turning it down means admitting that everything she believed, everything she taught me, was wrong. It means choosing a life that doesn't make sense on paper, has no guarantees, that requires me to trust something I've never trusted before."

"Trust what?"

"That I'm enough. That this whole thing is enough. That I can build a life here without screwing it up."

He's quiet for a moment, his jaw tight. "And what have you decided? Are you taking the job?"

"I don't know."

"You don't know?" He laughs, but there's no humor in it. "You've had two weeks, Eleanor. Two weeks to think about it, and you still… don't know."

"It's not that simple."

"It is that simple. Either you want this life, or you don't. Either you want us, or you don't." He crosses his arms. "I told you from the beginning I don't do casual. I can't give my heart to someone who's gonna leave. And you said you understood. You said you were falling for me. You said, 'I'm in it.'"

"I meant all of it."

"Then how can you not know? How can you stand there and tell me you're still deciding whether to move to another continent?"

I don't have an answer, because he's right. If I really wanted this, if I really wanted him, the choice should be obvious. So why isn't it?

"I think you should go," he says quietly.

"Wyatt—"

"I need space, Eleanor. Time to think. And you?" He shakes his head. "You need to make a decision. A real decision. Not because of me or the bar or anyone else. You need to figure out what you actually want."

"And if I choose to stay?"

"Well, then we'll talk. But right now…" He shakes his head again. "Right now, I can't look at you without seeing two weeks of lies. And I need that to stop hurting before I can think clearly."

I stand there for a moment, wanting to argue, explain, make him understand. But I can't, because he's not wrong. And even I don't understand. I kept it from him. I lied. And no explanation will change that.

"I'm so sorry," I say, "for not telling you sooner."

"I know you are."

But he doesn't say it's okay, because it's not.

I pick up my purse and walk out the door. I pause at the threshold.

"I do love you," I say without turning around. "I know I've never said it before, but I do. I just don't know if that's enough."

I don't wait for a response. I just walk to my car and drive away, leaving him standing in the door of his cabin.

CHAPTER 19

The drive back to The Rusty Spur is a blur. I'm crying, and it's the ugly crying, with the gasping sobs that make it hard to see the road. I have to pull over twice to wipe my eyes, catch my breath, and stop my hands from shaking.

What had I done?

I was so afraid of making the wrong choice that I made the worst choice of all. I kept secrets. I built walls. I pushed away the one person who's been honest with me from the very beginning.

And now I might have lost him.

When I finally get back to my apartment, I sit on the sofa in the dark and let myself fall apart. I cry for Wyatt. I cry for Meredith, who will be disappointed in me. I cry for Mavis, who believed I could be a real person and whom I've now proven wrong. I cry for my mother, who wanted me to be something I'm not sure I can be. I cry for myself, for the girl who grew terrible tomatoes and talked to her plants, for the woman who learned to love a honky-tonk bar in a mountain town, and for the version of Eleanor who was finally, finally starting to figure out who she was.

I don't know how long I sit there. Maybe hours. The moon rises and sets. The darkness deepens and then slowly begins to lighten.

And somewhere in the middle of the night, something shifts.

I think about what Meredith said about choosing the life that makes you happy, not the life that looks good on paper. And I think about what Presley said about making the decision for myself, not anyone else. I think about Mavis's letter, about being graceless and still being loved, about finding a place to be yourself.

But most of all, I think about Wyatt and the way he looked at me when I told him I loved him. The hope and hurt all tangled together.

I do love you. I just don't know if that's enough.

But what if it is enough?

What if love, messy, complicated, terrifying love, is exactly enough?

I pull up my laptop and open Genevieve's email.

And this time, I know exactly what to write.

Dear Ms. Ashford,

Thank you so much for thinking of me for this incredible opportunity. The position is everything my mother dreamed of for me, and I'm deeply honored to have been considered. However, I must respectfully decline.

Six months ago, I inherited a honky-tonk bar in the Blue Ridge Mountains of Georgia. I came here expecting to fulfill the will's terms, then sell the property and return to my real life. But what I found instead was something I didn't know I was looking for: a community that has welcomed me, work that matters to me, and people I've come to love.

My mother taught me that success meant prestige, accomplishment, and the approval of others. And while she was a remarkable woman and I will always be grateful for the skills she gave me, I've now learned that success can mean choosing happiness over ambition, choosing connection over advancement, choosing a life that feels right even when it doesn't look right on paper.

I hope you find just the right candidate for this position. The Institut is extraordinary, and whoever fills the role will be very fortunate.

With gratitude and respect,

Eleanor Whitfield

I read it three times, and then before I can second-guess myself, I hit send.

The email disappears into the digital void, and I sit back with my heart pounding in my chest. It's done. I just turned down two-hundred thousand dollars and a life in Switzerland. I just chose Copper Creek. Again.

I wait for the regret to come, the panic, the voice of my mother telling me I've made a terrible mistake. But it doesn't come. Instead, there's just quiet, the kind of quiet that must feel like peace.

The sun is rising over the mountains when I finally move from the sofa. I shower, change into clean clothes, brush my hair, and skip makeup because my face is still so swollen from crying that there's no hiding it. I look at myself in the bathroom mirror.

"You made a choice," I say out loud. "Now follow through."

Of course, this isn't the first choice I've made. When I turned down the Gary Allen deal, that was a pretty big choice too.

It's 6:47 a.m. when I pull into Wyatt's driveway. His truck is there. Smoke is not rising from the chimney. The cabin looks quiet, still, like a painting. I sit in my car for a moment, trying to gather my courage.

He may not want to see me. He may slam the door in my face. He may tell me it's too late and that I've broken something that can't be fixed.

But I have to try.

I get out of the car and walk to the porch. My hand is shaking when I knock.

Nothing happens.

I knock again, louder this time.

Still nothing.

"Wyatt," I call out. "It's Eleanor. I know you're probably still really mad at me, and you have every right to be, but I need to talk to you. Please."

Silence.

I lean my forehead against the door, closing my eyes. Maybe he's not here. Maybe he went to his grandmother's or the bar, or anywhere that wasn't here with memories of last night.

I'm about to go back to my car when I hear footsteps inside.

The door opens.

Wyatt is standing there in the same clothes from last night, crumpled like he slept in them—or maybe he didn't sleep at all. His hair is a mess. There are dark circles under his eyes, and his expression is guarded.

"It's not even seven in the morning," he says.

"I know. I'm so sorry, but this just couldn't wait."

He doesn't invite me in. He just stands in the doorway with his arms crossed, waiting.

"I made my decision."

Something in his eyes flickers—hope or fear. I can't tell which.

"And?"

"I turned it down. The job. I sent the email about an hour ago."

He doesn't move or react, just keeps watching me.

"Why?" he asks.

"Because I finally figured out what I want."

I take a breath.

"For thirty-four years, I've been living someone

else's life. Making choices based on what my mother wanted, what I thought society wanted, and what looked good on paper. And you know what? I was miserable. Successful, polished, and completely miserable."

"Eleanor—"

"Let me finish, please."

He nods.

"So when I came to Copper Creek, I thought this was just a detour. Six months I had to get through before I could go back to my real life. Somewhere along the way—gardening with your grandmother, learning to pour drinks without spilling, riding that stupid mechanical bull—I stopped wanting to go back. It stopped being home. Because this place is my real life. This messy, complicated, unpredictable life. It is the first place I have ever felt like myself."

My voice breaks, but I keep going.

"And you. Gosh, Wyatt, you're the first person who's ever really seen me, maybe other than Mavis. Not the version I perform for other people, but the real me. The one who's scared and uncertain and makes terrible decisions like hiding a job offer for two weeks because she was too afraid to face it."

"That was a pretty terrible decision," he says, a faint hint of softness in his voice.

"I know, and I'm so sorry. I should have told you the moment I got that email. I should have trusted you enough to work through it together instead of just shutting you out." I step closer. "But I'm telling you now, I'm choosing this. I'm choosing Copper Creek. I'm choosing The Rusty Spur." I reach out and take his hand. He lets me, though his fingers don't close around mine. "I'm choosing you," I say, "if you'll still have me."

For a moment, he doesn't speak. He just looks at me with an expression I can't read. I realize, with a little bit of fear, that I might have waited too long, that the damage might already be done.

"You hurt me," he says finally.

"I know."

"Two weeks, Eleanor. Two weeks of you lying, of watching you pull away and not knowing why, of feeling like I was losing you and not understanding what I did wrong."

"I know, and I hate myself for it."

"I don't want you to hate yourself," he says. "I just want you to understand. Why didn't you tell me?"

"Because I was afraid that if I said it out loud, I'd have to make a choice. And I just wasn't ready. I was scared of choosing wrong, scared of giving up the life my mother wanted for me, scared of—" I stop and swallow hard. "Scared of wanting this too much. Wanting you too much. Because if I let myself want it and then it didn't work out…"

"You'd be devastated."

"Yes."

He's quiet for a moment. Then, slowly, his fingers finally close around mine.

"I know something about being scared," he says. "About wanting something so much it terrifies you. About building walls because it feels safer than being vulnerable."

"I know you do."

"And I know something about making mistakes. About hurting people you love because you're so wrapped up in your own fear."

"Wyatt—"

"Look, I'm not saying it's okay what you did, keeping the secret. It's gonna take some time for me to trust that you won't do it again." He steps closer. "But I also know that you're here at seven in the morning after staying up all night making the hardest decision of your life. And you chose this. You chose us."

"I did."

"Then I think," he pauses, and a small smile tugs at the corner of his mouth. "I think I can work with that."

I feel so relieved that my knees go weak.

"Yeah?"

"Yeah."

His free hand comes up to cup my face, his thumb brushing across my cheekbone. "But Eleanor…"

"Yes?"

"If you ever keep something like that from me again—"

"I swear, I promise, I won't. No more secrets, no more walls. We'll figure that out, figure everything out together."

"Together," he repeats.

We're standing so close now, close enough that I can see the exhaustion in his eyes. And some hurt, but underneath it all, the hope, the love.

"I meant what I said last night," I whisper. "I love you."

"I know," he says, his voice rough. "I love you too. Even when you're infuriating. Even when you make the most terrible decisions. Even when you scare the heck out of me."

"Wyatt—"

"Eleanor, I really want to kiss you right now."

"Then kiss me."

"Are you sure? Because we said we'd wait until it was October, until you were sure about everything."

I think about the email I sent an hour ago, about the door I closed and the door I opened.

"I'm sure," I say. "I've never been more sure of anything in my life."

He doesn't wait for me to say it again.

His mouth finds mine, and everything else falls away.

The kiss starts soft, tentative. His lips brush against mine like he's asking permission, like he's giving me one final chance to change my mind. But I don't want to change my mind. I want this. I want him.

I wrap my arms around his neck and pull him closer, and the kiss deepens into something else, something hungry and desperate and full of everything we've been holding back for months. His hands slide into my hair, angling my head so he can kiss me deeply, and I make a sound against his mouth that I might be embarrassed about if I were thinking clearly—but I can't think clearly. All I can do is feel. Feel his hands in my hair, his chest against mine, his heart pounding fast, matching mine, the scratchy stubble of his chin, the taste of him, coffee and something sweet underneath.

When we finally break apart, we're both breathing hard.

"Wow," I manage to say.

"Yeah." He rests his forehead against mine, his hands still tangled in my hair. "Definitely worth the wait."

"Definitely."

We stand there for a moment. The sun is fully up now, painting the mountains in golds and pinks, and somewhere I hear a bird in a tree singing.

"Come inside," Wyatt says. "I'll make breakfast."

"I'm not hungry."

"You need to eat. You've been up all night making life-altering decisions." He pulls back just enough to look at me. "And then you can tell me everything. The whole story. No more secrets."

"No more secrets," I agree.

He takes my hand and leads me into the cabin.

We eat eggs and toast at his table by the window, and I tell him everything about Genevieve's email and how I felt when I read it, about the two weeks of agonizing over my decision, about the responses I never sent, about lying awake at night trying to figure out what I wanted, about the conversation with his grandmother in the garden and how afraid I was, and am, of choosing the wrong thing. He listens without interrupting, just eats his eggs, and watches me with those steady blue eyes.

"Your mom really did a number on you, didn't she?" he finally says when I'm done.

"She loved me, in her way."

"I know, but love isn't always healthy, you know? The way she raised you to value achievement over happiness, to perform instead of actually having feelings, to see everything as a ladder to climb." He shakes his head. "That's a lot of stuff to unlearn."

"I'm trying."

"I know you are." He reaches across the table and takes my hand. "And I'll help you, however I can. Even when it's hard. Even when you make me want to tear my hair out by the roots."

"That might be often."

"Probably. But you're worth it."

I squeeze his hand. "So what happens now?"

"Well, now we finish breakfast, and then you're gonna go home and get some sleep, because you look like you're about to fall over." He grins. "And then tonight we celebrate."

"Celebrate what?"

"You choosing this life, choosing to stay here." He stands up and starts clearing the dishes. "I think we should tell everyone. Make it official. Let Dolly spread the gossip so the whole town knows by tomorrow morning."

"Everyone's going to have opinions."

"Everyone always has opinions. That's what happens in small towns." He smiles. "But they're good opinions. They want you to stay, Eleanor. They've wanted that since you walked into town with your pencil skirt and pearls and tried to order fancy wine at a honky-tonk bar."

I laugh. "That was so embarrassing."

"That was so adorable." He comes around the table and pulls me to my feet, wrapping his arms around me. "You're adorable. Infuriating, but adorable."

"You keep calling me infuriating."

"Because you are. It's one of your best qualities."

I tilt my head up and kiss him, just a soft brush of the lips. "I should go," I say reluctantly, "before I fall asleep standing up."

"Go. Sleep. I'll pick you up at seven."

"For what?"

"It's a surprise," he grins. "Trust me."

"I do," I say.

And I do trust him, completely. It's the strangest, most terrifying, most wonderful feeling in the world.

I drive back to The Rusty Spur in a daze. Everything looks brighter, somehow, more real. The mountains are greener, the sky bluer, the air sweeter. Or maybe I'm seeing it all for the first time, without the filter of fear and uncertainty. I park in the lot and sit for a moment, watching the building's weathered wood and the big neon sign with its cowboy boot and spinning spur. This is mine, not because I inherited it or am obligated to run it, but because I chose it and want to be here now.

I get out of the car and walk to the side entrance, but before I can go inside, I hear someone calling my name.

"Eleanor!"

I turn to find Dolly hurrying across the parking lot, her platinum hair catching the morning sun.

"Dolly, what are you doing here so early?"

"I could ask you the same thing." She stops in front of me, slightly out of breath. "I was driving past and saw your car, and I've been worried about you, sugar. You've been kind of off all week."

"I know. I'm sorry." I stop to take a breath. "I had something to figure out."

"And did you figure it out?"

"I did." I smile. "I'm staying, Dolly. I turned down a job offer in Switzerland, and I'm staying in Copper Creek for good."

Her face transforms. There's surprise, then joy, and then something that looks like tears about to fall.

"Oh, honey." She pulls me into a tight hug, and I'm having a hard time breathing. "That's just wonderful. So wonderful."

"I'm sorry I didn't tell you sooner. I should have."

"Hush. You told me now, and that's what matters." She pulls back, studying my face. "Does Wyatt know?"

"He knows. I told him this morning."

"And?"

I can feel myself starting to blush. "And things are really good."

Dolly's grin is triumphant. "I knew it. I knew you two would work it out. Mavis would be so happy."

"You think?"

"Oh, honey, I know it. She wanted this for you. All of it. The bar, the town, the people. You belong here, Eleanor. You always did. But you had to figure that out for yourself."

"Thank you, Dolly, for everything. For being patient with me while I figured it out."

"Well, that's what family does." She releases me and steps back. "Now, go get some sleep. You look like death warmed over. Tonight we're celebrating. I'm telling everybody."

"Wyatt said the same thing," I say, laughing.

"Great minds think alike." She winks. "See you tonight, sugar."

She walks back to her car, already pulling out her phone, probably to start the gossip chain that will have the entire town informed by lunchtime. I watch her go, then turn back to The Rusty Spur.

My bar. My home. My life.

I climb the stairs to my apartment, collapse on my sofa, and fall asleep within seconds. I don't dream about Switzerland or my mother or impossible choices. I dream about mountains and music and a man with blue eyes who loves me.

CHAPTER 20

I sleep until four in the afternoon. When I finally wake up, my phone is full of messages.

From Presley: *OMG Dolly told me! I'm so happy you're staying!*

From Boone: *Good news travels fast. Glad you're sticking around!*

From Meredith: *I knew you'd make the right choice. See you Saturday for gardening. Bring your appetite, I'm making pie!*

And from Wyatt: *Hope you slept well. Still picking you up at seven. Wear something comfortable.*

I smile at the phone and type back. *Slept great. See you at seven. Can I have a hint about the surprise?*

His response is immediate. *No.*

Then another message pops up. *But you'll like it, I promise.*

At seven o'clock sharp, his truck pulls up into the

parking lot. I'm waiting on the porch in jeans and a soft green t-shirt, comfortable like he said, but nice enough that I don't feel underdressed for whatever it is he's planning. My hair is down, still a little damp from the shower, and I'm using just enough makeup to hide evidence of my sleepless night.

He gets out of the truck and stops when he sees me.

"You look beautiful," he says.

"I look like a woman who slept for twelve hours."

"You look beautiful," he repeats.

He opens the passenger door for me, as he always does, and I climb in. The cab smells like him, cologne and something underneath that's just Wyatt.

"So where are we going?" I ask as he pulls out of the parking lot.

"You'll see."

"You know I hate surprises."

"No, you don't. You hate not being in control. There's a difference."

He's not wrong.

We drive through town, past Dixie Diner and the Sweet Tea Bakery and Grits and Grind, past the town square with its white gazebo and towering oaks, past the church where Pastor Dale preaches on Sundays. And then Wyatt turns onto a road I haven't been on before, a very narrow one that winds up into the hills behind town.

"Wyatt, where—"

"Patience."

We climb higher as the trees press in on both sides until it opens into a clearing at the top of a ridge. And I understand.

The clearing is full of people.

Dolly is there, setting up a folding table laden with food. Presley is stringing lights between two trees. Boone is manning what looks like a portable grill, turning burgers. Meredith is sitting in a lawn chair, directing everyone. And beyond them, the view. The entire valley lies below us, Copper Creek nestled in the center like a jewel. The sun is just beginning to set, painting everything in warm light.

"Wyatt," I breathe, surprised.

He's grinning so much. "This is the overlook. Best view in the county. We do picnics up here sometimes for special occasions."

"And this is a special occasion?"

"You chose to stay. That's about as special as it gets."

I'm out of the truck before I can think about it, walking toward the group. These people who have become my family.

Dolly sees me and lets out a whoop. "She's here! The guest of honor has arrived!"

And then I'm hugged by Dolly, who smells strongly of perfume and hairspray. By Presley, who squeezes me so hard I can barely breathe. By Boone, whose hug is gentle for such a massive man. By Meredith, who cups my face in her soft hands and says, "I'm so proud of you, my dear."

"How did you arrange all of this?" I ask Wyatt when I finally pull myself away from the group.

"I made some calls while you were sleeping. Turns out people were pretty motivated to celebrate."

"You did all of this in a few hours?"

"We did all of this," he says, gesturing at the group. "This is what community looks like, Eleanor. People showing up for each other."

I blink rapidly. I refuse to cry again.

"Thank you. All of you. I just don't know what to say."

"Don't say anything," Dolly says. "Just eat. Boone's been slaving over that grill for an hour, and he'll be offended if you don't try his burgers."

The evening winds down around ten o'clock. People drift away in twos or threes, carrying leftover food, tired children, and calling goodbyes across the clearing. Meredith fell asleep in her lawn chair an hour ago, and Boone gently carries her to Wyatt's truck as if she weighs nothing.

"I should help clean up," I say, but Dolly waves me off.

"You've done enough. Go be with your man. Enjoy the stars."

So I do.

Wyatt and I end up on the tailgate of his truck after

he returns from taking his grandmother home, legs dangling, looking out at the valley below. The lights of Copper Creek twinkle in the darkness.

"Heck of a week," he says.

"Heck of a few months."

He laughs softly and pulls me closer. I lean into him.

"Thank you," I say, "for all this, and for not giving up on me."

"Couldn't if I tried." He presses a kiss to my temple. "You're stuck with me forever now, Eleanor Whitfield."

"Good."

We sit there until the last car pulls away, until the clearing is empty and quiet. The only things we can hear are the sound of crickets and the distant murmur of the creek.

And I think, this is it. This is home.

It's not just the place, but the feeling.

The weeks that follow settle into a rhythm. Summer deepens into fall. Leaves begin to turn, splashing the mountains with color. The bar stays busy with the last of the tourist season, and I find myself looking forward to the quieter months ahead. Time to plan, improve, and dream about what The Rusty Spur could become.

Wyatt and I don't talk about October fifteenth. We don't need to. The decision has been made. The only thing left is the paperwork.

As the date approaches, I think about my great-aunt Mavis more and more. About the woman I never met who somehow knew me better than I knew myself.

About the gift she gave me, not just the bar, but the permission to become myself.

I sure hope I've made her proud.

October fifteenth arrives on a Tuesday. The morning is crisp and clear, the kind of fall day that makes you want to go sit in a stack of hay and drink cider. I wake up early in my apartment above The Rusty Spur and lie there for a moment.

Six months ago, I drove into Copper Creek with no idea what I was getting into. Six months ago, I walked into a honky-tonk bar expecting to hate every minute of my time there.

And today, The Rusty Spur officially becomes mine.

My phone buzzes with a text.

Wyatt: Big day. You ready?

Me: Nervous, excited, all of it.

Wyatt: I'll pick you up at 9:30. We'll go to Harlan's together.

Me: You don't have to do that.

Wyatt: I want to. This is important. You shouldn't do it alone.

I smile at my phone.

Me: See you at 9:30.

I shower and dress, not wearing the pencil skirt and pearls I arrived in, but nice jeans and a white t-shirt, complete with my new hiking boots. Something that feels like me, the real me.

At 9:30 sharp, Wyatt's truck pulls into the parking lot.

I meet him outside, and he pulls me into a hug before I can say anything.

"You've got this," he says against my hair.

"I know. I just…" I pull back and look at him. "It feels like the end of something, you know? And the beginning of something else."

"And that's exactly what it is."

He opens the door for me. "Come on. Let's go make it official."

Harlan's office looks exactly the same as it did six months ago. Same stacks of paper, same creaky stairs, the same smell of old books and coffee. But I'm differ-ent. Everything about me is different.

Wyatt waits in the truck. This is something I need to do alone.

I climb the familiar stairs one last time as a visitor. The next time I come here, whenever that will be, I'll be a true citizen of Copper Creek. A property owner and a member of the community in every sense of the word.

Harlan is waiting behind his desk, a folder open in front of him.

"Ms. Whitfield," he gestures to the chair across from him, "please sit."

I sit, my heart pounding.

"Well," he says, looking at me over the reading glasses sitting at the tip of his nose, "it's been quite a six months."

"That's one way to put it."

"Developers, health inspections, community work-days, apparently a relationship with Mr. Wyatt Rivers himself that has the whole town talking." He chuckles. "Mavis would have loved every minute of that."

"Do you think so?"

"I know so. She never did anything the easy way. Why should you?"

He picks up a pen. "Now, are you ready to make it official?"

He slides a stack of documents across the desk. I read them carefully. Transfer of ownership, the final release of the estate, the confirmation that all condi-tions of the will have been met.

"Sign here," Harlan says, pointing. "And here. And here."

I sign. My hand is steady.

Eleanor Whitfield.

"Congratulations," Harlan says when I'm done. "The Rusty Spur is officially yours, free and clear."

I stare at the papers, at my name, at the reality of what I've accomplished.

"I did it," I whisper.

"You did," he leans back in his chair, winking. "Oh, there's one more thing."

He reaches into his desk and pulls out a cream-colored envelope, slightly yellowed around the edges, with my name written on the front.

"Mavis left this for you. Instructions were to give it to you on this day, if you made it through."

My hands tremble as I take it. "She wrote me another letter?"

"She did. Left it with me for safekeeping."

I turn it over in my hands, almost afraid to open it, because Mavis has been known for surprises. But whatever's inside, it's the final word, the last thing Mavis will ever say to me.

"You want some privacy?" he asks.

"Oh, no. You can stay."

I open the envelope and pull out two sheets of paper covered in her familiar handwriting.

My dearest Eleanor,

If you're reading this, you made it. You stayed. You fought through whatever challenges came your way, and I'm sure there were many. You became part of Copper Creek, just like I knew you would.

I have a confession to make. This was never really about the bar. I mean, the bar matters, don't get me wrong. It's been my life, my life's work, my greatest joy, the place where I found myself after leaving Atlanta all those years ago. But I could have left it to anyone. I could have sold it and donated the money to charity. I could have left it to the church outright.

I left it to you because I wanted to give you what no one else ever gave me. Permission to fail.

Your mother, my sister's daughter, was raised the same way I was. Taught that perfection was the only acceptable outcome, that mistakes were something to be ashamed of, that showing weakness was the greatest sin of all. I escaped that world, but your mother embraced it, and she passed it on to you.

I watched that from a distance, Eleanor. All those years, I watched. I saw a little girl who grew tomatoes in secret because her mother thought gardening was beneath her. I saw the young woman who gave up her dreams to run her mother's business. I saw a polished, perfect exterior and the loneliness underneath.

And then I thought, she needs what I found. She needs Copper Creek. And if I don't help her, she's never going to find it on her own.

Here's the part I haven't told you yet.

She also needed Wyatt Rivers.

I stop reading, catching my breath, my throat tight.

Yep, I planned that too. Or I hoped for it, at least.

I've known Wyatt since he came back from Afghanistan, broken and lost and convinced he could never be whole again. And I watched him rebuild himself, piece by piece. I saw the man he was becoming, kind, steady, loyal. And I saw how alone he was, how he'd closed himself off after Laney left, how he'd convinced himself he didn't deserve love.

Two broken people, I thought. Two people who've been taught that they're not enough. So what if I put them in the same place and let nature take its course?

It was a gamble. You might have hated each other. You

might have sold the bar on day one and gone back to Atlanta without ever even giving Copper Creek a chance. But I had a feeling.

Call it intuition, or meddling, or the instinct of a woman who's watched a lot of love stories unfold in that bar over the last almost forty years.

I knew you'd be good for each other. I knew you'd challenge each other, frustrate each other, and push each other. And I hoped you'd see what I saw. Two people who fit together like puzzle pieces, filling in each other's empty spaces.

If I was right, if you and Wyatt have found your way to each other, then I die happy. Truly happy. Because I didn't just save my bar. I saved two people I love, even if I never met one of them.

And if I was wrong, if you're reading this and thinking, Wyatt Rivers, that stubborn, infuriating man, well then, I do apologize for meddling. But somehow I don't think I was wrong.

Take care of him, Eleanor. Take care of the bar. Take care of yourself, most of all.

And remember what I told you before.

You can be graceless and still be loved.

You can fail and still be worthy.

You can let that mask slip once in a while and discover that the person underneath is someone worth knowing.

You are enough. You always were.

All my love, now and forever,

Mavis

P.S. The bourbon in the barbecue sauce was always the secret. But the real secret is love. Love is the same way. It's not one ingredient that makes it work. It's everything mixed together, given time to develop into something rich and beautiful. Be patient with yourself and each other. The best things take time.

I'm crying before I finish the first page, and by the end, I can barely see the words through my tears. She knew it and planned it. She saw two broken people and decided to give them a chance to heal each other. And it worked.

"Ms. Whitfield?" Harlan's voice is gentle. "You all right?"

I wipe my eyes with the back of my hand, laughing. "She's impossible. Even gone, she's absolutely impossible."

"That was Mavis," he says with a smile. "Three steps ahead of everyone else, always."

I fold the letter carefully and put it back in the envelope, then tuck it into my purse, close to my heart, where I'll carry it always.

"Thank you, Harlan, for everything."

"Thank Mavis. She's the one who believed in you."

He stands and extends his hand. "Welcome to Copper Creek, Ms. Whitfield. Officially and permanently."

I shake his hand and then surprise us both by pulling him into a hug. "She was lucky to have you," I say.

"We were lucky to have each other," he replies, patting my back awkwardly. "Now go on. I believe there's a young man waiting for you outside who will want to hear about this."

~

I find Wyatt leaning against his truck, his arms crossed, watching the door.

"Well?" he says as I approach.

I don't even answer with words. I just walk straight into his arms and hold on tight.

"That good, huh?"

"She planned it," I say into his chest. "All of it. She knew about us before we even met."

"What are you talking about?"

I pull back and look at him. "Mavis. She left me another letter. She said she saw two broken people who needed each other and decided to put us together in the same place and see what happened."

He's quiet for a moment, processing this new information. Then a slow smile spreads across his face.

"That crafty old woman."

"The craftiest. So we were just puppets in her grand scheme."

"Apparently."

I reach up and touch his face. "Do you mind?"

"Mind that the woman who saved my life also managed to guide me to the love of my life?" He turns his head and kisses my palm. "No, Eleanor, I don't mind at all."

He pulls me close and kisses me softly, right there on Main Street in front of Harlan's office, where anyone walking by can see.

I don't care. Let them see. Let the whole town talk. I'm home.

EPILOGUE

One year later, the first Fall Festival since I officially became the owner of The Rusty Spur is everything I dreamed it would be. The weather is perfect, crisp and clear, with gold and red leaves dotting the mountains.

The crowds are bigger than last year, and the pie contest is fiercer than ever. I place third with my apple crumble. I consider that progress.

The Rusty Spur is thriving. Revenue is up forty percent thanks to some changes I've made and the reputation we've built. Gary Allen disappeared into oblivion when every property owner in town declined his repeated offers. Last I heard, he'd moved on to developing some resort in Tennessee. I sure hope those communities fight as hard as we did.

Wyatt and I are taking things slow, the way we promised we would. Sunday dinners at Meredith's.

Saturday mornings in the garden. Long walks through town where we hold hands and talk about everything and nothing. We're building something real.

The festival is winding down when Wyatt finds me near the pie booth.

"Come with me," he says, taking my hand.

"Where are we going?"

"It's a surprise."

I let him lead me through the thinning crowds, past the craft booths and the stage, up the hill toward the overlook where they threw my welcome party over a year ago. The sun is setting, painting everything gold. The whole valley is spread out below us. Copper Creek is glowing in the last light of day. I can see The Rusty Spur from up here, just the neon sign starting to flicker on.

"It's beautiful," I say.

"You're beautiful."

I turn to look at him and find him on one knee.

My heart feels like it stops in my chest.

"Eleanor," he says, his voice shaking a bit. "A year and a half ago, you walked into my bar in a pencil skirt and pearls, and I thought you were the most annoying woman I'd ever met."

I laugh through sudden tears.

"You were stubborn as a mule, lost and completely out of your element. You were also brave and kind and much stronger than you knew."

He pulls a small box from his pocket.

"Mavis thought we'd be good for each other. Turns out she was completely right about everything."

He opens the box. Inside is a ring, simple and beautiful, with a stone that catches the last light of the setting sun.

"I want to spend the rest of my life with you. I want to wake up next to you every morning and fall asleep next to you every night. I want to build a life with you here, in this place we both love."

He looks up at me with those blue eyes full of hope, and maybe just a little fear.

"Eleanor Whitfield, will you marry me?"

I'm crying so hard I can barely speak, but I manage the only word that matters.

"Yes!"

He slides the ring onto my finger. It fits perfectly.

And then he's on his feet, pulling me into his arms and kissing me like we're the only two people left in the world.

"I love you," he says against my mouth.

"I love you too."

We stand there at the overlook as the sun sets and the stars come out, wrapped up in each other. And I think about Mavis. About her letters, her scheming, her faith in two broken people who needed each other.

I think about how she saw something in me that I couldn't see in myself, and how she gave me the greatest gift anyone has ever given me.

Permission to become who I was always meant to be.

Thank you, I think, *for all of it.*

Somewhere, I'm certain she's smiling, maybe in one of the stars starting to twinkle above.

"Oh my gosh! They just got engaged!" I hear Presley squealing and turn to see half the town running toward us, clapping and cheering.

I'm definitely home.

~

Come join my FREE Patreon to learn about giveaways, new releases, and read bonus scenes from my books: https://www.patreon.com/cw/Rachel HannaBooks

Join my newsletter list to get special discounts in my store: https://store.rachelhannaauthor.com/ pages/newsletter-sign-up